My Heart from Inside

By

Aviva Gat

Text copyright © 2019 Aviva Gat
All Rights Reserved

This work is protected under the Copyright Act of the United States. No part of the publication may be used, copied, distributed, or transmitted in any form or by any means, including electronic or mechanical, except with the permission of the author, except for brief quotations included in critical reviews and articles.

My Heart from Inside

To Elia, who made my dreams come true when she turned me into a mother.

"No one else will ever know the strength of my love for you. After all, you're the only one who knows the sound of my heart from the inside."

Chapter 1

March 28, 2019

Sometimes all your options are the wrong ones. I've been thinking a lot about decisions lately. Sometimes the right choice just pops right out at you, but other times every choice seems wrong. And even if you do think the right choice is obvious, five years later you may find yourself questioning why that decision seemed so obvious back then, when it was so obviously wrong. But was there a right decision? This question keeps rolling around in my head, bouncing from side to side—there was a right decision, there wasn't. We made the right one. No, the wrong one.

I'm debating with myself for the millionth time when I see her. She walks through the gate with her pink backpack that has a glittery unicorn on it. Her sandy blond curls pulled back into a ponytail and frizz lines her face like a mane blowing in the breeze. She's skipping, her hands hooked on her backpack straps.

I crouch down a little lower and push my large sunglasses up my nose as my hands make their way to the fence in front of me. I hold it tight as though I may blow away. I'm far enough away that she won't see me, but close enough that I can see the freckles on her nose. As she skips through the courtyard, I have to move to maintain my view through the bushes. I'm still on the fence, my hands scaling the bars as I slide around. She hugs a dark-haired girl with a purple backpack and they hold hands as they start walking toward the building. I imagine that the other girl must be her best friend. They smile at each other; their lips moving as quickly as only a five-year-old's can.

Now I can only see her back as she starts to disappear in a crowd of children making their way into the school. The bell rings and the sea of backpacks starts to flow faster through the open doors. I start moving fast toward the gate, trying to maintain eye contact with her pink unicorn backpack as long as I can before it disappears.

"Can I help you?" One of the teachers has noticed me. She's standing in front of me now on the other side of the fence. "You know, I've seen you here before. If you were a man, they would have already called the police."

I smile at her and feel my sunglasses again to make sure they are still masking my face. She's right. If it were a man standing outside an elementary school like I was, crouching behind bushes, peering through the fence, the police would come straight away. The man would be labeled a pedophile and the neighborhood would be on high alert. Thankfully I'm a woman. I probably just appear pathetic, or weird. Crazy even.

"You should go," the teacher says to me. I stand up and take a last look at the school to try to find the pink backpack again. But I can't. She must already be inside, sitting in her kindergarten class. I bet she's a good student. Listens. Does her homework. Already writing her ABCs.

I stand up and quickly nod at the teacher. Even with my sunglasses I can't make eye contact with her. I'm too embarrassed. Embarrassed that I am here? No, just embarrassed that I was noticed. I turn around and start walking away from the school, my arms crossed in front of my chest and my head facing the ground.

I tell myself this is the last time I will go to the school, but I know I am lying. I say that every time. The problem is, I miss her. I miss her even though I never really got to know her.

Part 1

"Life is always a rich and steady time when you are waiting for something to happen or to hatch."

– E.B. White, Charlotte's Web

Chapter 2

January 4, 2013

Cameron lay on the table with her feet in the stirrups. She hadn't peed in four hours, the doctor told her to hold it because it would make it easier for him to see when he sticks the catheter with the embryo into her uterus. All she could think about was going to the bathroom and relieving herself. Funny how that was her only thought on this important day, the day when—hopefully—her wish would come true.

"Ready to be a mommy?" Andy said.

Cameron looked up at him and gave a half smile, while letting go of her breath. He was holding her hand tight, standing next to her in the operating room.

"Don't get too ahead of yourself," Cameron responded. She wondered where the doctor was, how long this would take and when she could go to the bathroom.

Then the door opened and Dr. Klein walked in wearing his sea green scrubs. He had a hat covering his head and a mask blocking his mouth.

"How are we doing today?" he asked as he sat in front of Cameron and turned on a big screen in front of them. The screen was positioned so Cameron could see what he was doing while she lay down.

"Doing great, doctor," Andy responded. "Very excited. How are you?"

"Also excited," Dr. Klein said. Cameron was silent. She let Andy speak for her when she was nervous or anxious. He was better under pressure. Then a nurse came in carrying a little box with three petri dishes. The nurse looked at the wrist band on Cameron's arm. "Can you tell me your name and birthday?" she said.

"Cameron Stevens. November 2nd, 1984."

"Stevens, yup," the nurse said looking at the label on the petri dishes. She handed them to the doctor. He separated the three dishes and slid the first one on to the tray of a microscope. Instantly, the image of the petri dish appeared on the screen. The grey blob seemed to vibrate with life in its little dish.

"This one has eight cells," the doctor said. "That's alright for day three."

Three days ago Cameron had her eggs retrieved. After three weeks of hormone shots to the belly, her body generated sixteen eggs. A normal female body generates just one every cycle. While she was still under anesthesia, Andy gave his sperm sample to the nurse and the eggs were fertilized. Then, the watch began. The eggs sat in a lab while technicians monitored them to see which ones would take and grow. Of the eggs, twelve had started to grow. The top three were now to be examined by the doctor. The rest, frozen until a later time when they may get a chance at life.

The doctor slid the petri dish off the microscope and put the second dish on. "Ten cells!" he exclaimed. "Now that's more like what I expected to see." Cameron and Andy looked at the blob on the screen. It did look bigger than the first. Then the doctor slid the third dish onto the microscope. "Also eight cells. Hm." The doctor seemed to be thinking something to himself. He looked at the couple, who was holding hands tightly. Cameron wondered if Dr. Klein was this friendly with all his patients. It must be exhausting, doing this all day. Pretending that each patient's embryos were so exciting. Cameron just wanted him to hurry up so she could pee.

"I recommend we only transfer one embryo and freeze the other two," Dr. Klein said. "All three look fine, you're young, and your hormone levels are perfect. I don't want to risk you getting pregnant with multiples."

"Whatever you say doc," Andy said. "We trust your judgment."

Dr. Klein slid the second petri dish—the one with the ten-cell embryo—back onto the microscope. "So, this is the guy," Dr. Klein said.

Andy looked back and forth from the screen to his wife. "That's our baby!" he said, his smile growing bigger with every passing second. "Hey doc, is it a girl or a boy?"

"I don't know," Dr. Klein responded. "It's a healthy embryo, that's all that we care about."

"Sure, of course," Andy said.

Cameron hoped it was a girl. She imagined them wearing matching outfits and styling her hair. She knew Andy wanted a boy. Someone he could toss a ball around with and share his love of football.

"Ready?" the doctor asked.

Cameron nodded. She just wanted to get this part over with. She wanted it to be ten days from now, when she would take a pregnancy test. The nurse lifted Cameron's hospital gown and squirted the cold jelly on to her stomach. Then she pulled out the ultrasound wand and started moving it around on Cameron's flat abs.

"Wow, your bladder is really full!" the nurse said, laughing as she started slowing down the movements of the wand and focusing on one place. "Here's your uterus, you see that? That is the lining, where we implant the embryo." The nurse was pointing to the screen. It looked like a black and white empty hotdog bun.

"This may feel a little uncomfortable," Dr. Klein said as he gently put the embryo on the end of the catheter. "Just watch the little guy go."

Cameron felt the doctor slide the catheter into her uterus. She watched intently at the screen, afraid to blink and miss it. She watched as the catheter approached her uterus and suddenly, the little embryo jumped off and swam right into the lining.

"Perfect," Dr. Klein said. "A good swimmer. Now you just need to sit still for fifteen minutes and then you're free to go."

"Wait, what if I pee and the embryo falls out?" Cameron said, the fear suddenly engulfed her.

"It won't, you can't pee it out," Dr. Klein responded, a knowing smile on his face. "Don't worry. Try to relax. Take it easy for the next few days and we'll see you back here for your pregnancy test."

The doctor and nurse left the operating room, leaving Cameron and Andy alone in the dark.

"So how does it feel to be pregnant?" Andy asked. He was still holding Cameron's hand.

"Like I have to pee!" Cameron said. She gave a nervous laugh. "I really hope this works."

"It will, I know it," Andy said. "There's no reason it shouldn't. You heard the doctor, your hormone levels are perfect, this little guy has ten cells and is a great swimmer. It's going to work."

Cameron kissed Andy's hand. She loved his optimism; it was one of the things that drew her to him. She was more of a realist, or as Andy liked to call it, a pessimist. But she would tell him, it's not pessimistic if it's the most likely outcome. He'd disagree.

Please work, Cameron prayed silently. They had been trying to get pregnant for three years. Cameron, thin, athletic, and healthy, had always feared that she would be infertile. There was no reason she should be—all the doctors said there was nothing wrong—but no matter what she and Andy tried, it just didn't work. For the first year, they didn't try that hard, they just didn't try not to get pregnant. Then, Cameron started tracking her cycle and when that didn't work they went to the doctors. She and Andy both had a bunch of tests performed, and everything came back perfect. You're young, the doctors told them, keep trying, it will happen. But now, Cameron was twenty-eight and still childless. Meanwhile, she had friends already on their second pregnancies.

"What are we going to call it?" Andy asked, waking Cameron from her thoughts.

"Peanut?"

Andy laughed. "Peanut it is. Maybe we'll even keep that name after he's born."

"You mean after *she's* born," Cameron joked. She was starting to loosen up. Suddenly the door opened and the nurse popped her head in.

"You can get up now," she said. "Good luck!"

Cameron pulled her legs out of the stirrups and sat up. Andy handed Cameron her clothes and watched his wife slip out of the hospital gown to put her dress back on. She suddenly felt self-conscious seeing her husband's eyes on her. His gaze drifted down to her small chest, tight waist, thin thighs.

"I have the most beautiful wife," he said. "How about we stay in here a little longer?" He wrapped his hands around her waist and kissed her neck, stopping her from pulling the dress down over her shoulders.

"Andy! They could walk in any moment!" Cameron said with a smile.

"What? Is it too much to ask to have sex with my wife when she conceives?"

Cameron lightly hit him on the shoulder and shook her head.

"When do you start getting horny from the pregnancy hormones?" Andy joked.

Cameron laughed as she pulled down her dress and threw the hospital gown in the bin. When she finished, Andy opened the door of the operating room and grabbed Cameron's hand as they walked out and through the doors of the clinic.

Chapter 3

January 14, 2013

Cameron hadn't been able to sleep, which is why she was surprised when she woke up in the morning. She was sure she had been awake all night. She felt nauseated, a pit in her stomach. Morning sickness? Probably too early for that. Most likely she was nervous about going to the clinic to get her blood drawn for the pregnancy test.

The night before, Andy came back from work with a home pregnancy test. He said he couldn't wait for the test in the morning, so why don't they just find out now? Cameron refused to try it. It had only been ten days since they transferred the embryo, she didn't know if a five dollar test from the drug store would be able to tell if it worked. She didn't want to get any false hopes, or any false disappointments.

Andy understood. He got her like that. He never pressed her to do anything she didn't want to do. Not even when they were on their honeymoon in Thailand and he wanted to go ziplining. Cameron was afraid of heights and preferred to see the jungle from the ground. She kissed him after they strapped him into the harness and took a jeep ride to meet him at the other side.

Andy was in the shower when Cameron woke up. She was usually out the door before him, she got up every day at six to run or go to a yoga class before work, but today she had taken the day off. No workout and no work. She didn't want to find out the news while sitting at her desk or in a client meeting. She wanted to be alone.

She rolled over to the side of their king-size bed. She had been sleeping in the middle. The right side was her side, but at night she always rolled over to be close to Andy. To feel his warmth. She thought about their first sleepover. It was after their fifth date, when he took her out to a nice steakhouse. He ordered a bottle of wine, even though they were both too young to legally drink. But with Andy's confidence, the waiter didn't card them—probably thinking about the tip he would get at the end of the evening. He just smiled at the couple, brought over the wine, opened it and poured a sip for Andy to taste. Andy took a thoughtful sip and smiled at Cameron. His smile made her heart flutter. They finished the wine over the next couple hours and then Andy walked her back to her apartment. Her roommates were already asleep, so they snuck in quietly to her bedroom. Cameron had only invited a few boys into her bedroom before. She wasn't like her roommates or her sorority sisters, who sometimes found themselves waking up in different fraternity houses or with strangers in their beds. Cameron didn't judge them for it, but it just wasn't for her.

She had agreed to let Andy come in because she was falling for him and she was pretty sure he liked her too. After all, they had gone out five times, which was pretty significant for two college students. He had taken her to nice places, made her laugh, treated her with respect. Or maybe it was just the wine. In her bedroom, Andy kissed her gently and then looked at the pictures on her wall. She had pictures of her friends from high school and from different sorority events. He asked about a few pictures, where were they taken, who were the other girls with her. She answered all his questions and then she wrapped her arms around him. She had enough of talking about her friends.

Cameron heard the shower stop. She got up and put on her white satin bathrobe, the one her mother had bought her for her wedding, and went into the bathroom where Andy was toweling off.

"Good morning," he greeted her, kissing her on the cheek. "How did you sleep?"

"Alright," she said while grabbing her toothbrush.

"It's going to be fine," Andy said. "Whatever the results. Call me right away, I'll come home if you want."

"Don't worry." Cameron spit the toothpaste into the sink. Andy slid past her through the bedroom and to their walk-in closet. She watched him standing in front of his small section, choosing which suit to wear. She eyed his dark hair, wet and messy from the shower, his shoulders, abs and the towel around his waist. He picked a dark brown suit with a blue shirt and a red paisley tie. Cameron liked that combo a lot.

As Cameron washed her face, Andy left the bedroom to make coffee. She could smell the roasted coffee beans while she dabbed lotion on her face. Anti-wrinkle cream. She wasn't old enough to have wrinkles, but she had been using the cream since she was twenty-one. She was sure her fifty-year-old self would thank her. She gently smoothed the cream around her blue eyes, then down her nose and across her high cheekbones. Then, she pulled the rubber band out of her hair, letting the straight strands fall around her face. A few brush strokes through her copper-colored hair and she was ready. She left the bathroom to meet Andy in the kitchen and poured herself a large mug from the French press.

"I have a light day today," Andy said. "So anything at all, just call me."

Andy worked at a hedge fund in Midtown. He spent his days researching stocks and companies and writing proposals for investments. Then, once an investment was made, he tracked it, to determine when was the optimal time to sell to maximize capital gains. He was good with numbers and was one of the top managers at the firm. He never had a light day at work. There was no such thing.

"I promise I will call you the minute I hear anything," Cameron said to him. She felt herself smiling as she sipped the hot coffee.

"Maybe only have one cup today," Andy said. "You shouldn't have too much caffeine. Or we could switch to decaf."

"Stop worrying!" Cameron rolled her eyes. She loved that he worried. That he thought of everything.

"Alright. Done worrying." He put his coffee mug in the sink and came over to her. He kissed her lips, lingering there for a few extra seconds. "Try to relax, enjoy the day off."

"I will," Cameron responded. "Have a good day. I'll talk to you soon."

Andy grabbed his briefcase and left their apartment, heading to the subway to take him from their Upper East Side apartment to his Midtown office. Alone, Cameron quickly finished her coffee and went to the bedroom to put on her clothes. She normally wore business casual clothes every day to work, but because she had the day off, she opted for something more comfortable. Faded jeans and a white T-shirt. She zipped up her tan boots and wrapped her down coat around her shoulders. She grabbed her Coach purse and a bottle of water on the way out of the apartment. Best to drink a lot before a blood test. It helped the blood flow. The nurses always had so much trouble finding her veins.

She walked the few blocks to the clinic. It was a sunny day. The cold air still bit her face, but she could feel the sun trying to warm her. For the three weeks before they retrieved the eggs from her, she had done this walk every other morning before work. She had cut her runs short or skipped yoga to make sure she could get to the clinic, do the tests, and get to work on time. At the clinic, they would take a blood sample to check her hormone levels and do an ultrasound to check the size of the follicles in her ovaries. In the afternoons, the doctor would call her and tell her whether to increase the dosage of the medicine she was taking or keep it the same. In the evenings, she would give herself a shot to the stomach with the medicine. She alternated sides every day, one day on the left of her belly button, the next on the right. By the end of the three weeks, her stomach was covered in bruises. Then the doctor told her it was time. Her hormone levels were high and she had enough follicles large enough to release eggs. The next day, they retrieved them. Three days later, they transferred one embryo into her uterus. Now, ten days later, it was time to check if it worked.

She got to the clinic and said good morning to the receptionist, who signed her in. Then, she followed a nurse in to one of the patient rooms. Cameron took off her coat and sat down in the chair, reaching her right arm out for the blood sample. She squeezed her hand into a fist a few times, squeezing and releasing, hoping to make one of her veins pop up. The nurse washed her hands, tied a rubber band around Cameron's bicep and started to feel the inside of her elbow for a vein.

"How are you feeling today?" the nurse asked through her face mask.

"Fine," Cameron responded. "How are you?"

"Can't complain," the nurse said. "Here's the vein." She started tapping the vein with two of her fingers. When the vein swelled, the nurse took the needle and pricked it, drawing blood to fill two vials. "All set. The doctor will call you as soon as the results are in. Good luck!" The nurse held a cotton ball over the needle as she pulled it out of Cameron's arm. "Band-aid?"

"No thanks," Cameron responded. Band-aids always irritated her skin. Better to just hold the cotton ball for a few minutes until the blood stopped. The nurse left the room, leaving Cameron to sit for a few minutes, before she put on her coat and left the clinic. Instead of going home, she started walking toward Central Park. She hoped that was the last time she would have to go to the clinic. If the IVF was successful, she would continue her care with her regular gynecologist. They only had to return if they were unsuccessful and wanted to try another round. Cameron hoped they didn't need to do that. Not only was it emotionally taxing, but it was expensive. Cameron and Andy had plenty of savings, they both worked hard at high paying jobs and didn't spend unnecessarily, but Cameron would have hoped to keep their savings for something else. Say, for private school for their children, or college.

Cameron spent the morning wandering around Central Park. At one point, she stopped in a Starbucks and ordered herself a second coffee. Decaf, just in case. She could check her test results from the clinic's app on her phone. She kept checking the app to see if the results were in, even though she knew it was early. She checked at 9:30 a.m. Then again at ten. Nothing. She told herself she wouldn't check again until eleven. But at 10:45, she broke.

She opened the app and to her surprise, she saw the test results were in. Her heart stopped as she clicked on the test. Her hCG level was 200 mUI/mL. What did that mean? She had expected the results to say positive or negative. A number? That told her nothing. Her heart was racing as she called the clinic. She knew the doctor was supposed to call her, but she couldn't wait. The secretary answered.

"Hi, this is Cameron Stevens. Is Dr. Klein available?"

"Hi Mrs. Stevens," the secretary answered slowly. She obviously didn't feel the urgency that Cameron was trying to transmit through the phone. "I'll put you through to his office. If he isn't with another patient, he will answer."

"Thank you," Cameron said as the holding music came through the line. The tune played through the phone, making Cameron wonder whether this music was supposed to relax her or build up suspense. She wasn't sure.

"Dr. Klein." He startled her when he answered, even though she was waiting for it.

"Hi Doctor, it's Cameron Stevens, I got my pregnancy test results today and I wasn't sure what they meant," Cameron said, trying to sound calm and collected when she felt anything but.

"Hi Cameron," Dr. Klein said, with the same coolness as the secretary. "I haven't had a chance to look at the results yet. Could you tell me what they were?"

"My hCG level is at 200."

"Congratulations Cameron. You're pregnant."

Chapter 4

January 14, 2013

Cameron wasn't an emotional person. She didn't cry in movies and she most definitely didn't cry in public. But now she couldn't stop the tears from coming down her face. Happy tears. She was so overcome with feelings, that tears seemed to be the only logical way to let them loose. She took note of it, that this was her first happy cry. After getting off the phone with Dr. Klein she sat quietly on a bench in Central Park while she composed herself and tried to figure out how to tell Andy. She didn't want to worry him, she also wanted to try to contain his excitement. After all, the pregnancy was so early and who knew what would happen. She didn't want to get too excited either, only to have something happen and end her motherhood before it started.

"Andy?" she said when he picked up the phone.

"Hi babe, how are you doing?" Cameron could hear him shutting a door, probably to his office. Background noise disappeared.

"Andy, I'm pregnant," she whispered, afraid to say it too loud.

"What!? I knew it!" he replied, about ten decibels higher than Cameron had spoken. "Where are you? Are you sitting down? Should I come home?"

"No, yes," Cameron spoke up a little louder. "I'm fine. I'm in the park. I'm going home. You don't need to come home. I'll see you after work."

"I'll try to get out of here as soon as I can," Andy said. "Let's celebrate tonight. I'm making reservations. Love you."

"Love you too," Cameron said before ending the call. She breathed deeply, closed her eyes. After a few minutes, she decided to walk back home. She didn't want to catch a cold from sitting outside all day, especially now when she knew she had another life to protect.

At home, she tried to read a book, but she couldn't concentrate on the words. Her mind wandered. She thought about how she could keep this secret until the end of the first trimester when it would be the only thing on her mind. She thought about what her friends would say when she ordered club soda during their weekly happy hour. Maybe she should try watching TV. But still, she couldn't focus.

She decided to check her work email. Maybe that would get her mind off the little bundle of cells growing inside her. She opened her laptop and watched the list of unread messages load. The first was from a client, E.I. Foods, which made baking materials. They wanted to meet to talk about doing a rebranding in light of the recent health food craze. The next was from another client, Clarin, a baby stroller maker. They were going to recall one of their products and wanted to get ahead of any bad press. How appropriate. Cameron made a note not to buy a Clarin stroller, even though she would do her best to ensure the recall didn't affect their business. The third email was from her boss, asking if she was interested in meeting with a new client, B.R. Pharmaceuticals. They were developing a new drug for diabetes and wanted to prepare materials for an upcoming conference where they would launch the drug.

Cameron responded to the emails one by one. She invited E.I. Foods to call and schedule with her assistant.

With Clarin, she suggested that they notify the press of the recall and spin it that they were doing it as a precaution. They could also offer all their customers who returned the product an upgraded version of their stroller. She said she would create the press release and schedule talks with the relevant media if they liked this strategy. To her boss, she responded that she would be happy to take on the new client and would start researching the diabetes drug market right away. The list of emails went on, that's what it's like for a senior manager at one of New York's leading public relations firms.

She spent the afternoon working from the kitchen counter. She didn't notice the time go by and she didn't think about her pregnancy until she heard the front door open. Andy came in with a bouquet of purple lilies—Cameron's favorite—and a small white teddy bear. He kissed her lips, pressing his hard against hers.

"How are you doing, mommy?" he asked.

"I'm not a mommy yet," Cameron answered, as she took the lilies and put them in a crystal vase on the counter. "We still have eight and half months to go."

"It will go by fast," Andy responded. "Before you know it, we'll be changing diapers and singing nursery rhymes."

"I hope so," Cameron said cautiously. She eyed the teddy bear still in Andy's hand. They had agreed that they wouldn't buy any baby things until at least halfway through the pregnancy. Cameron was afraid to jinx it. She also didn't want people coming over and seeing any new purchases that would give away their secret.

Andy followed her gaze to the bear. "I know," he said, reading her mind. "I just thought it would be a good memory to tell the baby. That we bought this bear the moment we found out about him. I'll keep it in the closet."

"It was very thoughtful," Cameron said. She couldn't help but smile.

"We have reservations in an hour at Bistro 86," Andy said. "Put on one of your beautiful dresses so I can show off my gorgeous wife."

Bistro 86 was the first restaurant they ate at after they moved to Manhattan together. They had both agreed that Manhattan was the place to go after they graduated from Boston University. With Andy's degree in business and Cameron's in communications, that seemed the best option for them to excel in their careers. A few weeks before graduation they took a trip together and found a cozy apartment on Second Avenue. It was a small place, one bedroom, a kitchen, and a bathroom so small that you had to sit sideways on the toilet. But it was perfect. They returned to Boston after signing the lease and putting down the security deposit and first and last months' rent.

After the graduation ceremony, with both of them still in their red caps and gowns, Andy got down on one knee and opened a small blue box. The sunlight hit the diamond, making it dazzle like fireworks, as he told her that he couldn't imagine his life without her. Cameron gasped and held her hands to her heart. She had known they would get married eventually, but wasn't expecting the ring just yet. Of course she happily accepted, letting him slip the square-cut diamond onto her finger. It was a beautiful ring, but she would have said yes had he proposed with a rubber band.

The next day, they packed up a moving van and drove down to New York, talking the whole time about their wedding plans. It would be the next summer, outdoors somewhere, with a Rabbi conducting a traditional Jewish ceremony. The conversation continued as they moved the boxes from the van to the apartment and immediately went to eat at Bistro 86.

Now, almost seven years later, they were in a bigger apartment—one they had bought with help from their parents—but still in the same Upper East Side neighborhood. Bistro 86 was their go-to for any celebration, birthdays, anniversaries, friends in town; it never disappointed.

Cameron slipped on a red dress that had long sleeves and a plunging neckline. The dress hugged her slim waist, accentuating her hips. She looked at herself in the mirror, thinking that this may be the last time she would wear this dress, at least for a while. She loved that dress and she made a promise to herself that she would wear it again, three months after having the baby. That would be plenty of time to get back in shape.

Then she flung her head forward to run her hands through her shoulder-length hair. Give it a little volume. She flung her hair back, and gently placed each runaway strand in place around her head. The red dress accentuated the highlights in her brown hair.

Last, she put on her black high heeled boots—another love that she probably wouldn't want to wear as the pregnancy progressed—and joined Andy in the living room. She gave a twirl and he wrapped his arms around her.

"You are so beautiful," he said. "I can't wait until you have a stomach."

Cameron laughed, throwing her head back. "Will you still think I am beautiful then? When I'm hormonal and crying and fat?"

"You will never be fat," Andy responded as he led her out the door.

At the restaurant, Andy ordered a bottle of San Pellegrino. Usually he would have opted for a Pinot Noir or a Merlot, depending on what they were ordering, but he wasn't going to drink alone. They both scanned the menu, even though they had their favorite dishes.

"Shall we start with the endive salad with blue cheese?" he asked.

"I can't have blue cheese."

"Carpaccio?"

"No raw meat." Cameron read down the menu, realizing that most of the dishes were now off limits to her. Egg yolk ravioli, foie gras, tuna tartare.

"So you tell me what you want to order," Andy said. "We're in this together, whatever you can't eat, I'm not eating either."

Cameron smiled as she gave another look through the menu. They ended up sharing a green salad, lasagna, and rosemary chicken.

Chapter 5

March 21, 2013

It was the first day of spring and the weather was starting to warm up. At this time of the year, Cameron would usually start putting her winter clothes in the back of her closet and bringing her spring wardrobe forward. Her spring wardrobe was full of bright colored dresses, high-waisted skirts, and slim-fit pants. She still hadn't bought any maternity clothing, but she knew that most of her wardrobe may be a little tight on her now. She was thirteen weeks pregnant. Starting the second trimester, and she was still too afraid of becoming attached to the pregnancy or the baby in her stomach. Baby. She wouldn't even call it that yet.

It was still early, before 7:00 a.m., but she had already come back from her run—the doctor told her she could continue exercising so long as she didn't push herself—and showered. She had slowed down her runs, cut the distance, but it was a habit she couldn't let go of. Not yet. She got out of the shower and examined herself in the mirror. She pinched the skin on her stomach, it was still flat, but she could feel a difference. Her hands rose to her face, feeling her cheeks that had grown fuller over the last few weeks.

They had an ultrasound appointment that day. They would find out the sex of the embryo—the baby—and they had agreed that if everything was going well, it was time to start telling people. Cameron and Andy had kept the secret completely between the two of them, at Cameron's insistence. She was afraid of telling people and then having to share her grief if something had happened. She thought maybe some people had started to suspect. Her mother often commented that she sounded more tired than usual on the phone, imploring her to tell her if something was going on. Her friends quietly eyed her club soda every Thursday when they met for happy hour. But maybe Cameron was just paranoid.

She put on a high-waisted A-line dress and blow-dried her hair so that it fell flat on her shoulders. She applied her make-up, a little foundation, eyeliner, mascara, and gave herself a last once over before leaving the bathroom. Andy was just waking up. She kissed him goodbye, reminding him to meet her at the doctor during lunch for their appointment. She slipped on a pair of black flats and was out the door by 7:30 a.m. She liked getting to the office early. It gave her a head start. She would read the news—checking for anything that could affect her clients—and then start going through her emails. By the time most of her colleagues were arriving, she would have already planned out her day, knowing exactly what tasks needed to be accomplished and who she would need to contact. That's what it took to get ahead in this business.

She had worked hard to get to where she was. Her career was built from late nights, early mornings, and the ability to always be ahead of her colleagues. A baby would change that. It wasn't fair, she thought, but it would be worth it. Telling her boss about the pregnancy would be difficult. It wasn't that her boss wouldn't understand—he would—but it would add a huge load on his plate. He would need to redistribute her projects for her maternity leave and make sure he was up to date with all her clients.

She took the subway down to Midtown and made her way to her office. It was in one of the tall high-rises on Madison Avenue. She swiped herself into the building, went through the metal detector, greeted Dexter the security guard, and took the elevator up to the eighteenth floor. She stopped in the kitchen first to brew a pot of coffee and then made her way through the cubicles to her office. There were a couple junior associates already in, trying to prove their worth and get on the fast track to manager. She appreciated their dedication, always choosing the early risers to work on her projects.

She was like them when she started out. Her first job out of college was a market analyst for a boutique advertising firm. It was an arduous job, she spent most of her time going through financial reports and writing summaries that she wasn't sure anybody actually read. After a few months, she had to get reading glasses because the font on the reports seemed to be getting blurrier. She made a few jumps from there, eventually landing herself at Lawrence Spector Communications. Jim Lawrence hired her after a process that included three interviews, an analytical test, and a presentation to the senior managers. He said she aced it, and she started out already halfway up the ladder as a junior manager. It didn't take long until junior switched to senior, and she had an office and assistant of her own. Next stop was partner.

She started reading the news, first checking her Google Alerts for all her clients. The Clarin recall had a few new hits—a blog post saying that a stroller recall should make the company close up shop and a human-interest story about a child who had gotten hurt when the stroller brakes didn't lock in place like they should. Maybe time for a rebranding of Clarin, Cameron thought.

After her morning news and email ritual, Cameron had a project status meeting with her associates working on the B.R. Pharmaceuticals drug launch and then a brainstorming meeting with executives from Kastron, a new company entering the hand tools market. She breezed through the meetings, giving feedback to her associates on their progress and bouncing out a few logo and motto ideas for Kastron. The whole time trying to ignore the clock ticking closer and closer to her ultrasound.

When she could finally break free—only after a junior associate tried to suck up to her by asking her opinion on a pamphlet mockup he made for one of his clients—she rushed outside, forgetting her leather jacket on the back of her chair. She debated briefly whether to go back up the elevator and get it or brave the cold for the ten-minute walk to the doctor's office. She'd brave the cold; the sun was shining and if she kept up her pace she would be warm enough when she got there.

Andy was standing outside the building when she arrived. He was in a dark grey suit with a maroon shirt. No tie today. He must not have any meetings, Cameron thought. When he saw her approaching, he instinctively took off his suit jacket and wrapped it around her shoulders.

"Aren't you cold?" he asked as he kissed her forehead.

"I forgot my jacket," she responded, happily accepting his. Ever the gentleman, she thought.

"I can't have you getting sick now, your immune system is weaker when you're pregnant."

"I know." Cameron smiled at him. Overprotection was something she had already gotten used to. He opened the door for her, and they went inside the building, navigating the halls to the doctor's office. This was their second ultrasound. At the first, six weeks earlier, the doctor showed them the little black beating dot on the screen, pointing out the heartbeat and assuring them that the embryo was growing at a healthy pace. Cameron wasn't sure what to expect this time. Would it look like a baby? Or still just a flashing blob?

Cameron signed in at the doctor's office and the couple followed a nurse into one of the rooms where Cameron changed from her dress to the smock they provided and lay down on the table, propping herself up on her elbows. A few minutes later, Dr. Lee came in.

"How are we doing?" Dr. Lee asked. Dr. Lee was young for an ob-gyn. Or at least she looked young. Cameron guessed they were probably about the same age, meaning Dr. Lee had probably just finished med school in the last few years. Cameron had started seeing Dr. Lee before the pregnancy, on a recommendation of a friend.

"Good," Cameron responded.

"Any morning sickness? Nausea? Weaknesses or pains?" Dr. Lee asked after a quick scan of Cameron's chart.

"No, everything has been pretty easy so far," Cameron said.

"Good. Let's take a look."

Cameron lay back, moving the gown so that her stomach was showing. While she was often proud of her body, at this moment she felt embarrassed. Like she should have more to show for being a third into her pregnancy. Dr. Lee squirted the cool gel onto Cameron's stomach and started to move the wand around. It only took a second for her to find the baby.

"Here it is!" she said. "We're going to do a full body scan today, starting with the toes. Here they are." Suddenly there were ten dots on the screen in front of them. "Ten perfect toes… And here are the feet, and the legs… Now you see the hips and the stomach… There's the liver, and you see the bones are starting to form around the rib cage. And there is the heart beating. A good strong heart." The doctor paused and looked at the couple. "Alright, and here are the arms...the right hand...and here is the left. Ten fingers, looking good. Now let's look at the head, you see the pulsing there? That's part of the brain. It's still developing now; at the next ultrasound the brain will be more in one piece. Overall everything looks good. Do you want to know the sex?"

Cameron and Andy had both been fixated on the screen. Even as Dr. Lee had been pointing out each body part, Cameron couldn't really recognize them. How did the doctor know that was the stomach? Or the liver? She went so fast, did she have time to count ten toes?

"Babe?" Andy called Cameron. "Do you want find out the sex?"

"At this point it is still a little early," the doctor said. "So whatever I tell you, it's not one hundred percent, maybe seventy percent at this point."

"Sure, what is it?" Cameron asked, still looking at the screen, trying to figure out what she was looking at.

"It's a girl."

Chapter 6

March 21, 2013

Scout's was always busy for happy hour. By 6:00 p.m. every weekday the bar would start to fill up with suits from the surrounding office buildings. Cameron and her girlfriends usually tried to meet there by 5:30 to make sure they got a table for themselves somewhere in the front. Great for people watching and easy to maneuver to when taking the necessary bathroom breaks.

When Cameron arrived, Beth was already sitting at the table reading the happy hour menu. She was usually the first to arrive, trying to escape work as early as possible. Beth and Cameron had been roommates in college and Beth was a bridesmaid at Cameron's wedding. What a day that was. It was in June—after their first year in New York—at the Central Park Boathouse. Cameron spent the night before the wedding at the Park Plaza with her sister Alexa (maid of honor) and three bridesmaids: Jen, her best friend growing up, Mandy, her sorority sister, and Beth. The girls spent the evening putting on face masks, reminiscing, and talking about when they knew Cameron and Andy would get married. Beth said she knew it the moment she heard Cameron sneaking him into their apartment all those years ago. Just before they went to sleep, Beth had said, "Cameron, I hope you know how lucky you are. Andy is one in a million, no, a billion. There are probably just six or seven other guys like him on the planet." Cameron did know how lucky she was. She wasn't jealous of watching the string of men parade in and out of her friends' lives and bedrooms.

Cameron laughed to herself as she approached the table, she knew Beth would order a Long Island iced tea, no matter what was written on the menu. "Thinking of changing it up?" Cameron asked as she reached down to give her friend a hug.

"Maybe." Beth smiled, putting the menu down. "How was your day?"

The girls went over their usual complaints about their jobs. Beth's boss was an idiot, always making her re-do things multiple times because he didn't know what he wanted, and Cameron's client thought they knew more about PR than she did. They ordered a round before the rest of their friends arrived. Beth got her usual Long Island iced tea, while Cameron ordered her club soda. Cameron watched Beth's eyebrows raise ever so slightly when she ordered.

"Cutting back?" Beth asked. Her tone just slightly judgmental.

Cameron tried to play it cool, even though she felt like a little kid caught with her hand in the cookie jar. She had been waiting for this moment though for the last thirteen weeks. Each week, she tried to whisper her order to the waiter, hoping her friends would just assume she had ordered her usual gin and tonic. "I have a presentation tomorrow," Cameron said. "How are things with Jim?"

Jim was Beth's latest love interest. Like the ones before him—and probably like the ones after him—he was a Wall Street type, cocky, ambitious, and not as good looking as he thought he was. Beth was an expert at picking the Wall Street guy out at a bar. It always started with a little flirting, a date over drinks which led back to his place or hers, and then a few months of dating when Beth complained that she didn't know where it was going, if he would get serious, or if she should just end it. Usually it ended with the guy pulling a Houdini—just disappearing.

"Ugh, don't get me started," Beth said. "Last night, he texted me at 11:00 p.m. asking if I wanted to come over. Does he think we're still on college?"

"Did you go over?"

"Well, yeah, I mean, I wasn't going to…"

Just then the rest of their happy hour group appeared, Samantha, another girl from college, and Cindy, who Cameron had met at her first job in NYC and absorbed into her group of friends. With the four of them together, Cameron sat back. Beth had lost interest in Cameron's drink of choice and was giving the girls details about her night with Jim and why she wasn't going to talk to him anymore.

"He actually asked me to leave," she said. "He said he had to get up early, but so what?"

The girls commiserated while giving each other sideways glances. When was Beth going to grow up? While Samantha may have been like her in college, she was now living with her boyfriend of two years, and Cindy had gotten married the previous summer. Cameron listened to the conversation, thinking about how she would jump in with her news. She hadn't told anyone yet, and while she was still afraid of saying it out loud, she was dying to tell them. Telling her friends would make it seem more real, not just a daydream belonging to her and Andy.

"So I have news," Cameron said when there was a slight pause in the conversation.

"You're pregnant!" Cindy blurted, clapping her hands in front of her chest.

"What!? How'd you know?"

"I'm sorry! You wanted to tell us, I shouldn't have said it!" Cindy slapped her hands over her mouth.

"Yes, I'm pregnant," Cameron told them, as if Cindy hadn't just said it a second ago. "It's a girl."

"I knew it! I'm sorry, hun, I just had a feeling, you know?" Cindy said. "You and Andy have been married for six years now, you know? I knew it would happen soon, I've been expecting it for a while, and well, you haven't ordered a drink lately, and you know, you get the picture!"

"Congratulations!" Samantha shouted. "This calls for another round on me!" Samantha motioned to a waiter. "Four margaritas, one virgin."

"This is so exciting!" Cindy's voice became louder when she was excited. "How are you doing? Have you been getting morning sickness? When are we going to start seeing that tummy?"

At first Cameron felt relief. And then, excitement. Letting the secret out in the open, in the crowded bar, allowed it to blossom. It made it real. Nothing bad can happen now, Cameron thought, now that I've said it aloud, this is really happening. Cameron answered her friends' questions. They asked about how Andy was doing—great—if the pregnancy was planned—very planned—if she was going to have a baby shower—she hadn't thought about that yet. With each answer, they cheered their drinks together. This was the first time Cameron felt pure excitement about the pregnancy; the first time she didn't guard herself from enjoying the miracle happening inside her.

When the girls left the bar, three of them drunk, they each hugged Cameron a little tighter than normal. They begged her to promise their weekly happy hour would continue through the pregnancy and after, even if she needed a few weeks off when baby Cam arrived. Cameron smiled and promised, knowing how unrealistic that would be. Beth hugged her last. She had been silent most of the evening, sitting back as her friends gushed over Cameron. Cameron squeezed Beth's hand before turning around to leave. She knew Beth was unhappy. She knew Beth wanted what she had. Sometimes Cameron wanted to apologize to her, say sorry that her life seemed so perfect on the outside, tell her that everything isn't as it seems. That she also had hard times, but Cameron was a private person. She hadn't told the girls about using IVF to get pregnant. It was something she preferred to keep to herself.

Cameron took a cab home, feeling too tired to trek toward the subway. When she walked in the door, Andy was sitting on the couch with the TV on. He looked up at her, muting the TV as she came over to curl up next to him.

"How was it?" He kissed her head as she snuggled into his chest.

"Fun," Cameron beamed. Telling her friends gave her adrenaline, energy, made her feel ready to take on her new role as mom-to-be. But as fun as it was, this was Cameron's favorite part of the evening. Sitting at home. On the couch. Snuggling with Andy.

Chapter 7

June 13, 2013

"Are you going to ignore me the whole trip?" Andy was exasperated. Cameron didn't respond. She just looked out the window, studying the weeds on the side of the highway. They rented a car for a weekend getaway to the Hamptons. A last romantic trip as just a couple, a 'babymoon.' They were going to stay in a secluded bungalow near the beach. Sleep late. Eat out. And lounge on the sand.

"Cameron, come on," Andy pleaded with her. "I'm sorry I upset you."

That struck a chord with her. "You're sorry you upset me or sorry about what you said?"

"Both. Whatever will end this fight and let us enjoy the weekend."

"You don't understand," Cameron said. "For you, this pregnancy hasn't changed anything. You just get to have fun anticipating a baby for nine months."

"That's not true…"

"Wait," Cameron cut him off. "For me, it's changed everything. My body is totally different, I can't do a lot of the things I used to. I have to watch everything I eat and drink. I can't get comfortable to sleep. I have to think twice about every single thing I do. You have no idea what that's like."

"You're right," Andy said. "I don't. But I am trying to be helpful. I didn't mean to hurt your feelings. I was just saying, that maybe you should stop exercising. Give your body a break, you've been going through so much."

"Maybe you should stop watching football," Cameron shot back at him. Sometimes she knew when the hormones were taking over, but she couldn't back down now. Admitting she was overreacting was not an option. She had to keep going. "Exercising is the one thing I do for me. It helps me relax, isn't that what you want me to do? Relax? Imagine how stressed I would be if I stopped exercising!" She was on a roll now. "And just so you know, what I do now, is barely exercising! I run so slow that you could probably walk faster. But I have to do it for my sanity!"

"What if you trip and fall on your stomach?"

"I won't." Cameron looked back out the window. There were clouds in the distance. She hoped it wouldn't rain during their trip. She had just bought herself a few maternity bathing suits. When she was trying them on in the store, the saleswoman commented on her figure, guessing she was still in her first trimester. Cameron gleamed as she told her she was finishing her second.

Cameron knew she wouldn't stay mad. She just needed to be mad long enough to prove her point and then she would calm down and things would go back to normal. Andy was so patient, she really did know and appreciate that, but she wouldn't tell him. That would prove her anger was unfounded.

They stayed quiet the rest of the drive. After a few hours and several bathroom breaks, they pulled up at the bungalow. Andy parked and walked up to the small lockbox by the door. He punched in the code and opened it, pulling out the key. Then he quietly unpacked the car, bringing in their two small suitcases. Cameron watched him. She was wearing a fluttery blue dress, her hair pulled back into a short ponytail at the nape of her neck. She was sweating.

After a few deep breaths, she followed Andy into the bungalow. It was quaint. A living room with wooden floors and a small fireplace. A kitchen nook facing the ocean. A bedroom with a king-size bed and floor to ceiling windows. Cameron sat on the bed and watched as Andy silently put their suitcases down. He looked at her, not sure yet if the fight was over. She smiled at him, signaling that it was.

"So can we have make-up and vacation sex?" Andy came over and sat down on the bed next to her. She looked into his eyes, placing her hand on his cheek and kissing his lips. He gently undressed her and moved her back down on the bed.

"Even at seven months pregnant, you still have the most amazing body," Andy said when they finished, Cameron lying in the crook of his shoulder.

"It's even more amazing that my body is making person," Cameron joked back, knowing that wasn't what he meant. They lay there in bed, enjoying the rest of the afternoon, reminiscing about other 'lasts' they had. Their last night in Boston, before moving to New York. Their last night together before their wedding. Their last dinner before the IVF, which included more alcohol than was good for them. Now, their last trip before the baby.

"What do you think about Juliette?" Andy said. "For the baby."

"What? No," Cameron smiled.

"We need a strong name," Andy said. "Something beautiful, memorable."

"I want to name her after my grandmother," Cameron said. Her mother's mother had passed away a year ago from cancer. When she was sick, Cameron would call her every week to check in on her, tell her about her job, life in New York. "When are you and Andy going to start a family?" she would ask. Cameron always kept a stoic tone, responding that they would, some day. Now she was sorry her grandmother would never meet her great granddaughter.

"We can't name our daughter Esther," Andy said.

"No, but something that starts with an E," Cameron responded.

Chapter 8

September 24, 2013

It was 3:00 a.m. when Cameron looked at the clock next to her bed. She was three hours into her due date and there was no sign that the baby was coming. She didn't feel any different than she had the day before, or even the week before. She felt a little kick, the baby squirming around inside of her. "Go down," she whispered to her, putting her hands on her belly. Cameron craned her neck to see if Andy was awake. His eyes were closed, he was breathing heavily. In a deep sleep.

Cameron sighed. Everyone was always telling her "Rest now because you won't get any rest when the baby comes," but what horrible advice that was. Like rest was something you could stock up for a rainy day. And anyone who said that obviously didn't know what it was like to be nine months pregnant. Unable to sleep. The discomfort and anxiety keeping her up.

She hugged the long pillow that ran the length of her body in front of her. Sleeping on her side had been tough. She had slept on her stomach for the first few months, then moved to sleeping on her back. When that was no longer comfortable, she started having more restless nights. In the last week, it got worse. She was awake at night more than she was asleep. During the day, at every moment, she was anticipating the baby coming. Every time she stepped outside. Got in the shower. Went for a walk. This will be it, she thought, but it never was.

She wanted nothing more than to be post-delivery. To be a mom instead of being pregnant. Andy kept telling her to savor these last few days, the last days of quiet, he called them. Maybe for him they were quiet, but Cameron's mind was screaming.

3:12 a.m. Andy still wouldn't wake up for another four hours. Cameron turned to look at him. Sometimes she would sigh heavily when she couldn't sleep to see if that would wake him up. It was her way of pretending she didn't want to wake him. Sometimes it worked, and he would snuggle up to her and ask why she couldn't sleep. She sighed again. A little louder this time.

When Andy didn't stir, she decided to get up. She could go read or watch TV. She really had nothing to do. She had stopped working two weeks ago, hoping to get in some 'me' time and finish up last minute things on her to-do list, like set up the nursery. Get a few things in the house fixed. Buy any baby things they may have forgotten. Those last two weeks she was frantic to get everything done. She was up at 7:00 a.m. every day, out the door to run errands and then back to organize and clean.

Their apartment had two bedrooms. The second had previously been an office and workout room. It had a small desk and a treadmill. Now, the desk and treadmill had been replaced with a crib, closet, rocking chair, and small changing table. The walls were painted a light yellow and decorated with flowers and birds. Clothes were organized in the closet by size, newborn clothing on one shelf, 0-3 months next to it, 3-6 months on the shelf above. 6+ on the top shelf. Towels, sheets, blankets on the bottom. Everything had been laundered in baby-friendly detergent.

Cameron slipped out of bed, wrapping herself in her bathrobe—which she could no longer close around her—and walked to the baby room. She opened the closet and reviewed each shelf, checking that everything was in order. Most of the items she got as presents at her baby shower.

In July she had flown to Atlanta for a baby shower. Her mother and sister Alexa had planned it. The shower was small, just ten women including three of her mother's friends. The rest of the guests were Cameron's old friends from when she grew up. Since living in New York, Cameron hadn't been in close touch with many people from her childhood, but seeing them always brought them back together like no time had passed. There was Jen, who now had two children of her own, a girl, age three and a boy, just ten months. The other guests were Jessica, whose oldest was already seven; Sarah, whose twins were five; Naomi, who was pregnant with her third; and Hayley, who had two boys and her tubes tied. Cameron was the only one of her old group of friends who was not yet a mother. The girls gabbed about how magical her life was about to become, how she would completely change as a person. "Only the first three months are hard, after that, it becomes a real pleasure," Jessica said. "A big sister is the best, you're lucky to start with a girl," Naomi said. "You can't even imagine the love you will feel," Sarah said. Cameron smiled and accepted all the thoughts and advice, while on the inside she felt belittled by it. She beamed as she opened their presents and thanked each one of them, promising to send pictures the minute the baby was born. When she was on her flight back to New York, she finally felt like she could breathe again, take off the fake smile plastered on her face. They meant well, but after traveling down a very different path for the last ten years, Cameron felt like they lived in a distant world.

Cameron sat down in the rocking chair, placing her hands on her stomach. She hummed a quiet tune, rock-a-bye baby, while thinking about how morbid the lyrics were. *Rock-a-bye baby in the treetops, when the wind blows the cradle will rock, and when the bough breaks, the cradle will fall, and down will come baby, cradle and all...*

Why would mothers sing that? She would need to learn some more optimistic lullabies.

She must have dozed off in the chair, because the next thing she knew a ray of light was shining on her through the window and Andy was standing in the doorway, already in his suit. He had two cups of coffee in his hands. When she fluttered her eyes open, he handed one to her.

"I was wondering where you were when I woke up," he said. "Happy due date."

Cameron smirked.

"How about we go out tonight, one last date night?" he asked. Every time they went out now it was their 'last date night.' They had been saying that for weeks.

"Sure," she said, taking a sip of the coffee.

"I'll try to come home early today." Andy kissed her, finished his coffee, and headed out the door. Alone again, Cameron looked around the nursery, trying to think if there was anything missing. She had extra sheets for the crib, the bassinet, and the stroller. She had pacifiers, mobiles, stuffed bears. Receiving blankets, diapers, baby wipes, Desitin. Everything was ready. So why wouldn't the baby come already?

It was 8:00 a.m. Ten hours until Andy would come home. She pushed herself out of the rocking chair and waddled to the living room. She stretched out her yoga mat and sat down in Child's Pose. Her knees open wide on the mat, stomach falling between them, arms stretched out. She flowed through a few Warrior poses. Warrior One, her body facing forward, her arms up high. Warrior Two, her body opening to the side, arms stretched wide. She felt wobbly; her balance was off. She had cut back on exercising. Not because of her fight with Andy, but because it was becoming difficult. Instead of running, she now walked, and instead of strengthening her muscles with yoga, she focused on stretching.

8:20. She went to the kitchen and opened the fridge. She hadn't been eating much lately. Everything she put in her mouth made her feel uncomfortably full. Gave her heartburn. She grabbed a yogurt and a banana and ate them slowly while reading the news on her laptop. She still checked her Google Alerts, even though she wasn't working. She saw a review of Clarin's new strollers. The company was now called BabySafe and their strollers had a whole new look, very modern. Cameron had bought a different brand, even though she really liked the new look. She read the review, very positive. Good, hopefully the company would still be around when Cameron came back from maternity leave.

10:05. Cameron left the apartment to go for a walk. That was supposed to help induce labor, right? She walked to Central park and circled the bridle path. The weather was warm but not hot. A breeze blew through her hair, drying her sweat. She was constantly sweating now, no matter the weather. When she finished her circle, she started to jog on the way home. If walking wouldn't induce labor, maybe jogging would.

12:18. Cameron stopped in a nail salon. It was a good time to get a pedicure. She couldn't reach her toes, and who knew when would be the next time she would have nothing to do. She chose a nude color for her toes. That way, when it chipped it wouldn't be as noticeable.

1:22. Cameron stopped at the grocery store. She could stock up on things, but then she changed her mind. She didn't want to have to carry everything back to the apartment. Instead she just bought a bag of pretzels and a bottle of lemon-flavored water. She ate the pretzels as she continued to wander the streets.

Somehow, the shadows started to get longer, the air cooled as the afternoon started to fade into evening. Cameron had been out all day, zipping in and out of stores, through different neighborhoods. She turned to head back home, feeling rushed in case Andy would make it there before her. She didn't want to explain that she had been walking all day.

When she arrived, the apartment was still empty. A sigh of relief left her lips and she jumped into the shower to get ready for the 'last' date night. Soon she heard the door open and a few minutes later Andy joined her in the shower after stripping off his suit.

When they finished the shower, Cameron toweled off and examined herself in the mirror. Her belly button was almost inside out and a faint line appeared below it stretching down. This would be gone soon, she thought, as she moved to her closet to slip on a dress. Even her maternity dresses were starting to become tight.

Andy had made reservations at a Vietnamese restaurant nearby; one they had been wanting to try. It was a short walk, that Cameron waddled with Andy at her side. The restaurant was quiet, the food rich and the evening uneventful.

By the time they made it back to the apartment, Cameron was exhausted. She quickly brushed her teeth, took off her makeup, and put on her pajamas, hoping for a good night's sleep. She closed her eyes and hugged her body length pillow. When she opened her eyes, it was dark. 11:58, the clock said. Her due date was over.

Chapter 9

March 28, 2019

When I get home, I throw my keys onto the counter next to the picture of my daughter. She was four months old when the picture was taken. It's a close-up on her face. She's smiling, her eyes like crescent moons, totally oblivious to the circumstances around her. My daughter. I start to think what it means to be a daughter. Is it DNA? Is it the nine months when you nurture her in your womb? Or is it the moments you hold her, comfort her, tell her everything will be OK even when you know it won't?

Every time I look at her I feel a wave of sadness, loss. It's not her fault, the circumstances in which she came into this world. That her birth started a perpetual cycle of 'what-ifs' that never ends.

Now, I'm alone. I can be myself, let my feelings loose. I walk to my closet and move my mess of clothes aside. In the back corner is the box. I made the box when I was angry. When I first found out how cruel fate could be. Maybe I thought if I hid those things away, then I could pretend everything happened the way I wanted it to, the way it should have happened. And with the years, maybe I would continue pretending, and eventually my mind would forget and start believing that the way it should have happened were the real memories. But I know that's not possible.

I open the box. It's full of pictures. Memorabilia. The first picture is of me at the hospital, lying on my back, my huge stomach like a globe above me. My arms are up covering my face. The next picture is from the delivery room, just minutes after the baby was born. She's on my chest and I'm holding her as though I were afraid to break her. The next picture is of my husband holding her. His eyes sparkle at the camera. Back then, we didn't know what was coming. How everything would be turned upside down.

The box also has the hospital bracelet that was wrapped around the baby's ankle. It has my name on it, like she belonged to me. I finger the bracelet; it always mesmerizes me how small it is. Then I touch the hat the hospital gave us when we left. I suddenly feel anxious, afraid of getting sucked into the contents of the box, so I quickly close it and put back in the closet, moving my clothes to hide it.

They said parenting was hard. But the hard part isn't the nighttime feedings or the crying. The hard part is knowing that things could have been different. If only...

Chapter 10

October 4, 2013

"Why won't you help me!" Cameron screamed at Andy as the pain shot through her abdomen and around her back. The contractions were getting stronger now, the pain unlike anything she could have imagined. With each contraction—just about every five minutes—Cameron bent forward, grabbing on to the end of the bed in their hospital room. Andy rubbed her stomach and lower back, like their doula had taught them. When this contraction hit, Andy was sitting with his phone and hesitated a moment before coming to her.

"I'm sorry! I'm here," Andy yelled back, throwing his right hand on her tummy and his left on her back and quickly rubbing circles.

"Not like that! Slower! More gentle. No!" Cameron winced as she berated Andy's massaging. "It's over now, you can stop. Next time you have to help me!"

Cameron had been having contractions for almost twenty-four hours already. They started very delicately, a slight cramp in her lower abdomen, barely noticeable. She didn't even tell Andy about them until five hours had passed and she was sure about what was happening. She didn't want to excite him, or panic him, too early. She was sure labor would start somewhat dramatically. Like in the movies. Her water would break while she was at the supermarket and strangers would help her catch a cab to get Andy and zip to the hospital. Or the contractions would strike her like lightning, leaving no doubt that the baby was coming. But it wasn't like that. It happened so slowly, so gradually, that at first Cameron wasn't sure why people always talked about how painful childbirth was. But now, she was starting to understand.

The contractions had started in the late afternoon, while Cameron was walking in the park. Andy was still at work. When Cameron came home from her walk, she started to time them. At first eleven minutes apart. Then seven. Then back to twelve. Each lasting only ten to fifteen seconds.

Then Andy came home with takeout. They sat and ate it out of the carton boxes while talking about two of Andy's co-workers who had slept together and now made for a lot of interesting gossip. Every time a contraction came, Cameron subtly took out her phone and logged it in her app. Andy poked fun, asking what on her phone was more interesting than his office drama, but Cameron just smiled lightly and told him to continue. They cleaned up, sat in front of the TV for a while and then made their way to the bedroom.

"Tomorrow's the day," Cameron said.

"What's happening tomorrow?" Andy asked. They had been waiting so long that they had gotten used to the fact that the baby wasn't coming. It almost seemed more likely that things would continue as they were, Cameron pregnant, passed her due date.

"The baby!" Cameron laughed at Andy's surprise.

"What? How do you know?"

"I'm having contractions. Since this afternoon."

Andy's eyes grew wide. "Should we go to the hospital? Why didn't you tell me?"

"Not yet." Cameron promised herself she would stay calm when it happened. No need to go to the hospital too early. "I didn't want you to worry. There's still time."

They went to sleep, tried to at least. Another last for them, the last time they could sleep through the night. Cameron dozed, waking every once in a while when a contraction shocked her between REM cycles. In the morning, her contractions were still sporadic, not seeming to get any stronger or closer together.

Andy called in sick. It was a Friday, the slowest day of the week for him, anyway. It was a warm autumn day, so they went out for brunch, sitting at a small round table on the sidewalk outside a café. They sat silently, unsure of what to talk about. Talking about the baby seemed to raise panic between them, but everything else seemed too mundane a topic for such an occasion. "Are you ready to go to the hospital?" Andy asked when they finished eating.

"Not yet," Cameron said. The contractions were getting stronger, now consistently about six to seven minutes apart. "Let's go for a walk."

"A walk? How about we go home and rest?"

"We can rest after we walk."

Andy knew better than to argue. He walked next to her, maintaining her slow pace as they weaved toward the park. The walk took longer than normal, Cameron could feel herself getting slower, but she pressed on, thinking about the fact that walking could help the baby come quicker. It was early afternoon by the time they got home and Cameron finally said, "It's time."

Andy grabbed their hospital bag, which had been packed and sitting by the door for weeks, and flew out the door, running down the four flights of stairs to catch a cab. Cameron waddled out behind him and pressed the call button for the elevator. When Cameron walked out of the building, Andy ran to her, ushering her into the backseat of a cab. By then it was rush hour, Friday evening, when everyone was leaving work or trying to get out of the city.

Andy kept urging the cab driver to try different routes, try to get around someone, but it was no use. They would inch along until they made it to the hospital. By then, Cameron was in pain. Andy helped her out of the cab between contractions and threw two twenties at the driver without bothering to look at the meter. They went straight to the maternity ward—they remembered where it was from their tour of the hospital—and checked in. Cameron gave a urine sample and they were admitted to a room where a nurse came in to check her. "Three centimeters," the nurse said. "You still have a long way to go."

"That's not possible!" Cameron retorted. She was sure she was already at eight or nine. How could the pain get any worse?

"Do you want an epidural?" The nurse asked matter-of-factly, unsympathetic to the fact that Cameron was being ripped open from the inside. Cameron nodded, feeling disheartened. It could be hours. The nurse left the room, leaving Andy to comfort Cameron.

Andy took out his cellphone and snapped a picture of Cameron lying on the bed. "What are you doing!?" she screamed as she looked up at him.

"Don't you want to be able to show this to our daughter one day? What you went through for her?" Andy started a video. "Tell her something."

Cameron covered her face and Andy pointed the camera at his. "Hey little peanut! We can't wait to meet you! Your mommy isn't feeling so well right now, but it will be worth it when she sees you!" He clicked the camera off and looked at Cameron, who had now gotten up and was pacing the room. Her contractions were getting stronger and somehow it seemed logical that yelling at Andy would make the pain go away.

"Where is the anesthesiologist!?" Cameron screamed after the last contraction when Andy hesitated with his phone.

"I'll go look for him," Andy suggested, slipping out the door. Cameron could hear him trying to sound calm as he urged the nurses to get Cameron an epidural as soon as possible. He came back a few moments later, assuring her he was on the way.

"I need it before the next contraction," Cameron said desperately. "That's in three minutes." But it wasn't three minutes. The contractions were getting closer and closer together. With each one, Cameron yelled at Andy that he had exactly two minutes to find the anesthesiologist and drag him to their room. It seemed, to Cameron, that it was hours before the anesthesiologist waltzed into the room.

"How are we doing today?" he asked nonchalantly as he started to set up the needle for the epidural.

"Not so good," Andy said. "She's in a lot of pain."

"Well that's what I am here for. Where are you guys from?"

"Here, Manhattan," Andy responded.

"No, like where are you from originally? Most people aren't from Manhattan," the anesthesiologist seemed more interested in small talk than doing his job.

"Can you please just give me the epidural," Cameron whined to him. She was struck by the sound of her voice, so cantankerous.

"I need you to sit down and don't move," the anesthesiologist said. "Even if you are having a contraction, don't move at all." With a swift movement the epidural was in and Cameron instantly felt a wave of relief. She lay down on her back and closed her eyes. She couldn't sleep but she rested. The pain of the contractions didn't disappear, but it was dulled. Instead of writhing with pain, Cameron breathed through each one, letting is pass through her. Every so often a nurse would come and check her. After the epidural she was at six centimeters, and then at seven, then eight. At some point, Cameron lost track of time, she didn't know if she had been laying there minutes or days.

Dr. Lee's appearance startled Cameron. "Are you ready to have a baby?" the ob-gyn said as she checked Cameron's opening. "Ten centimeters dilated, it's time to get this baby out." Cameron squeezed Andy's hand as she pushed. She pushed with every part of her body, with her stomach, her shoulders, her eyes. She pushed until she felt the doctor slide the baby out of her and place it on her stomach. Cameron gasped as she looked down and saw the purple little thing wriggling on her stomach. She felt the slimy hands and feet rub her skin as the baby took its first few breaths.

"Look at her!" Andy said. "She's so perfect! Can you believe it?"

Cameron cried. Her second happy cry. She held the baby on her stomach, unable to stop the sobs escaping from her throat.

Chapter 11

October 5, 2013

After the baby was born and Cameron held her on her stomach, the nurse took her and cleaned her up, weighed her, pricked her heel to get a blood sample, and swaddled her before returning her to Cameron to hold. Cameron cradled the little bundle in her arms, mesmerized by her little eyes, nose, and her tongue which she kept sticking out of her mouth. It was two in the morning when the baby arrived, and while Cameron was exhausted, she wanted to hold her for a little while before she would hand her off to the nurses and sleep. She couldn't believe that little thing came out of her, that it was alive, a new person in the world. She and Andy marveled at the baby for an hour before Andy recommended they try to sleep. "We have the rest of our lives to hold her," he said. "Let's let the nurses take her for a little bit."

Cameron didn't have the energy to disagree. She was still in the bed, her legs a little numb from the epidural, and she allowed the nurse to take the baby to the nursery while she and Andy tried to get some sleep. When Cameron woke up, Andy was sitting in the chair in their room with two coffees and a bag of croissants. Cameron hadn't realized how hungry she was until she smelled the warm butter. She eagerly ate one while slurping down her coffee. "Not so fast, speed racer," Andy joked. But Cameron was in a hurry. She wanted to go to the nursery and pick up their daughter.

Cameron wanted to stand up. She motioned to Andy to help her—she still felt wobbly—and leaned on his arm as she pulled herself out of the bed. She continued to hold on to Andy's hand as they walked out of the room through the corridor to the nursery, where newborns were lined up neatly in rows.

"Do you recognize which one is ours?" Andy asked, smiling at her. Cameron looked down the rows and felt a pang of sadness when she realized she couldn't. She felt lost in the nursery, like she didn't belong. An imposter who wasn't really a mother.

"It's OK," a nurse said, coming up behind her. "Most parents can't tell which baby is theirs right away. But your name is written on their bassinets and on their armband and ankle band. What is your name?"

"Cameron Stevens."

The nurse smiled as she pointed the couple to a baby in the third row. Cameron and Andy weaved through the babies, making their way to the bassinet. The baby was sleeping, her eyes closed peacefully. She had short blonde hair on her head, which felt like peach fuzz as Cameron rubbed her hand on it. The baby's tiny hands were down by her sides, closed in tight fists, and her legs splayed open creating a tiny diamond between them. On the card inserted on the end of the bassinet, it said:

Mother's name: Cameron Stevens

Baby's birthdate: Oct. 5, 2013, 2:04 am

Baby's birthweight: 6 lbs 4 oz

Blood type: B-

At first Cameron didn't think anything of it. She continued to stare at the sleeping baby, she was so still it was almost scary. "Can you believe it?" she asked Andy, seeing that he was also mesmerized by her.

"I can," he said. "I knew we would get here one day. Even when you thought you'd never get pregnant. I knew you would."

What Cameron said next, she would never know why she asked it, why the thought came into her head. Why she needed to know right then. "Andy, what blood type are you?"

"A positive," he responded, still looking at the baby. "Same as you."

"Are you sure?"

"Of course I'm sure, every time I donate blood they check it and tell me," he said.

"Is it weird that we have the same blood type and the baby has a different blood type?"

"We're in a hospital, why don't we just ask one of the nurses," Andy suggested and motioned to a nurse in the room. The nurse came over to them, a smile plastered on her face.

"We just have a general medical question," Andy started. "Let's say two parents have the same blood type, A positive. What blood type could their baby have?"

"Well, if they are both A positive, the blood type would be A or O. Positive or negative."

"Not B negative?"

"No, that wouldn't be possible."

"So I think they may have been a mistake with the blood test of our daughter," Andy said, pointing out the blood type on the baby's bassinet. "We're both A positive."

"Hm," the nurse looked at the card on the bassinet, studying it with her eyes. "We can do another test to be sure." The nurse walked away, coming back a moment later with a small needle. She removed the baby's pants, sanitized one heel with a piece of gauze and pricked the heel, taking just a small amount of blood. The prick woke the baby, making her eyes burst open and a weak cry escape her mouth.

"Oh, no, my baby," Cameron whined, holding on to her hand. "Poor thing." When the nurse went away, Cameron lifted the baby from her bassinet, hugged her to her chest and started rocking her. Her cries became fainter and soon stopped. Andy looked at the baby and at Cameron. He was silent. "I'm sure it was a mistake," Cameron said, although she was also worried about the blood test. The results would come back in a few hours, the nurse said, leaving Cameron and Andy to sit with the baby and wait.

"I should try to feed her," Cameron said. She put the baby back in the bassinet and wheeled it out of the nursery, down the corridor back to their room, where she lifted the baby to her chest and tried to get her to latch on to her breast. Andy had followed her back in silence and sat quietly watching Cameron struggle to get comfortable and get the baby to eat. "I can't tell if there is anything coming out," she said to Andy, but his blank stare made her understand that he was somewhere else. Probably tired, she thought, deciding to just let him be. She focused on the baby, who had wrapped her lips on Cameron's nipple, but seemed to be sleeping. Cameron tried to nudge her awake. She didn't know how much the baby needed to eat or whether she had eaten anything at all. I'll try again later, she thought, and placed the baby back in the bassinet. The couple sat in silence; Cameron didn't know what to say, she could feel the tension in the room rising, she knew Andy's mind was racing. But she had to stay calm.

An hour later, the baby woke up and Cameron again tried to feed her. When the baby latched on and began to suck, there was a knock on the door. Andy got up to open it and a nurse stepped in.

"Hi, I just wanted to bring you the results from the blood test we just ran," she said. "The baby's blood type is B negative."

"You see, that's not possible," Andy said. "We're both A positive."

"Are you sure?" the nurse said, reviewing the chart that was tucked in the box in the room's doorway. "I see Cameron's blood type is A positive. How about we do a blood test for you?"

"Sure," Andy said. "But I am A positive."

The nurse stepped out and came back wheeling a small cart. She tied a rubber band around Andy's arm and cleaned the inside of his elbow before sticking a needle into his vein. She drew a small vial of blood and promised to return as soon as she could with the results. Cameron could feel Andy about to explode. Whenever he was angry or upset about something, he would purse his lips. He started shaking his leg, and his eyes narrowed as he focused on the empty bassinet.

"She's not our baby." His voice was cold. "Something must have happened. Maybe they switched her in the nursery. Remember how you couldn't recognize her when we went in? They must have switched her."

"How could that happen?" Cameron responded. "They put the bracelet on her leg in front of us. See? It says here, Cameron Stevens." She pointed out the hospital bracelet on the baby's leg. Andy breathed out heavily and a silence fell over the room. Cameron continued to hold the baby to her breast and Andy started pacing around the room.

Later, the nurse came back with Andy's blood test. "You're A positive," she said, confirming what the couple already knew. "Did you use any assisted reproductive technology to get pregnant?"

"IVF," Andy said, raising his hand to his head. "I'm going to kill them."

Part 2

"A mother's joy begins when new life is stirring inside... when a tiny heartbeat is heard for the very first time, and a playful kick reminds her that she is never alone."

– Author unknown

Chapter 12

January 4, 2013

"Can you turn that thing off?" Avery snapped when Graham's cellphone rang for the fifth time.

"I am sorry, it's Aiden this time," Graham said, checking the phone. "Maybe I should answer it."

Avery and Graham didn't often leave their two boys home alone, but they were in a pinch. They only scheduled this appointment a few days ago and were unable to find someone to come over. They didn't need a babysitter, the boys were eight and twelve already, but leaving them home alone was a gamble. Last time they did it, Aiden had toilet-papered the living room and Maddox graffitied his name all over the walls.

"Hello?" Graham answered. Then paused. "In the cupboard. Middle shelf on the right." He then hung up the phone. "He wanted to know if we had any more pretzels."

Avery rolled her eyes and smiled. "I knew it wasn't an emergency."

The couple was waiting in the dark room, Graham by the door—he would have been pacing if there was more space—fidgeting with the change in his pocket, and Avery lying on her back on the bed. She checked her watch, ticking her tongue at the time. "I still need to make it to the grocery store today," she said when Dr. Klein walked in.

"How are we doing today?" He asked the couple as he sat down in front of Avery and turned on the screen in front of her.

"We're great, doctor," Avery said hurriedly.

A nurse then entered the room, carrying a small tray with three petri dishes. She set the petri dishes down and looked at the label. "Can you tell me your name and birthdate please?" she asked.

"Avery Stephens. November 22nd, 1974."

"Stephens..." the nurse repeated slowly as though she was having difficulty reading the label. "All right."

"We have three embryos here," the doctor said as he slid the first one on to the microscope. Immediately a quivering blob appeared on the screen. "Since you are a little older, I recommend we transfer two, just to increase the chances that one will take. Worst case scenario, you have twins."

"Sure doctor, whatever you say," Avery said. "Just do what you need to do."

"This one looks good," Dr. Klein said. "It has twelve cells already. Pretty impressive for three days. Let's see how the others did."

Avery looked at Graham, whose hands were in the pockets of his brown corduroy pants. She could hear the jingle of the change in his pocket. The doctor slid the second petri dish onto the microscope. "Also twelve cells! You have very healthy embryos." Next, he moved the third dish onto the microscope. "Wow, ten cells. We don't usually see such fast-growing embryos with people your age. This is very good."

A smile started to grow on Avery's face. She suddenly felt proud of her embryos, growing so fast just days after her eggs were retrieved from her uterus and combined with Graham's sperm. "Of course they're growing fast! They want to join our family!" she laughed.

"They sure do," Dr. Klein said. "We're going to transfer the two twelve-cell embryos." The doctor took the petri dish off the microscope and inserted the two chosen embryos into a catheter. In the meantime, the nurse squirted gel onto Avery's stomach and rubbed the wand on the gel. Immediately her uterus appeared on the screen. Avery felt the catheter being inserted into her and on the screen they saw it approach her uterus. Suddenly, the two embryos jumped from the catheter into the uterus lining.

"Look at them go!" Avery said, her eyes wide. "Graham, did you see that?"

"Sure did, amazing little buggers."

The nurse and doctor left the room, telling Avery to stay lying on her back for the next fifteen minutes. After that, they were free to go. In ten days, she would return for her pregnancy test.

"Ugh, I hope this works," Avery said, letting out a huge sigh. She was already thirty-eight and really wanted a baby girl. This would probably be her last chance, she thought. Thirteen years ago, when she got pregnant with Aiden, she would have laughed if someone had told her she would be in fertility treatment. Aiden was an accident; she and Graham had only been dating for a few months when she found out she was pregnant. Hell, she wouldn't even have called it dating. But Graham, ever the chivalrous gentleman, insisted they get married. She remembered telling him about the pregnancy. It was late one evening, he came to meet her when she got off work. She walked out of the restaurant, still smelling like the fries she had been serving all night, and there was Graham, sitting on the curb reading The New Yorker. She gave him a light kick to get his attention, he looked up at her and removed his glasses.

"I'm pregnant, you fucker," she screamed at him, blaming him for what happened. She was on the pill, and she took it almost every day. He scrambled to get up, almost tripping on the curb.

"What? That...that is wonderful." He gasped.

"I'm getting an abortion," Avery told him. "You have to pay for it. I hope your NYU salary can take care of that!"

"No," he said, almost like a prayer. "This is amazing. Let's have a baby. You would be a great mom."

"Please," Avery responded. "You don't even know me."

The next afternoon, Graham showed up at Avery's apartment—the first time he had been there in daylight. She was on her way out, she had another evening shift at the restaurant, and when she opened the door, Graham knelt down on one knee and held out a shiny ring. One that he had probably bought from a street vendor in Washington Square Park. He was a first-year literature professor at NYU, which meant his salary was barely enough to live in New York, let alone buy a ring.

At first, Avery brushed by him, calling him crazy, out-of-his-mind, and a few other things, but then she thought, why not? He was different than every other guy she had ever been with. For starters, he had an 'adult' job, one with a salary instead of shifts. He also had a college degree, a few degrees even.

Graham followed her down the stairs of her fourth-floor walkup. By the time they got out to the street, Avery agreed. She figured they would probably get divorced—most couples seemed to—so why not. It wasn't permanent, she had nothing to lose.

A month later, they were at city hall in Manhattan. Avery wore a white bohemian dress she bought at Forever 21 the day before and Graham wore his only suit. It was a little wide in the shoulders, long in the sleeves, but he looked good in it, Avery thought. Afterwards, they sat in Battery Park and ate hot dogs.

At first, Avery kept living in her apartment. Sure they were married, and having a baby, but did she have to live with him? She stayed in her fourth-floor walkup with her two roommates, until it started getting difficult for her to walk up and down the stairs. Then, Graham convinced her to move into his apartment—in Brooklyn. At first Avery scoffed at Williamsburg, complaining about living off the island, but she soon realized his Brooklyn apartment was closer to her job than her Manhattan apartment.

It wasn't easy getting to know each other with Avery's hormones raging. Avery seemed to go from elated to completely desolate in seconds, but Graham was patient and did everything he could to keep her comfortable. When Avery got to seven months, he convinced her to quit working at the restaurant and he started tutoring failing students to make ends meet.

When Avery had the baby—Aiden James they called him—Graham cancelled all his classes for two weeks to stay home with her and help. Avery cried constantly— more than the baby—she hated Graham for convincing her to have it, and she hated herself even more for being so easily convinced that they could raise a child. Why didn't she have the abortion, she thought daily. Then one day, when Graham was home taking care of the baby, Avery woke up from a nap and walked into their living to see Graham cradling the baby in his arms and singing to him. He wasn't singing a lullaby or a nursery rhyme, he was singing Backstreet Boys, of all things. Avery burst into laughter, startling Graham, who looked up at her with a big smile on his face. It was at that moment that Avery first felt love for Graham. That she first felt like everything would be all right.

From there, things changed. She, Graham, and Aiden became a family. Three years later, they decided to have another child. Avery became pregnant easily—the first month they tried—and nine months later Maddox was born. Avery had been hoping for a girl and they agreed to keep trying until her dream came true. For some reason, when they decided to try again Avery had a hard time getting pregnant. They tried for two years, and finally she got pregnant, but two months later she miscarried. A year later, she had a second miscarriage. They continued trying, but she just didn't get pregnant. They agreed to try IVF as a last resort.

When fifteen minutes had passed, Avery got up from the bed and put her clothes back on.

"Do you think the house is still standing?" she laughed as she grabbed Graham's hand on the way out of the clinic. "Or we'll come home to a huge pillar of smoke?"

"Definitely smoke," Graham laughed back. "Unless there were enough pretzels to keep them busy."

Chapter 13

January 14, 2013

Avery didn't need an alarm clock to wake up. Every weekday she was up at 6:30 to make lunch and breakfast for the boys. She quietly slid out of bed, careful not to wake Graham whose snoring had become endearing. She went into the bathroom and pulled her fluffy blond hair back, securing it with a scrunchy she'd probably had for longer than she had been a mother. Two minutes to brush her teeth and another to wash her face, and she was on the way downstairs to the kitchen.

She set out three brown paper bags, labeled each one, and toasted six slices of whole wheat bread. Three turkey sandwiches, Graham's with lettuce, tomato, and mayo, Aiden's with lettuce and mustard, and one plain, just turkey and bread, for Maddox. She cut off the crust on Maddox's sandwich, and wrapped each one in wax paper and then tin foil before slipping them into the brown paper bags. Each bag got an apple, washed and wrapped in a paper towel. Then Avery went to the cupboard to look around. She usually gave them pretzels, or a granola bar, but today she grabbed chocolate chip cookies, making three Ziploc bags with three cookies each. It was Graham's first day back after winter break, and hell, it was a big day for Avery also. The boys deserved to be spoiled a little bit, even Graham, although he was starting to get a little soft around the middle. With the cookies in the bags, she took a stack of sticky notes and a pen. *Hope you're having a great day!* she wrote on one and slipped it into Aiden's bag.

Don't forget to smile! she wrote on Maddox's post-it. *Wish me luck*, was the note for Graham.

With the lunches made and set by the door, she went back upstairs to the boys' room. She gently opened the door, letting some light in to the dark room. The boys were both in a deep sleep in their two twin beds, Aiden with one arm and leg hanging off the side and Maddox curled up on his side. This was a precious moment every day for Avery; she loved watching them sleep. She stood for a moment in the doorway—the calm before the storm—and then walked through the room to the window, pulling the shade and letting the sunshine in.

"Moooooooooommm," Aiden yelled stuffing his head under his pillow.

"Good morning," she said in an upbeat tone, one she too would have hated at 7:00 a.m. when she was their age. "Time to get up for school." Maddox stirred, turning over onto his other side. Avery went to Aiden's bed, pulling his New York Knicks comforter off him. "Aiden, it's your turn to choose breakfast, what do you want?"

"Pancakes."

"Again!" Maddox apparently was awake.

"I like pancakes!"

"Maddox, tomorrow you can decide," Avery said. "Hurry up and come downstairs." She left the boys to get ready and hurried back down the stairs to get the pancakes started. The boys came down and each sat at their respective spot at the kitchen table. Avery had already set each one a glass of orange juice, syrup, and a bowl of grapes. She brought them their pancakes, hot from stove.

"Anything going on at school today?" she asked, sitting down to watch them eat. She grabbed a grape from Maddox's bowl.

"No," Aiden said.

"Maddox, I know you have a math test this week, we can study together after school," Avery said. He hadn't been doing so well in math.

"I don't need to study," Maddox answered.

"You said that last time and you brought home a C."

The boys gobbled up their breakfast—too fast, Avery thought, as though they wanted to minimize quality time with their mom in the morning. Then, they grabbed their lunches and their backpacks and headed out the door. Their schools were next to each other and Aiden always dropped his brother off at the elementary school before going to middle school.

With the boys gone, Avery put on a pot of coffee and took out her laptop to check her orders. She already knew she had a busy day; she had several orders she needed to drop off at the post office and she needed to get more supplies. When Avery stopped working at the restaurant at seven months pregnant with Aiden, she needed something to fill her time. She started making jewelry, just for herself and for friends, something to keep her occupied. She kept getting compliments; people on the street would ask her where she got her necklace or her earrings, so she decided she wanted to start selling them. She remembered how afraid she was to tell Graham—she needed his money to buy supplies for the jewelry; she hadn't been good at saving. She was sure Graham would tell her it was just a hobby and she should just continue making for herself—especially because he was also tight on money—but he surprised her. He loved the idea, called her an "entrepreneur" and told her he considered the money an investment. She didn't know where he got the money for the investment—she didn't ask when money came her way back then—but she used it wisely, buying beads, hooks, chains, and other pieces she needed. He helped her set up an online store on Etsy and she was in business. At first it was slow, but after a few years it became profitable. Now, thirteen years later, she was getting tens of orders daily and barely had enough time to make the jewelry to fill her orders. She wasn't going to pay their mortgage with the business, but it did give them some wiggle room. In fact, it was what paid for the IVF treatment. One of the reasons she wanted a daughter so badly was so she would have someone to share her business with. She imagined sitting at home on Saturdays, teaching her daughter how to make the different pieces she sold. Her daughter would love it and even come up with her own designs, which Avery was sure would be best sellers.

Avery did receive a few new orders overnight. She took note of the pieces she needed to make, planning when she would get around to them. A few minutes later, Graham came down the stairs. He was wearing a blue plaid button-down shirt and khaki pants, his curly hair still looking like he just got out of bed. He poured himself a cup of coffee and sat down at the kitchen table next to Avery. He looked especially tired for someone who just woke up.

"Ready for today?" he asked. The night before, Avery reminded him that today she would be taking her pregnancy test. When she said it, Graham reacted like he had completely forgotten that they were doing IVF. Avery couldn't blame him; she knew he has been stressed at work. At the beginning of the school year in September, Graham had been appointed head of the literature department at NYU. At the time, they rejoiced at the huge promotion—it was quite a prestigious position—but Graham soon realized the prestige came with a lot of headaches. Professors complaining about having to teach general education classes, teaching assistants who seemed to disappear into thin air, and endless interviews of PhD candidates. But Graham invested his all in the position, ensuring he still always had time for students who took his seminars. At least as the department head, he could teach anything he wanted. He liked to teach graduate level seminars—those students were actually interested in literature and often had intelligent things to say.

"Yup," Avery said abruptly.

"Whatever it is, our family is perfect," Graham said as he stood up, kissed Avery's head and put his mug in the sink. "Let me know how it goes." He grabbed his lunch, giving Avery a small nod of thanks and went out the door.

Avery went back to checking her Etsy account. She had a few messages to respond to and wanted to update some of the pictures of the pieces she was selling. When she finished, she cleaned all the dishes stacked up around the sink and went back to their master bedroom to get dressed. A pair of old jeans and a baggy sweater. She didn't have time to think about what she wore. Then she was out the door. She would first go to the fertility clinic to take the pregnancy test, then she would head downtown to the Garment District to visit her jewelry supplier. Hopefully she would make it home in time before the boys came back from school.

It was a long ride on the subway to get to Manhattan. She had to take the J/Z train and then switch to the 6 once she got to Manhattan. Poor Graham did the commute every day. But it was a small price to pay in order to live in a house instead of in an overpriced, tiny apartment. Their first apartment together in Williamsburg was so close to Manhattan, that it didn't seem like the end of the world to Avery to live there. Once she was pregnant with Maddox, they decided they couldn't raise two boys in their one-bedroom apartment—it was tight enough already with a three-year-old running around. So they moved deeper into Brooklyn, finding a small three-bedroom house in

Highland Park. By then, Graham had gotten tenure at NYU, and saved just enough for a down payment. They moved in a month before Maddox was born.

Avery sat on an orange subway seat and put her earphones in. She started listening to the soundtrack of the play *Rent*. She liked listening to musicals and singing along. On her and Graham's first wedding anniversary he took her to her first Broadway show, *Chicago*. It was the first time they had gotten a babysitter and been alone together since Aiden was born.

Today she couldn't focus on what she was listening to. She was zoned out, so much so that she was surprised when she arrived at the fertility clinic for her blood test. She walked in, checked in with the receptionist and followed the nurse into a patient room. The nurse drew her blood and said the doctor would call her as soon as they got the results. Avery was out the door less than twenty minutes after she arrived. She then hopped back on the subway for her next stop, spending a few hours with her supplier ordering pieces they didn't have in stock and grabbing a few things that were available in the shop. She was back on the subway by 2:00 p.m. It was a gamble whether she would make it home by three when the boys got off school. Hopefully she would be there by 3:30 and meet them at home. She usually greeted them with bagel bites or chicken tenders for their after-school snack.

She got lucky with the trains and was opening her front door at 2:58 p.m. when her cellphone rang. Still standing on her porch, she rummaged through her purse and pulled out her phone. "Hello?"

"Avery, it's Dr. Klein. Congratulations, you're pregnant."

Chapter 14

February 7, 2013

7:12. Avery startled when she looked at the clock. How was she still asleep? Walking up at 6:30 had been getting harder. Maybe it's time to set an alarm clock, she thought. She was seven weeks pregnant and already feeling sluggish and tired all the time. She knew she needed to jump out of bed, she had lunches to make, the boys to wake up, not to mention a huge order that came in through Etsy a few days ago that she needed to fill. But she stayed still, another moment. Then, with a deep breath, she dragged herself up, sitting hunched over on the side of the bed for a second before pulling herself the rest of the way up.

She quickly threw her hair back into a ponytail, brushed her teeth, and washed her face. Then, before going downstairs she hopped over to the boys' room to wake them up. "Rise and shine!" she said as she drew the curtains. "We're running late today, so you need to get up quickly." The boys groaned in unison. "Come on, no time for this today." Avery walked to each bed, giving each boy a little shake before turning to step out of the room.

"Wait! Mom, it's my turn to pick breakfast," Maddox whined when Avery was in the doorway. Right, she forgot.

"Sure, honey, what do you want?" She looked at him, pleading in her head that he would choose something simple.

"Can we have waffles?"

"Eggo OK?"

"Sure."

Great, Avery sighed with relief and bolted down the stairs. She grabbed three brown paper bags and made three turkey sandwiches, filling the bags with an apple and a small bag of pretzels. Then she grabbed the waffles from the freezer and popped a few in the toaster. When the boys came down, she served them their breakfast, taking one waffle for herself. She was hungry.

The boys were out the door quickly, leaving Avery alone in the kitchen. She made a pot of coffee and sat at the kitchen table. She had about an hour until she had to leave for the doctor appointment. Today was her first ultrasound and Avery was nervous. By now, the fetus (or fetuses because they inserted two embryos) would have a heartbeat. They would be about the size of a blueberry already.

Soon Graham came downstairs and poured himself a cup of coffee. He didn't have any classes that morning and wouldn't go to the university until later. "How are you feeling?" He asked, munching on a half-eaten waffle sitting on the table.

"Good, tired." Avery said. "What if it's twins?" She was afraid of twins. There were so many complications, so much risk. After having two miscarriages, all she wanted was one healthy fetus, one that would kick and grow until it would join their family.

"We'll manage," Graham said. He didn't understand her fear, she thought. He thought she was worried about dealing with two newborns, not the high-risk pregnancy. They never knew why Avery miscarried twice. The first one happened when she was twenty-one weeks—more than halfway. Everything seemed fine, she felt the baby's kicks like bubbles blowing in her stomach, and then one day she didn't feel them. They went to the doctor for an emergency checkup—they were sure everything was fine, but why not go settle their nerves? The doctor tried to calm them, telling them that sometimes babies are more active and sometimes they rest; it was hard to feel them anyways at this stage, depending on their position. Then the doctor squirted the ultrasound gel on Avery's stomach and searched around for the fetus. It was there alright—but there was no heartbeat. A few days later, the doctor performed the procedure to take out the dead fetus. It was a girl. Avery cried for weeks.

The second miscarriage was more dramatic. At ten weeks, Avery woke up one morning in a pool of blood. Graham rushed her to the hospital, but there was nothing they could do. They took out the fetus, again leaving Avery feeling empty. And guilty—like she killed the two babies. What was wrong with her that she couldn't carry a baby to term? Especially after having two healthy pregnancies with her boys.

"Don't worry," Graham said, waking her from her daze. "Everything will be alright." He rubbed her back and massaged her shoulders. She hoped he was right; she couldn't handle losing another baby.

After they finished their coffee, Avery took all the dishes to the sink. "I'll clean today," Graham said as he kissed her forehead. "You just sit and relax." Avery didn't argue. She knew when to accept a little help.

She went upstairs to get dressed. Some of her clothes were already getting a little tight on her. Pregnancy at age thirty-eight just wasn't the same as pregnancy at twenty-five, nor was a fifth pregnancy the same as a first. Avery had always been a little curvy, she had wide hips, large breasts, but she was never fat. In her twenties she had a body that could get her anything she wanted, all she had to do was open the top button of her blouse. It was why she was always the best tipped waitress at the restaurant she worked at.

During her first pregnancy she didn't start showing until she was already three months. Even then, she didn't look pregnant, so much as she looked like she had just started to let herself go. She was six months pregnant before strangers felt comfortable enough to ask her about it. After Aiden was born, she bounced back quickly, wearing her pre-pregnancy clothes in just two months. With her second pregnancy, she started gaining weight a little earlier, and there were a few pounds she never took off. But she accepted it. She thought her body was always perfect—it got her exactly what she wanted before she got pregnant, and after it gave her exactly what she wanted with her family. So what if she wasn't sexy like she once was?

Now, seven weeks into this pregnancy, she felt bloated, like her stomach was already starting to puff out. Time to start wearing stretchy pants—until she was ready to unbox her maternity clothes. She pulled on a pair of leggings and threw on a large sweater and headed downstairs. They were ready to go.

The couple hopped in their car—Graham drove—and went to their doctor's office. Avery was relieved they no longer had to trek to Manhattan for appointments at the fertility clinic. They chose that clinic because of its great recommendations and success rate, but it was a hassle to go back and forth. Now she was under the care of her regular ob-gyn, just a ten-minute drive from their house.

At the doctor's office they checked in with the receptionist and were immediately brought into one of the patient rooms. A nurse came in to check Avery's blood pressure and weight and told them the doctor would be with them shortly. A few minutes later, Dr. Walker came in. He greeted them politely, asking Avery if she had any pain or felt anything unusual. He was the same doctor she had been seeing for years—the same one who cared for her during her two miscarriages. She told him she had been tired, more so than with the other pregnancies, but he didn't appear to be concerned. He just asked her to lay back for the ultrasound.

Avery complied, placing her feet in the stirrups in front of her. The doctor squirted the gel on her stomach and soon they could see her uterus on a small screen.

"Here we are," the doctor said. Suddenly a pulsing sound came through the ultrasound machine. "That's the heart. Very strong heartbeat."

Avery felt relief. A heartbeat. The doctor continued to study the fetus for a few moments before pulling the wand off Avery's stomach. "Everything looks good," he said.

"It's just one?" Avery asked.

"Yes, just one," Dr. Walker responded.

Avery finally felt like she could stop holding her breath. She smiled and grabbed Graham's arm. "It's just one!" she repeated and started to laugh.

"We'll see you again in eight weeks for the next ultrasound," Dr. Walker said before he walked out of the room.

"Graham! I was so worried!" Avery said, still laughing. It was something she did when she felt uncomfortable or relieved. Graham chuckled; her laugh was contagious. The couple returned home and said goodbye to each other. Graham had a lot of work to do at the university and Avery had a lot of jewelry pieces to put together. When Avery was alone in the house, she went upstairs to one of the bedrooms which had become her studio. It had a square table in the middle with all the tools she needed: wire cutters, round- and flat-nose pliers, crimp pliers, needles, and even a magnifying glass—her eyes just weren't what they used to be. Along the wall she had several sets of drawers organized with beads, wires, chains, clasps, earrings, and types of adhesives. As she sat down to get to work, she wondered what they would do when the baby would need its own room. She would have to get rid of her studio.

When Avery got in the zone, she didn't notice the time pass. She could work for hours without moving, without eating or going to the bathroom. That's what happened to her today, she was so focused on her jewelry that she was startled when she heard a knock on the open door.

"Mom?" Maddox said quietly. Avery jumped. She hadn't heard the boys come home. She didn't realize how long she had been working.

"Hi honey, how was school?"

"It was OK," Maddox said. "Mom, is everything alright?"

Avery was struck by his question. Did he suspect something was not alright? They hadn't told the boys about the pregnancy; they didn't want to say anything until they felt more comfortable that Avery wouldn't miscarry.

"Of course honey, why do you ask?"

"You didn't put a note in my lunch today," Maddox said. "I wanted to make sure you were OK."

Sweet Maddox, Avery thought. They would have to tell the boys soon.

Chapter 15

March 26, 2013

"Be a girl, be a girl," Avery said, standing in front of her mirror with her hands on her stomach. For the last few weeks she had been doing this every morning. She knew it wouldn't make a difference—but some superstitious part of her thought it might.

The boys were on spring break, so she didn't need to get them up for school that morning. She let them sleep in, watch a little TV in the morning and then she wanted to take them out for some fun. Quality time before the baby was born. She promised she would take them to Coney Island this week—they went together every spring break. But later in the week; today, she had a doctor's appointment. She would find out the sex of the baby.

A month ago, Avery and Graham sat the boys down one Saturday after breakfast and told them about the baby. Avery started with "we have a surprise for you!" and both boys grinned each imagining what the surprise could be. Neither were prepared to hear what came out of Avery's mouth next.

"You're getting a little brother or sister," she said, watching both boys' mouths drop open. It wasn't the type of surprise they were hoping for, Avery knew, but she wanted them to see a new sibling as a good thing. Something that would make their family better.

"Your mom could use a little help these days," Graham said. "We would both really appreciate it if you could chip in more around the house. The pregnancy has been tough on your mother."

The boys smiled, agreeing that they would do what they could. They would keep their room clean, try to listen better. Avery smiled, hoping those commitments would last longer than a week. And they did. While Avery still had to remind them sometimes, the boys cleaned they room, picked up around the living room and kitchen, and tried to settle disagreements between them without getting Avery involved. One Sunday the boys even got up early to make breakfast, which they served to Avery and Graham in bed. It was a nice gesture, even if it left a lot of clean up for Avery in the kitchen.

This morning Avery had also slept in. After standing in front of her mirror repeating her mantra "Be a girl," she went downstairs to make coffee. While the pot brewed, she toasted a bagel and lathered it with a thick layer of cream cheese.

Soon Graham joined her, pouring himself a cup and sitting at the table next to her. He was also on spring break, but for him that just meant he had a week to catch up on work when the students were gone. "How'd you sleep?" he asked.

"Fine," she responded. "I had that dream again." Every few nights for the last month she had been having a recurring dream. In the dream it was Christmas, she and Graham were older, maybe in their sixties and they were sitting around the tree opening presents. Aiden and Maddox were there, as were Avery's parents. When it was Avery's turn to open a gift, she grabbed a large box from under the tree and gently tore the paper. Inside was a naked baby, who squealed so loud it woke her up. It was a strange dream and Avery didn't know what to make of it. She often had weird dreams when she was pregnant, but this one seemed different. She couldn't stop thinking about it, what it meant about the baby growing inside her. Where was this new baby in the dream? Why wasn't he or she with them opening presents? Why would she be given a baby in a box? When she first told Graham about the dream, he told her not to think too much of it, it was the pregnancy hormones. There was no use reading too much into it. But Avery felt differently. She believed that dreams often embody someone's deepest fears and anxieties. Did it mean the baby was a gift to her? It seemed like a good dream, but it always left her with a bad feeling.

"It's natural that you're worried about this pregnancy," Graham said. "After everything you've been through—everything we've been through—it makes sense."

When they finished their coffee, it was time to go to their doctor's appointment. The boys were still sleeping, so Avery left a few bagels on the counter with a note. *Enjoy! We'll be back soon.* Avery hoped the boys would eat the bagels without toasting them. She wasn't sure if she trusted them with the toaster yet.

At the doctor's office, a nurse checked Avery's blood pressure and weight—she'd gained ten pounds already since the pregnancy—and told her to wait for the doctor for the ultrasound. When Dr. Walker came in, he smiled at the couple and took his place next to Avery at the ultrasound machine. "How have you been feeling?" He asked while squirting the gel on her stomach.

"Good, better now in the second trimester," Avery responded, her eyes fixated on the small screen that now showed her uterus and the little fetus. She could already see its little arms and legs, like strings of yarn attached to a huge head. Dr. Walker scanned the fetus from toe to head, pointing out the feet, vital organs, hands, the face, and brain.

"Everything looks good," he said. "Do you want to know the sex?"

"Yes!" Avery screamed abruptly. She held her breath, her strong 'yes' still vibrating in the air.

"It's a girl," Dr. Walker said. "Congratulations."

"A girl! Graham! Finally!" Avery said, a laugh escaping her mouth. Graham joined her laugh with a little chuckle and held Avery's hand a little tighter.

"Amazing," Graham said. "And a lucky girl to have two big brothers to protect her."

Dr. Walker finished the ultrasound, asking the couple if they had any more questions before leaving them alone. Avery's heart was fluttering. A girl! Finally! She couldn't have been happier.

When they left the doctor, Graham went to his office in Manhattan to catch up on work and Avery went home to the boys. She found them in the living room, sitting in front of the TV with their empty plates sitting next to them on the couch. She grabbed the plates and did the dishes while the boys were still mesmerized by the cartoons in front of them.

"Want to go get ice cream?" she asked them from the kitchen.

"Yes!" Maddox yelled.

"After the show," Aiden responded.

"Sure, just get me in the studio when you want to go." Avery went upstairs to her jewelry studio. She wasn't sure when she would have time to keep up on orders once the baby arrived. She was trying to build up a stock of her most popular pieces to so she wouldn't fall too far behind. A fast turnaround was something her customers valued.

An hour later, the boys were at the door. "We're ready," Aiden said, just as Avery was closing the clasp on a necklace. She smiled at them and put down her tools. "Let's go," she responded.

She grabbed a light jacket and followed the boys out to the porch. It was a beautiful spring day. Not hot, but sunny enough that she didn't feel cold. It was the kind of day that you could even wear short sleeves after getting used to a winter of snow. They walked a few blocks to a small ice cream shop. Aiden tasted about every flavor before settling on rocky road. Maddox went straight for his favorite—plain vanilla. Avery usually didn't get anything for herself when she took the boys out for ice cream, but today she got herself a cone of mint chocolate chip. It was a good day to spoil herself.

"So are we going to sleep at all when the baby comes?" Aiden asked. "Tommy's dad just had a baby and Tommy said the baby cries all night."

"Some babies have a hard time sleeping, but she'll be in our room so hopefully you won't hear her," Avery said. "It's a girl, by the way."

"What's her name going to be?" Maddox asked.

"I don't know yet, have any ideas?"

"How about Hermione?" Maddox suggested. "Or Katniss!" Whether Maddox preferred Harry Potter or Hunger Games changed daily.

"Those aren't real names," Aiden responded sarcastically. "People would make fun of her. Maybe something like Rachel or Jennifer."

"All great ideas," Avery said, licking the ice cream that was starting to drip down her cone. "Are you guys excited to have a little sister?"

Maddox smiled and nodded; his mouth surrounded with the white ice cream like clown lips drawn on him.

"She's lucky she will have us," Aiden said, suddenly sounding much older than twelve. "I'll make sure nothing happens to her."

Chapter 16

March 28, 2019

After drinking my third cup of coffee, I grab my purse and leave the house again. I have therapy today. I've been going once a week for the last five years. Since it happened. Sometimes we talk about who I am angry at. Why I can't let go, forgive myself. Forgive the world. Sometimes we sit in silence for the full hour. I don't think it helps, but I'm afraid of what my husband will say if I quit. Last time I brought it up, he threatened to leave me. I used to not believe he would, but now I am not sure. If there is one thing the last five years have done to me, it's made me less sure of where I stand.

When I get to the therapist's office, I sit down in her small waiting room. The room is meant for one. How fitting. I wonder if everyone who sits here is as lonely as I am. The windowless room has just two brown leather chairs and a coffee table covered in magazines.

The door to Dr. Moore's office is closed, meaning she's with a patient. Her patients leave her office through a door on the other side so they never cross paths with anyone. I pick up one of the magazines. Cosmopolitan. I read the headlines. *Hot Sex Skills. Spring clean your skin. Look hot naked.* Who reads this stuff? I wish my biggest problems were my skin or my sex skills. Once upon a time I may have opened the issue and read it, but today, the magazine just makes me angry. Why not an article about dealing with real life problems? I grab a different magazine, Parents.

Nursery trends we love. Stress release tips for moms. I laugh to myself, flipping to the page on stress release tips. As if any of these will relieve my stress. If someone else recommends I get a massage I may scream.

I haven't told Dr. Moore about my plan. About what I've been doing; what I am going to do. It's none of her business anyways. I can imagine her response. She'd look at me with those piercing eyes and ask if this is what I really want. Why this is the only solution. She'll try to make me second guess myself, think again about my plan. It's better she doesn't know. Some things are better not disclosed to therapists.

Suddenly Dr. Moore's office door opens. It catches me by surprise. I look up at her, she's smiling. I always try to read her face. I imagine when she sees me, she thinks, not this again. I bet I am the kind of patient she complains about to her therapist—all therapists have therapists right?—or maybe she laughs about me at dinner parties when they ask her about her craziest patients. I imagine her sitting over drinks with a group of friends, telling them all about my situation and how five years later I haven't made any progress. Her friends probably laugh and say how pathetic I am, how sad. I sigh. I'm tired of giving her material for her dinner parties.

"Come in," she says in her ever-calm voice. I put the magazine down and walk in through her open door. She has a beautiful office. It's large, with big windows draped with sheer curtains. A mahogany desk sits on the far end, leaving space for a couch and two plush chairs. Sometimes I sit on the couch, sometimes in one of the chairs. I try to think if maybe she reads into it, where I choose to sit. If she thinks it means something. It doesn't. I just want to keep her on her toes.

"How are you feeling?" she asks.

Chapter 17

June 16, 2013

Physical pain is bearable. But the panic that comes with it is not. When Avery felt a sharp throbbing in lower abdomen, below her belly, where her right leg reached her hip, the panic overtook her. The physical pain caused her to keel over, almost all the way to the ground. But it was just pain. She breathed through it. The thoughts that accompanied the pain, the unknown, was what broke her. She was alone at home. Graham was working through the summer at the university. The boys were out, Aiden with his friends, Maddox at baseball camp. Avery was on her way up the stairs when it started. She braced herself, placing her hands on a stair two up from her feet. She slowly lowered herself down onto her left side while holding her belly, trying to find a comfortable position to sit. But with every movement, the pain grew sharper. When she was still, it throbbed harder. *I need to call Graham*, she thought. Memories of her last two miscarriages started to pop through her brain. How she felt, how they happened. *Not again, please not again.*

Avery slid herself down the stairs, one hand below her belly where the pain was and the other on the banister. At the bottom, she pulled herself up, but only halfway, she couldn't stand straight. She stood hunched over while she tried to remember where she left her phone. She had been in the kitchen earlier, eating breakfast, cleaning dishes. Then she was in the living room, relaxing on the couch for a few moments before she decided to go upstairs to her studio. *It must still be in the kitchen*, she thought.

The kitchen felt like miles away, but when she made it, her phone was there on the table. She grabbed it, quickly calling Graham. The phone rang. No answer. She called again. Again no answer. Where was he?

"Graham! Something is wrong!" she screamed into his voicemail. "My stomach, I don't know what it is. I'm going to the hospital." She hung up the phone, threw it in her purse and ran—still hunched over—out the door. A cab. She needed a cab, but this wasn't Manhattan. There weren't cabs driving around looking for customers. Here you had to call one. But what cab driver would take her? She was bent over, her eyebrows wrinkled in pain. She looked like she could die in their backseat.

Avery eyed their car parked in the driveway. Could she drive herself? She started shuffling toward their car, before second guessing that decision. No, it wouldn't be smart. By some miracle, a cab turned onto her street. She hailed it, trying to stand up as straight as she could while still holding the spot below her belly. A second miracle. The cab stopped. Avery jumped in the backseat before the driver could change his mind.

"Brookdale University Hospital," Avery said to the driver. "As fast as you can." The cab driver didn't respond. He just stepped on the gas. Avery called Graham again. When she reached his voicemail, she yelled another message. "I'm on the way to Brookdale, I'll keep you posted." She thought she sounded calm based on how frantic she was actually feeling.

When the cab pulled up, she threw $40 at the driver and jumped out, toddling as fast as she could—still hunched over—to the emergency room entrance. She approached the reception, where a small crowd was standing around waiting their turn. She couldn't wait her turn, she pushed through to plead with the receptionist.

"Please! I'm pregnant and something happened," she pleaded. The receptionist told her to go to the maternity ward, where there probably wasn't a wait. Avery nodded and turned around. She started wandering around the hospital looking for the maternity ward. Why are things always so hard to find? What do they expect pregnant women to do when they go into labor? Search the hospital until the baby falls out? Finally she saw a sign with a directory next to an elevator bank. The maternity ward was on the third floor. Great. She called the elevator, pressing the up button over and over until the doors opened. The elevator was slower than ice melting in winter, but it eventually reached the third floor. Avery waddled out and followed the signs to the maternity ward. The reception was empty and Avery leaned over at the counter.

"Hi, my stomach is hurting, something is wrong!" she pleaded again.

"How many weeks are you?" the receptionist asked. Her voice calm and quiet, she didn't seem to catch Avery's panic.

"Twenty-five," Avery said, starting to worry that all the minutes adding up would be the difference between life and death. "I need to see a doctor right now."

"One moment," the receptionist picked up the phone, speaking quietly into the receiver. Then a nurse came to escort Avery into the ward. The nurse took her blood pressure and then led her to a room with an ultrasound machine.

"Have you felt the baby kick?" the nurse asked as Avery lay down on the bed.

"I don't know. I can't tell." The question made Avery panic. Had the baby kicked? She couldn't tell through the pain.

"Don't worry, we'll check in a second," the nurse squeezed the gel on Avery's basketball sized stomach. Don't worry, Avery repeated sarcastically in her head. Don't worry was the worst thing to say. As if Avery could just stop worrying on command. The nurse took the wand and started moving it around Avery's stomach. "There's the heart. It's beating fine." She moved the wand. "Here is the head, the hands, the feet. Look she's already with her head down. Everything looks fine."

Avery was relieved, but not relaxed. "So what is this pain?"

"Probably a muscle spasm," the nurse said. "The doctor will come see you shortly." The nurse left Avery in the room to wait alone. Thank God the baby was alright, Avery thought. She could endure the pain. She didn't mind having the pain for the next fifteen weeks if it meant the baby would be OK. Avery was lying on the bed in the fetal position when the doctor came in. He pressed on her stomach a few times, asked her about her medical history and calmly asked if they could give her a painkiller through an IV. The doctor seemed unconcerned, echoing the nurse's suspicion that it was a muscle spasm. "Happens all the time," he said. "Try to take it easy," he advised. The nurse returned to give Avery the IV and soon the pain seemed to weaken. The throbbing turned to a pulsing, then it disappeared. Avery closed her eyes.

"Avery!"

She was startled awake by Graham who had just leaped into the room. "What's going on? Is everything OK?" She hadn't realized that she had fallen asleep. "I'm so sorry, I was in a meeting and I didn't have reception. I tried to call you back and you didn't answer, so I just jumped in a cab."

"You took a cab from NYU to here?" Avery yelled, calculating in her head what the tab must have been.

"I didn't know what else to do!" Graham defended himself. "It doesn't matter. As long as you are alright and the baby is fine. It's just money." Graham kissed Avery's head. "What happened?"

"I don't know," Avery said, suddenly feeling silly for getting so worked up over nothing. "I just felt this pain and I freaked out. I was so worried!"

"It's OK, you did the right thing," Graham responded. "You need to rest more. From now on, I will do more at home. I will talk to the boys; they will help more too. You cannot keep going at your same pace now."

She really couldn't argue.

Chapter 18

September 1, 2013

In her dream, Avery was swimming. She was in a lake surrounded by trees. The water was warm, not bathtub-warm, but warm enough that she preferred the feeling under the water than above it. Overhead, the birds were chirping and flapping their wings as they flung from tree to tree. She was gliding through the water on her back. She was weightless. No one else was around.

When her eyes fluttered open, she realized she was soaked.

"Graham!" she whispered sharply, tapping his back. "Graham! My water broke!"

"What?" Graham was groggy, hard to wake up in the night. "Aren't you at thirty-six weeks?"

"Almost thirty-seven, but that doesn't matter! The baby is coming now!" Avery suddenly felt a contraction. A weak one, just a few seconds before it dissipated. With the boys, her labor had started the same way. First her water broke, and then the contractions started. But both boys came around their due date, Aiden a day after forty weeks and Maddox a day before. Avery hadn't expected this baby to come so early. "Graham! Get up!" She nudged him harder. Graham had already fallen back asleep. "We have to go!"

Avery looked at the clock. It was 2:09 a.m. The boys were sleeping. What should they do? She didn't want to wake them up. She'd leave them a note. Maybe they'd even get home with the baby before the boys woke up. They usually slept late on Sundays.

Avery jumped out of bed and ran to the bathroom to dry herself off. She put a pad in her underwear and brushed her teeth. Then she threw on some comfortable clothes. Graham had just sat up, rubbing the bridge of his nose before turning on the lamp on his bedside table and putting on his glasses. While Graham slowly pulled himself out of bed, Avery grabbed a duffel bag and started packing it. They had discussed packing a hospital bag, but they didn't feel the urgency to do it yet. They thought they had more time.

Avery threw a bathrobe and few pairs of underwear and bras in the bag. A change of clothes for her, for Graham. She grabbed a few pairs of socks—she remembered how cold her feet were when Maddox was born—and her toothbrush. Another contraction.

They hadn't even set up the crib yet. Graham said he would do it this weekend, Labor Day weekend, because he was free from work for once. It sat in pieces leaning against their bedroom wall. At least Graham had already brought it down from the attic. The baby clothes they bought were still in bags piled up next to the crib. The clothes still needed to be laundered before the baby could wear them. Avery sighed, trying not to think about all the things that had to be done when they would come home from the hospital.

Avery ran down the stairs with the duffel bag and was scribbling a note on the kitchen table when Graham came down. *Baby's on the way! Call us if you need anything* she wrote to the boys, leaving the note on the table. Graham grabbed the bag from Avery and the two of them stepped outside to the car. It was dark out aside from the streetlights lining their block. The air was still warm, the remnants of summer still in the air. A contraction hit when she slid into the car.

The roads were empty. Avery had three contractions during the ride, each about five minutes apart. Her body was ready for the birth. It didn't drag the labor like it had when Aiden was born. Back then, it took a while from when her water broke until the contractions started. Even after they started it was still almost twenty-four hours until the baby came. Now, her body knew what to do. The water broke and the contractions started getting stronger quickly, charging her body to push the baby out as quickly as possible. Avery winced during the last contraction as they arrived at the hospital.

By the time they got to the maternity ward, the contractions were four minutes apart. The pain electrifying Avery for thirty seconds each time before disappearing. It's happening quick, she kept thinking, guessing she was already four to five centimeters dilated. A nurse led Avery into a hospital room and checked her cervix. Five centimeters, she confirmed. "Do you want an epidural?"

"Yes please!" Avery said, a little too desperately she thought. She didn't understand those women who said no to an epidural. Why not take advantage of modern medicine? The nurse left, telling them the anesthesiologist would be coming soon. Avery paced the room, pausing every three minutes when a contraction hit her, feeling like it was splitting her open from the inside. It's good pain, she kept repeating to herself. Good pain. Graham stood in the corner of the room with his hands on top of his head. He was watching Avery pace. "Do you want water? Something to eat?" he kept asking, but Avery declined. She felt like she could throw up.

She kept pacing. Now, the contractions were even stronger. She felt her bones ripping from her organs, her flesh stretching open. There wasn't much time left, she knew it, and she didn't have the epidural yet. "Graham!" she yelled. "It's happening. There's no time for the epidural, get the doctor!" She felt a sudden urge to push. Graham darted from the room, running back in moments later dragging a doctor by his shirtsleeve. Two nurses followed.

Avery lay on the bed as a nurse checked her cervix. Ten centimeters, said the nurse. It was time to push. When the next contraction shot through her, Avery squeezed her eyes shut and screamed as loud as she could. This birth was unlike the ones before it. With the boys, the epidural had numbed her, allowing her to enjoy pushing the baby out. Now, the pushing made her head spin, she started to see black spots around the room. The sweat dripped down her back and chest, pooling on the bed below her. "Another push," the doctor said. "The head is already out."

"I can't do it," Avery cried. "It's too much!"

"You're doing great," Graham consoled her. "You're amazing. It's almost done."

The next contraction shot through her and Avery screamed again, pushing with her head, her shoulders, her eyes. And then she felt the baby bulldoze through her. She looked down to see the doctor raise the baby up and place her on Avery's chest. Purple and covered in slime, the baby started to whimper as she burrowed her head in Avery's sweaty neck.

"I did it!" Avery yelled. She felt dizzy, still seeing black spots around her. But then, the laughter took over. "Oh my God, I did it!" Her laughter growing so loud it overtook her pain. Her whole body was throbbing, she felt weak, about to faint, but she held on, not wanting to miss a moment.

"Amelia May Stephens," Avery said, clasping her hands around the baby. The name she and Graham had settled on. Amelia after Amelia Earhart, the first female pilot, someone Graham admired, and May, after Avery's late grandmother. "You're going to change the world."

Chapter 19

October 6, 2013

"Hush little baby don't you cry, mama's gonna sing you a lullaby..." Avery was singing to Amelia when her phone rang. She was sitting in her rocking chair in their master bedroom, which was now so full of furniture that Avery felt like she was navigating through a maze whenever she entered. Between the bed, Avery and Graham's nightstands, the crib, changing table and rocking chair, there was just so little room to walk. It wasn't permanent, Avery consoled herself every time she bumped a hip on something. She was still adjusting to her new body and she wasn't as agile as she had been before.

The last month had been a whirlwind. After Amelia was born, Graham rushed home to tell the boys. Avery stayed in the hospital for another day with the baby. She had lost a lot of blood and the doctors wanted to keep her under observation. The baby passed all her checks perfectly. Her Apgar score and her hearing were perfect. When Avery was released, Graham picked her and the baby up and took them home, where he and the boys had worked hard to clean and set everything up for Amelia's arrival.

It had been nine years since Avery had a newborn. She had forgotten the feeling after those sleepless nights, the feeling of helplessness when the baby cried, the desperation to console her, the pain in her engorged breasts as milk seeped out through her nipples. But whenever Amelia fell asleep in her arms, it was all worth it. Avery would study her face, her puffy little eyes, button nose, thick lips. Not to mention Amelia's little hands, balled up like fists in front of her chest. At five weeks old, Amelia was just starting to observe the world that she so violently entered. The first few weeks, she rotated between eating, sleeping, and crying. But in the last week, she started to open her eyes and look around. She started to focus her eyes on her mother, as though trying to understand her face, the meaning of the smile on Avery's lips, the gleam in her eyes.

When the phone rang, Amelia startled, opening her eyes a moment to see herself still in her mother's arms. Avery looked over at the phone on the nightstand next to her. Normally she wouldn't answer the phone when she was with the baby. She never wanted Amelia to feel like she was distracted, not focused on her. But when she saw it was the fertility clinic calling, her curiosity got the better of her.

"Hello?"

"Hi Mrs. Stephens, this is Rachel from Klein Fertility Center. Dr. Klein would like to set up a meeting with you and Mr. Stephens." Rachel was one of the nurses at the clinic. She was the one who tested Avery's blood and uterus every morning while preparing for the IVF treatments. She was older, caring, reminded Avery of her own mother. Her voice quivered ever so subtly, but Avery caught it. It made her instantly alert and started a race of thoughts in her head.

"For what purpose?" Avery asked. She started to think about the reasons Dr. Klein could want to meet with them. It had been nine months since they had any contact with the clinic, since Avery's positive pregnancy test. From Avery's understanding, they didn't need to keep in touch, unless they wanted to use the embryos the clinic had kept frozen for them. Under the package Avery and Graham paid for, the clinic would keep the embryos for three years.

If the couple wanted them frozen longer, they could pay an annual fee. What if something happened to the embryos? Avery had heard of things like that happening before. An accident in the lab, a fire, a burglary. Avery and Graham probably wouldn't use the embryos anyway.

"The doctor would rather speak with you in person," Rachel said. "Could you come in today?"

Avery sensed the urgency and agreed that she and Graham would come to the clinic that afternoon. It was Sunday and Graham was at home, downstairs reading the paper. Strange, Avery thought, that the doctor was in on a Sunday. Avery cradled Amelia in her arms and went downstairs to tell Graham about the phone call. He calmly sipped his coffee.

"Something is off," Avery said, trying to explain the panic she heard in Rachel's voice. "Something doesn't make sense."

"So let's go and find out what is going on," Graham said between sips of coffee. Avery agreed. They decided to take the car into Manhattan and test their luck with parking. They didn't want to spend hours on the subway with the baby. The boys were in front of the TV and barely noticed as their parents explained to them that they were going out for a few hours.

The couple sat silently in the car as Amelia slept in her car seat. But Avery's head was anything but silent. Their IVF treatment went perfectly, it ended in a beautiful girl as Dr. Klein would soon see. So why could he need to meet them so urgently?

When they arrived, Graham parked in an overpriced lot and the couple entered the clinic. It was empty, aside from Rachel waiting for them in the reception. Only half the lights were on, creating an eerie look like the clinic was still sleeping.

"Thanks for coming in," Rachel said, standing up. She had been sitting down, biting her nails when the couple entered. Avery was wearing the sleeping baby in a sling wrapped around her body. It sometimes felt like she was still pregnant, tying the baby tight around her. "Right this way." She led them to the back, to Dr. Klein's office, where the lights were fully on. When Graham and Avery were inside, Rachel quickly closed the door, slamming it just loud enough that Amelia jumped in her sleep.

Avery and Graham sat down in front of the doctor, waiting for him to speak.

"Thanks for coming in on a Sunday," he said, repeating Rachel's sentiment. "I would like to speak with you about doing DNA testing of your daughter." Dr. Klein nodded at the sleeping baby.

"Why?" Graham asked. "Is this routine for babies born from procedures in this clinic?"

"Not exactly," Dr. Klein said, hesitating before he continued. "We had a little mishap in the lab and we just want to check everything. I am sure everything is fine."

"What do you mean 'a mishap'?" Avery piped in.

"Nothing major," Dr. Klein remained calm. "There is no reason to worry. We just want to check."

"If you want to do a DNA test of our daughter, you're going to have to tell us why," Avery said.

"Well that's the thing," Dr. Klein said. "We want to make sure she is your daughter."

"I do not understand," Graham said. "You retrieved Avery's eggs, used my sperm. Avery carried the baby for nine months…" Graham's voice drifted off.

Dr. Klein studied the couple's faces. He paused, holding his palms together in front of his nose before speaking. "The day we did the IVF transfer, there was another couple here who received the wrong embryo." He paused. "We've checked all our records, and there are no embryos missing from our other patients and we have been unable to locate that couple's embryos." Another pause. "We decided we want to do a DNA test on any baby born from a transfer on that day. Solely as a precaution, of course."

"You think that Amelia is not our baby?" Avery said, her hands instinctively touching the sleeping baby on her chest.

"There is a very slight chance," Dr. Klein said.

"Don't you have procedures in place so things like this do not happen?" Graham asked.

"We do, of course," Dr. Klein said. "We will be doing a full review of all our procedures. This type of thing has never happened to us before."

"We're not doing a DNA test," Avery said resolutely. "Amelia's our daughter. I don't care what happened in your clinic or whatever." Graham put his hand on Avery's shoulder.

"I understand your hesitation," Dr. Klein said. Avery suddenly noticed the bags under his eyes. They were puffy and purple, lined with red. "It is a very simple procedure; we would just need a quick swab from her mouth. And of course, swabs from your mouths as well to ensure a match."

"It's not about that," Avery said. With the lack of sleep over the last month, her patience had been severed short. "It's not our problem that your clinic made a mistake. Our family is perfect and we don't want to be involved in your malpractice."

"Avery," Graham said, instantly calming her. Then he turned to the doctor. "May we have a moment?"

Dr. Klein nodded. He stood up and walked out of the office, closing the door behind him. Avery watched him leave, studying his jeans and polo shirt. She'd only seen him in scrubs before.

"We should do the test, Avery," Graham said. "I know you do not want to; I do not want to either. But just to prove everything is fine. The doctor will not leave us alone otherwise. I do not want to get involved with lawyers who may force the test on us."

Avery nodded. He was right. "No matter what, Amelia is our daughter," she said.

"She is," Graham responded as he got up and opened the door for the doctor. "By the way Dr. Klein, how many couples did an IVF transfer that day? Are you DNA testing all of them?"

"Four couples," Dr. Klein responded. "You, the couple that found the issue and two others."

"We will do the test on one condition," Graham said. "No matter the outcome, Amelia is our daughter and there is no fighting that. We do not want to be involved with any media or lawsuits or any other circus that may ensue from this."

"Yes, yes, of course," Dr. Klein said. On his desk there were three DNA test kits. Avery hadn't noticed them before, but now she saw them stacked perfectly on top of a manila folder. Dr. Klein grabbed a pair of latex gloves from his desk, opened the first DNA kit and pulled out a cotton swab. "Mrs. Stephens, could you just open Amelia's mouth?" Avery agreed and gently moved the sling away from Amelia's face. She pressed lightly on her cheeks. Dr. Klein slid the swab in her mouth and moved it around for two seconds before taking it out and dropping it in a small zip lock bag. He then handed the other two kits to Avery and Graham and asked each one to swab their own mouths. They did and handed their DNA back to the doctor.

"We'll call when we have the results," Dr. Klein. "The lab is closed today, but we are going to try to rush delivery of the tests tomorrow."

Chapter 20

March 28, 2019

"Shit," I respond to my therapist. "I feel like shit." I hate those stupid questions. She knows how I feel, isn't it her job to know how I feel better than I do?

"Do you want to elaborate on that?"

Now there is an even stupider question. If I wanted to elaborate, I would. But I don't. I don't want to talk to her any more than she would want to talk to a tree. It is pointless and meaningless. I start thinking about how I'm going to pass this hour. I have things to do today. Things I need to get done before enacting my plan. I've just walked in the door, so I probably have a good fifty-eight minutes left. At least.

"I went to go see her this morning," I blurt out and immediately regret it. I can't believe I've just told her. It's the type of information she can use against me. To prove that I'm crazy or dangerous even. Dr. Moore touches the side of her glasses with her thumb and index finger. I call her Dr. Moore, no matter how many times she tells me I can call her by her first name. But then it would be like we are friends. And we are definitely not.

She has large glasses that surround her eyes like picture frames. Behind them, her eyes are a deep gray and lined with dark mascara and eye shadow. I wonder why she bothers, putting on so much makeup in the mornings when everyone she sees all day is crazy. Psychotic.

"How did she look?" she asks me.

"Happy," I say. She did look happy. With her glittery pink unicorn backpack. Her best friend. Why shouldn't she be happy?

"And how did that make you feel?"

I think for a moment, picturing her again in my head. The slight curve of her nose. The way her hair bounced when she skipped. Her smile, which showed two little front teeth. "Sad," I say as I start feeling it all over again. "Sad."

"Why do you think that is? That seeing her happy makes you sad?"

"Because I'm not there. I'm not a part of it. She doesn't even know who I am!" I'm working myself up. Going from sad to angry. "How is that even fair!?"

"What would make your situation fair?"

I smirk. I learned long ago that fairness doesn't exist. Not in adulthood. With kids, we pretend that things can be fair. We give each kid the same number of cookies or we buy each one the same number of presents. But why do we do this? Why do we teach them about fairness just to rip it away from them when they start to understand the world? It's cruel.

"Nothing," I respond.

"If fairness is off the table, what could make this situation acceptable to you?"

Again I smirk. Acceptable. Like this was offered to me and I could choose to accept. Like it wasn't just thrown at me, hit me like a tornado and catapulted me upside down to view the world from a perspective I didn't recognize.

"Nothing." I look around the office, scanning the walls for a clock. But of course there isn't one. She doesn't want anyone in here watching the minutes go by as she tortures them with her moronic questions. But I've tricked her. I have a watch. A quick glance at it and I sigh. Forty-nine minutes to go.

Chapter 21

October 8, 2013

Two nights Avery didn't sleep, waiting for the call from the doctor. When he didn't call yesterday, she was sure everything was fine. If it wasn't, he would have felt the urgency to talk to them right away. He was probably focused on the couple that had the wrong baby, he couldn't waste time on talking to Avery and Graham. By the end of the day, Avery had convinced herself of this, but after she got in bed she second guessed herself.

"Graham," she whispered, tapping his shoulder to wake him up. She had already been lying in bed for a few hours without a wink of sleep. "Graham!" She whispered a little louder. She didn't want to wake Amelia, who was sleeping in her crib next to them. Graham grunted. "What if the DNA test comes back that Amelia isn't our baby?"

"She is our baby."

"You don't know that."

"Avery, there is nothing we can do about it right now. Let's talk in the morning."

"What if they try to take her away from us?"

"They cannot. We are her parents. Legally we are. It's on her birth certificate."

"Are you sure?"

"Avery, try to sleep." Graham's breathing returned to its deep rhythm. But of course Avery couldn't sleep. She lay in bed, staring at the ceiling until Amelia woke up. Avery lifted her from the crib, fed her, and returned the sleeping baby to her crib. Then she continued staring at the ceiling, until Amelia's next wake up. Again, she lifted her from the crib, fed her. This time, the sunlight was already starting to peek in through the window. Avery studied Amelia's face. Her features. Did she resemble Avery and Graham? Whenever Avery took her places, everyone always said the baby looked just like her, but Avery didn't see it. It's a baby, she thought, it's too early to see what she looks like. When Amelia finished eating and fell back asleep, Avery gently placed her in the crib. She couldn't continue staring at the ceiling. She decided to get up. Start making lunch for the boys.

She was in the kitchen when her mother called. Avery hesitated a moment before answering the phone. "Hello?"

"Good morning!" her mother said through the line. "How's our little princess doing? Is she awake?"

"She's great, still sleeping," Avery responded. She decided not to tell her about the weight that was pressing down on her shoulders. The weight that seemed to be getting heavier and heavier, pressing her down to the ground. No need to worry anyone. "You want me to call you when she wakes up? We can video chat."

"That'd be wonderful, darling," her mother answered. "But before 11:00. I'm meeting with the girls today for lunch." Avery's mother, Sophie, was still a socialite in her old age. Ten years ago she had moved to Florida with her boyfriend, a widower a few years older than she. He was a homebody, but Sophie spent most of her days out—book clubs, luncheons, water aerobics, any activity to keep her busy. She even had a group of girlfriends that met often to gossip over cocktails. Sophie called her daughter weekly, mostly she relayed gossip about her friends, told her about all her activities, and asked about her grandchildren. She hadn't come to visit since the new baby was born, but promised to come soon. She was just all booked up for the first few months.

After hanging up the phone, Avery went to wake up the boys. They groaned like usual, but agreed to get up. Avery went back downstairs to make breakfast. Then her phone rang again just as she was about to flip the batch of pancakes. Who is this time? She first thought, forgetting that she had been waiting for a call for two days now. Then her heart stopped. It was the clinic.

"Hello?" she answered.

"Hi Mrs. Stephens," Dr. Klein said. Avery could sense the gravity in his voice. "Would you and Mr. Stephens be able to come in today?"

"Why? What were the results?"

"I think it is best we discuss in person," the doctor said.

"You can't do that," Avery yelled into the phone. "We've been holding our breath for two days and now you won't tell me?"

Dr. Klein sighed. Then cleared his throat. Avery remained silent, waiting for him to talk. He cleared his throat again. "You and Graham are a zero percent match to Amelia. You're also a ninety nine percent match to the baby the other couple gave birth to."

There are times in life when the earth stands still. Other times, the earth seems to spin so fast that you need to hold on or else you will fall off. At that moment, Avery felt the world stand still and spin at the same time. Her feet were grounded on the still earth, while her head spun. She was dizzy, nauseated. She held on to the counter in front of her.

"Mrs. Stephens?" the doctor said when he heard no reply. "I would greatly appreciate it if you and Mr. Stephens could come in today. Any time. We are not working with any patients at the moment."

"Are you sure?" Avery said as soon as she had gathered enough air. "Can you test again?"

"We're sure."

"Maybe you made another mistake and Amelia is our genetic daughter."

"No. Please let me know when you can come," Dr. Klein said. "We need to discuss the next steps."

Avery agreed to come in as soon as possible. Then she hung up the phone and ran to her bedroom. Amelia was sleeping peacefully in her crib while Graham stood in the master bathroom brushing his teeth.

"Graham!" Avery yelled, forgetting about the sleeping baby. "They got the results. We're not a genetic match for Amelia. But we are for the other couple's baby!" She yelled it like it was one long word instead of a few sentences. Graham stopped, his mouth dropped open, letting a few drops of toothpaste slide out.

"Are they sure?"

"Yes!" Avery yelled, exasperated. "What are we going to do if they try to take Amelia away from us!? She's our baby, I don't care what anyone says."

"Dr. Klein said they could not do that. Let's go speak with him."

Avery ran back downstairs. The pancakes were burnt in the pan and the boys had already helped themselves to cereal. She dumped the burnt food in the trash, scratching the pan before she threw it in the sink. "Mom and Dad have an urgent meeting," she told the boys. "When you finish please bring your dishes to the sink and go to school." She didn't wait for a response. She ran back up and got dressed. Then she picked up Amelia. The baby was awake in her crib, looking at the mobile turning above her. Such a sweet baby, Avery thought. She loved her so much, knowing that they weren't genetically related didn't change any of that. She kissed her head and brought her downstairs where Graham was waiting for her. They hopped in their car to drive to Manhattan. Sure it was rush hour, it could take a while, but Avery wasn't getting on the subway in her state.

"What do you think the doctor will say?" Avery asked Graham.

"I do not know," Graham said in his ever calm and rhythmic tone. "We need to tell him that we want our privacy. That he cannot tell the other couple who we are. That Amelia is ours and that is that."

Yes, Avery thought. He was right. They needed to be firm. No one could break up their family. After a long drive in traffic, they arrived at the clinic. The office was bright, all the lights were on this time, but it was empty. The couple walked through the reception and led themselves to Dr. Klein's office. The door was open, and inside Dr. Klein was sitting at his desk. Across from him was a tall man in a suit, who stood up when he heard them enter. The tall man offered them to sit down, which they did, Avery holding Amelia on her lap.

"This is Chase Greenberg, my lawyer," Dr. Klein said. "He's here to help out."

"Nice to meet you," Chase said, smiling and reaching out his hand to shake Graham's and then Avery's. To Avery, the handshake felt like an ambush. Why was a lawyer here?

"Listen doctor," Avery started. "We understand you made a mistake, but we want to move on. We would prefer that you leave our family alone. Our daughter's genetics don't matter to us."

"I see," the doctor started. "We have several things to discuss. First of all, our malpractice insurance will be discussing a settlement with you. That's what Chase is here for. You may also want to get a lawyer to help you with the settlement discussions."

"I'm sure we can come to a very fair agreement," Chase chimed in, his smile a bit too big for Dr. Klein's office. Avery's lips curled up in disgust.

"Second, I want you to know that you will be fully refunded for your IVF treatment here," Dr. Klein continued. "And your embryos that you still have frozen here will be kept safe free of charge for as long as you like. If you would like to use them, we will provide any treatments to you free of charge. Of course, that is, if you want to work with us again. If not, we can transfer your frozen embryos anywhere you choose." The doctor paused, looking back and forth between Avery and Graham. "As you can imagine, we will also be completely overhauling all of our procedures here. We're doing a full investigation of the lab and of course anyone at fault will be replaced. We can provide you with a report of our investigation as well."

"We won't be doing any more treatments," Avery said. She would be thirty-nine in November; she didn't think she would be able to handle another pregnancy. "And I don't care how it happened. We just want to be left alone."

"I understand," Dr. Klein said. "There is one more issue." He paused.

"What?" Avery said impatiently.

"The other couple," Dr. Klein said. "They want to switch babies."

Part 3

"Babies are bits of star-dust blown from the hand of God. Lucky is the woman who knows the pangs of birth for she has held a star."

– Larry Barretto

Chapter 22

January 4, 2013

Sydney had to drag herself to work today. She didn't want to go, but she knew that if she called in sick, she would look weak. Pathetic. And she was anything but pathetic. She would show Mark—Dr. Klein she was supposed to call him—that she didn't care. That he was the loser.

The night before, she and Mark were lying in bed together. She was still naked, her black lace bra and panties lying on the floor next to her bed. He had come over around 10:00 p.m., the usual time he made an appearance, and Sydney opened the door in just her lingerie. She felt bold, sexy. A real woman. Before saying anything, Mark wrapped his arms around her and pushed her backwards to the bedroom, where they made love. When they finished, they lay silently in bed, Sydney curled up on her side next to him.

She always wondered what he said to his wife when he came to her place at nights. Probably he pretended there was some sort of emergency at the clinic. His wife must be a silly woman, if only she knew there were no late-night emergencies for fertility doctors. But what could his wife say? Sydney could only guess how much money Mark was taking home. He owned the clinic, meaning the profits were all his. At twenty thousand dollars a month per patient, he probably made more in a month than Sydney made in a year. So his wife couldn't complain, Sydney thought. She had met his wife a couple times at the clinic. She was tall, blonde, the kind of thin that suggested she didn't eat more than a few grapes per day. Her body was always draped in designer wear, her fake nails long and painted according to the season. Sydney wondered what exactly Mark saw in her. He was such a sophisticated man, he should have ended up with someone a little more...she didn't know exactly, but someone different. Mark gently lifted her arm off his chest and sat up.

"It's over Syd," he said, his eyes at the floor. "I can't do this anymore."

"You're leaving your wife?" Sydney's heart leaped in joy. Finally! They could be together for real. Maybe someone a little more like her, someone with life experience. Who had to work hard to get to where she was. She was significantly younger than him in years, but that was just a number. If you counted her life experience, her knowledge, they were more like equals.

"No," Mark said. "Us, you and me, we're over. I can't keep sneaking around like this. And it's wrong. We work together."

"We work great together," Sydney said.

"It's unethical."

"You think the unethical part of all this is that we work together?" Sydney questioned. "Not that you're married? Or lying to your wife?" Her tone was snide, cynical. She couldn't stop that side of her from coming out when something angered her.

"Sorry, Syd," he said, getting up from the bed and gathering his clothes. "If you want to find a new job, I can help you. I know other clinics that can use a great lab technician like you."

"Whatever, Mark," she said. "I'm fine. Go home to your wife." But she wasn't fine. As soon as he left— quietly slipping himself out the door—she started crying, bawling. Still naked in the bed. How could he do that to her? She thought he loved her. He never exactly said those words, but he sure acted like it. She got up and threw on a pair of pajamas on her way to the kitchen where she grabbed a pint of ice cream. Brought it back to bed with her. She turned on the TV, there were always corny movies on late at night. She tried to watch, but her mind wandered. How could this happen? She wasn't the type of girl to get so upset over a guy. But she had never been broken up with before. She'd also never been with a married guy before. All the previous guys she'd been with were losers. Real losers. Guys with no ambitions. Guys who lived in their parents' basements or on their friends' couches. She tried dating 'good' guys, but they were just so boring. Until Mark.

At 6:00 a.m., she was still watching TV, the empty pint of ice cream sitting next to her, dripping on the sheets. She had to get up for work. She was going to show Mark exactly how much she didn't care about him. She jumped in the shower, turning the hot water all the way to the end, burning her skin. It felt good, like she was cleansing herself of the mistake she made. Then she blow-dried her hair, pinned it back—the way Mark thought she looked the best—and put on some makeup. More than she usually wore for work. She looked good, she thought as she blew a ruby red kiss to herself in the mirror.

She arrived at the clinic just before 8:00 a.m. She walked through the doors and made her way through the reception to the lab in the back. First she popped into to one of the patient rooms, where the other lab technician, Rachel, was giving blood tests and ultrasounds to women getting ready for their egg retrievals. Women preparing for having their eggs retrieved had to come into the clinic daily for about two weeks. They would have their hormone levels checked and the follicles in their ovaries measured so that the doctor could retrieve the eggs at the optimal time. Sydney greeted Rachel and smiled at the patient who winced as the needle poked the inside of her elbow.

Then Sydney started her morning routine, first checking on all the eggs that had been retrieved in the last few days. She checked to see which of the newer eggs became fertilized—called zygotes—and started to split into multiple cells—embryos. For the embryos that had already started growing, she checked to see their rate of growth. Then she checked the files to see which patients were coming in that day for an embryo transfer. If the person coming in for the transfer had their embryos frozen, Sydney would retrieve them from their specified compartment in the freezer to defrost. If the person only had their eggs retrieved in the last few days, she would check on the embryos and decide which would be used for the transfer and which would be frozen.

On that day there were four women coming in for embryo transfers. Two with fresh embryos and two with frozen. Sydney checked the patient ID numbers for the patients with frozen eggs to find the compartment with their embryos and took them out for the defrosting process. Then she looked at the fresh embryos for transfer. She looked at the first patient of the day, Cameron Stevens. She had twelve eggs that had started to grow. Sydney examined the embryos to choose the best three. The rest would be frozen. She must be young and healthy, Sydney thought to herself. Her embryos were growing fast and all twelve could have been good candidates for a transfer. Sydney chose the top three and packaged the rest to be frozen and filed away.

Then she looked at the embryos of the second patient of the day, Avery Stephens. An older patient, Sydney recognized immediately based on the number of cells in each embryo. Although there were three that weren't bad.

The rest—to be frozen—probably wouldn't make it through a defrosting, she thought. Sydney often fantasized about the patients and their future babies. It made her smile to think about the families she was helping. The people who existed because of the work she did. Maybe this embryo would cure cancer, she thought. And that one, a Nobel laureate for literature.

Sydney had all the embryos organized for the day when Rachel came into the lab. Rachel was older than Sydney, she had been working as a fertility lab technician for more than twenty years, the last five with Dr. Klein. When Sydney was first hired two years ago, fresh out of nursing school, Rachel taught her everything. Today, the two women worked together as partners, Rachel never acted more senior to Sydney.

"Look at you all made up today," Rachel said as she came in and put a face mask over her mouth. "What's the occasion?"

Sydney smiled. She hadn't told Rachel about her relationship with Dr. Klein, but she had a feeling Rachel suspected. Maybe she was just paranoid, but she felt that Rachel watched her closely whenever the doctor was around.

"No occasion," Sydney responded. "Just wanted to feel pretty."

"A girl like you in New York City," Rachel said. "I'm sure there are plenty of men who can make you feel pretty."

Sydney blushed. Just then Dr. Klein came in. "Good morning ladies," he said. "Sydney, Rachel." Sydney. So formal. He only called her that at work. "How are we doing this morning?"

"Just fine," Rachel answered first. "And yourself?"

"Great," Dr. Klein smiled. Then he walked out of the lab. Sydney watched him through the lab windows as he entered his office and took off his coat. Her blood started to boil. How could he be great? He could at least say he was fine, or alright, or anything a little less than great. She was supposed to be feeling great. Unphased.

"Everything OK?" Rachel asked, her eyes glued on Sydney.

"Great, everything is great," Sydney said. Soon patients would start arriving for egg retrievals—which they did in the morning—and then embryo transfers in the afternoon. Rachel assisted Dr. Klein with the retrievals, while Sydney spent the morning in the lab with the embryos. She then assisted Dr. Klein with the transfers.

The morning dragged on. Sydney kept looking out the lab windows as Dr. Klein walked back and forth between his office and the operating rooms. She willed him to look at her. Give a wink like he did sometimes, or a smile. But he didn't. He looked straight ahead as though his head was screwed on too tight. Every time he walked by she felt her hands get clammy. Her throat dry. Why won't he just look at me, she yelled in her head. She felt like she would explode when the first patient arrived for their egg transfer.

The receptionist notified her that the patient was ready in room three. With a big breath in, Sydney checked the patient file for the first patient. Cameron Stevens. She would show Dr. Klein. She would show him how over him she already was. She grabbed the file and went to the embryos stacked ready for the transfer. Dr. Klein, he would be sorry. Sorry he ended it with her. Sorry he even started seeing her. He was the one who started it after all. Sydney grabbed the petri dishes—Stephens—and walked out of the lab to room three.

She entered the room where a petite brunette was laying on the bed. She looked nervous, but calmed when her eyes drifted up to her husband. He was holding her hand. A big smile plastered on his freckled face. Sydney studied him quickly, trying not to look like she was staring. Tall, muscular. Thick styled hair. She should be with someone like that. She gave a quick, flirty smile. Sometimes the husbands smiled back, how easily men stray even when their wives are so vulnerable. This husband didn't seem to notice.

"Can you tell me your name and birthday?" Sydney said glancing at the wristband on the woman's arm before looking back at the husband.

"Cameron Stevens. November 2nd, 1984."

"Stevens, yup," Sydney said looking at the label on the petri dishes. She handed them to the doctor. He separated the three dishes and slid the first one on the tray of a microscope. Instantly, the image of the petri dish appeared on the screen. Sydney tuned out as the doctor reviewed the embryos, enthusiastically narrating his process to the couple. He chose an embryo to insert into the woman's uterus and Sydney prepared the ultrasound machine so they could see in the patient's uterus.

"Wow, your bladder is really full!" Sydney tried to joke. She looked at Dr. Klein, but his eyes were glued to the embryo. "Here's your uterus, you see that? That is the lining, where we implant the embryo." Sydney pointed to the screen. Dr. Klein still didn't look at her.

"This may feel a little uncomfortable," Dr. Klein said as he gently put the embryo on the end of the catheter. "Just watch the little guy go."

When he finished, Sydney took the other two embryos back to the lab, her anger boiling inside her. He didn't even look at me, Sydney thought. Was he just going to ignore her? Pretend like she was nothing? The nerve!

Soon the second patient arrived for the embryo transfer. Sydney grabbed the patient file and the embryos to bring to the room. Again, Dr. Klein ignored her. He didn't even notice when the husband winked at her! That would have driven him crazy yesterday.

When the third patient arrived, Sydney went through the motions. She grabbed the patient file, the embryos and went into the room. "Can you tell me your name and birthdate please?" she asked.

"Avery Stephens. November 22nd, 1974."

"Stephens..." Sydney repeated slowly. She suddenly felt like she was having déjà vu. The lack of sleep must be getting to me, she thought. "Alright."

Chapter 23

October 7, 2013

"This isn't our baby," Andy said for the fifth time. "We need to get our baby and give this one back. You have to fix this."

Cameron and Andy were sitting in Dr. Klein's office after receiving the DNA test results. Not surprisingly, they were not matches to the baby that Cameron just birthed. What did surprise them, was that Dr. Klein told them that another baby born from this clinic was a genetic match to them.

"This is a very complex situation," Dr. Klein said. "I will need to speak with the other couple."

"Won't they want their baby?" Andy said impatiently. "Just tell us who they are and we'll talk to them."

"Ethically I cannot do that," Dr. Klein said. "It's against doctor-patient confidentiality clauses."

"Well I think we're past medical ethics, doctor," Andy said, standing up. "You need to fix this somehow." He turned to Cameron, who was still sitting, the newborn lying next to her in their stroller. "Cam, let's go."

Cameron followed Andy out, pushing the stroller. She was torn. Looking at the peaceful baby in the stroller; she felt connected to her, affection. But love, she didn't know if she felt that. Maybe that's how all new moms feel, or maybe it was because it wasn't her baby. Maybe if it were her baby, she would have felt love instantly. Maybe her body sensed that something was wrong.

"We're going to sue the clinic, put them out of business and we're getting our baby back," Andy said when they walked outside.

"What about this baby?" Cameron asked.

"We'll give her to her parents," Andy said.

"And what if they don't want her?"

"Then I don't know," Andy said. "I don't want to raise someone else's kid. I want to raise ours."

Cameron nodded. It felt strange to be stuck with a baby they would be giving away. At the hospital, they hesitated to put their names on the birth certificate, but the hospital required it. As for the baby's name, they put an X. It wasn't for them to decide, they agreed. Her real parents could name her and amend the birth certificate once everything was sorted out. Their name—the one they choose—would be saved for their baby. When Cameron was released from the hospital, they took the baby home. The nurses said they couldn't leave her there. They could leave her at a fire station to become a ward of the state, but they didn't want that either. They wanted to return her to her real family. Was that so difficult?

Before they had even left the hospital, Andy had already started making calls to lawyers and setting up meetings. They were now on their way to meet with a medical malpractice lawyer and later they were meeting with another lawyer who specialized in reproductive rights.

They arrived at the first lawyer's office. According to Google, Kevin Conway was the top lawyer in his field in all of New York. When Andy had called and explained their situation to him, he agreed to see them right away.

"This is a very easy case," he said as they sat down in his office. "We're going to sue them for medical malpractice and breach of contract. They will be desperate to settle since they know it's something they cannot win. So we just need to decide what you want out of it."

That was easy enough. They wanted to make sure Dr. Klein never practiced medicine again. The money, no amount could fix what happened, but Kevin thought that five million dollars was a good starting point. With the lost earnings the couple would experience dealing with this case, future medical bills, pain and suffering the couple was going through, and the loss of consortium—strain on the couple's relationship—Kevin thought that amount could easily be reached in front of a jury. Cameron and Andy shook Kevin's hand when they finished the meeting. Kevin's confidence put Cameron at ease. At least he would fix one of their issues.

Then, it was time to meet with their second lawyer. This was the more complex issue. They didn't know anything about the other couple or their own baby for that matter. They didn't know if the baby was a girl or a boy, when it was born, whether the mother was as careful about protecting her health as Cameron had been, how they were caring for the baby, or what they would do with it once they found out.

"It will be easy to find out who they are," Alicia Black said. Alicia was a tall woman with thick dark hair that fell perfectly styled to her shoulders. She was wearing a black Armani suit, with a pencil skirt, blazer and a white blouse with ruffles along the neckline. She looked fierce, Cameron thought. The kind of woman who struck fear into men and elicited jealously from other women. She was sitting behind her desk in her corner office on the fortieth floor of a downtown high-rise. She was the Black in Frank Black LLP, a firm specializing in reproductive rights. After Andy explained their situation to her, Alicia gave them a little background on herself. Reproductive rights law was a broad topic—she represented families when surrogates broke their contracts, with complex adoption issues, egg or sperm donation cases, and a rare custody battle. While she had never heard of a case like Cameron and Andy's, she assured them that her experience was as close as they could find. "We'll just need to subpoena the doctor if he refuses to provide their information."

"We have to review all of our possibilities here," Alicia said. "Of course, we'll start by sending a letter to the couple with our request—that they agree to hand over custody of your baby and accept custody of theirs. Best case scenario, they agree and we will draw up the papers needed for that. From there we will need to file a request with the court to amend your baby's birth certificate."

"Sounds easy enough," Andy said, his mood lightening.

Alicia smiled. "We also need to prepare for alternative scenarios."

"What other scenarios?" Andy said, his eyebrows narrowing.

"There may be a chance that they refuse to give up your baby. Or maybe they agree, but they want visitation rights. You'll need to decide what is acceptable to you. Or there is the possibility of negligent parenting, you don't know them, you don't know how they have treated your baby," Alicia said. "In that case we may need to seek damages as well."

Cameron's heart stopped. It hadn't crossed her mind that the other couple could have harmed her baby. What if they were bad parents? Let the baby cry, forget to feed it, or leave it alone to feel neglected in its crib. Cameron was careful to take good care of their baby, as though she were their own. She breastfed her, held her, even took pictures that she would give to her mother. Fear that her baby wasn't receiving the same treatment overtook her.

"What do we do if they don't want to switch?" Andy asked.

"We will sue for declaratory judgment declaring that you are the baby's legal parents," Alicia said. "We'll also sue for damages, psychological pain and suffering and the baby's future medical expenses if we find evidence of any negligence."

There was that word again. Negligence. How could the parents not treat the baby well? Didn't they understand they were in the same boat as Cameron and Andy? If they were doing IVF, they must have really wanted a baby. But of course they probably wanted their own baby. Cameron prayed they wouldn't take out any anger on her poor baby.

"But a court case, that could take weeks, months even," Andy said.

"Yes, likely months," Alicia said. "We'll do everything we can to speed it up in light of the circumstances."

"If it's months, what do we do with this baby?" Andy said, pointing to the newborn resting quietly in the stroller.

"Either you can take care of her, or we can petition to put her in foster care for the time being," Alicia said. "But let's hope it doesn't get to that. I'm sure the other couple is just as distraught as you are and will want to fix things as soon as possible."

Chapter 24

October 11, 2013

A knock on the door startled Avery awake. She had been nursing Amelia in her rocking chair and had dozed off. She hadn't been sleeping the last few nights. Even those few hours when the baby was sleeping, she lay awake. How could she sleep after what Dr. Klein had told them? She wanted to forget it all, return to how things were before she got the call from the clinic. When she was just enjoying her new baby like every other new mother.

Three days ago, when they left Dr. Klein's office, Avery and Graham discussed what they wanted to do. They agreed to meet with the clinic's lawyer to discuss a settlement. Maybe they'd get a lawyer of their own after their first sit down, but they just wanted to settle things quickly. The fewer lawyers, the better, they thought.

Regarding the other couple, they decided to write them a letter. They would give it to the doctor to pass along to them.

Hi,

We are strangers but it seems that fate has decided to intertwine our families. Both of us began a journey to grow our families with the help of Dr. Klein, who we trusted with our most prized possession—a piece of ourselves. While Dr. Klein betrayed our trust, it seems we were both lucky enough to be blessed with a baby.

Our baby joined our family five weeks ago and she has brought so much joy. She is happy and healthy, and with her, our family is complete. We love her more than words can express and will raise her with strong family values that will ensure her lifelong happiness and success.

We understand that your perspective may differ than ours in how you want to proceed, but we hope that you will respect our family and keep it whole.

We wish you the best in raising your new baby and hope you feel the same joy we do.

They gave the letter to Dr. Klein, asking him to pass it on to the other family. They pleaded with him not to betray their identity, to respect their privacy, and not contact them again. Avery hoped that with that, they would be done with this mess. They would meet during the week with the lawyer and agree on a settlement and move on.

When the knock on the door woke Avery, she startled. Amelia was asleep on her breast, her eyes closed and lips curled. Avery put the sleeping baby in her crib and went to answer the door.

"Mrs. Stephens?" It was a young boy, probably in his twenties, wearing glasses and a white collared shirt that was wrinkled and untucked. He had a bicycle with him, which he held steady with one hand. In the other hand, he had an orange envelope.

"Yes?" Avery answered.

"You've been served," the boy said, handing her the envelope. He turned around, hopped on his bicycle and disappeared before Avery processed what she had just heard. She held the orange envelope in her hands. It was stiff from the papers inside. Turning back in toward the house, she ripped it open and headed toward the kitchen. She pulled a thick stack of papers from the envelope, *Complaint for Declaratory Judgment*, was the headline. Then she started reading. The words jumbled on the page as Avery concentrated hard trying to translate the legalese on the paper. There were phrases like *rights and*

obligations of the legal and biological parents...sole and exclusive custody...amendment of the birth certificate...parental intent...best interest of the child.
Avery felt herself getting hot as she kept reading. Her breath quickened and she felt lightheaded. I need to call Graham, she thought.

She ran upstairs and grabbed her phone, which she had left on her nightstand. Amelia had woken up and has started to cry.

"Graham!" Avery screamed when he answered the phone. "We're being sued!" She could barely hear herself over Amelia's shrieks.

"What? By whom?" Graham responded.

"I don't know!" Avery felt frantic. "A kid came to the door with some papers. He said I was served. I tried reading the papers. It's about Amelia. Something about a judgment, custody, or something like that."

"I am coming home," Graham said. "Do not do anything." He hung up the phone before Avery could say any more. She started pacing the room, she couldn't be still. She had to do something. She picked up Amelia and held her close to her chest. The baby immediately started to quiet down.

"Don't worry baby," she said. "I'm here for you, I'll protect you. I won't let anyone take you away from me no matter what." No matter what, she would fight whatever lawsuit came at them. She'd die before anyone took away her baby girl. She started to feel confidence in her resolve by the time Graham came home.

"Avery," he called for her as he entered the house. "Come down here." Avery was still in their bedroom holding Amelia. She ran down the stairs as quickly as she could while being careful not to trip. Graham was in the kitchen with his phone to his ear. When he saw her, he put the phone down, pressing the speaker button. "Avery this is Brad Sandfeld. He is a family lawyer who helped John win his custody battle." John was a colleague of Graham's who had two kids and a nasty divorce.

"Hi Avery, nice to meet you," Brad said through the phone. "Graham was just telling me about your situation."

"Our situation is that someone wants to kidnap our child," Avery said cynically.

"Yes, this is a very unique case," Brad responded. "But we can beat this. It is obviously in the child's best interest to stay with her parents. Any judge will see that. We will ensure that no one can take away your child." Brad paused for a moment. "I need to read the complaint you were served. And I think we should meet in person to discuss our strategy. Can you come to my office?"

Avery and Graham agreed to meet right away. No use wasting any time when their family was at stake. The couple jumped in the car, putting Amelia in her car seat for the ride.

"What about the other baby?" Graham said. "Did the complaint say anything about it?"

"I don't know," Avery said. She read the complaint, but she couldn't make sense of it. Why couldn't they write in plain English what they wanted? "You think they want both babies?"

"I assume if they want Amelia, they do not want the other one," Graham said. "The other has our genetics."

"So we will raise both," Avery said resolutely. "We can handle it. It will be like Amelia has a twin."

Chapter 25

January 31, 2013

Sydney was late. She sat on her bed, deciding what she would say when she got to work. What she would say to Dr. Klein. Since he broke up with her a few weeks ago, work had been torture. Sydney knew she had to stay professional. She continued with her daily routine working with the embryos, smiling at patients and aiding Dr. Klein during the transfers. All the while, she was burning inside. Waiting for Dr. Klein to say something to her other than "Please hand me that petri dish," or "Can you check on so and so's embryos," but he never did. Yes, he would come in the lab every morning and ask, "How are you?" but that wasn't directed to her. It was directed to Rachel and her. And since the breakup, Sydney let Rachel answer. Silence was better than lying, Sydney thought. She couldn't tell him everything was all right.

What's wrong with me? She thought to herself. She was dressed and ready for work, holding the white stick in her hand. She missed her period a couple weeks ago. Probably due to stress. Since the breakup—if she could call it that—she hadn't been eating as much. She'd been drinking more, going out with friends multiple evenings a week. A couple times those happy hours turned into a late night with a stranger and a shameful walk home at sunrise. Both times it happened, she told herself she would stop drinking so much. Stop making poor alcohol-induced decisions. That was how things had started with Dr. Klein and now look where she was.

When Sydney first started working for Dr. Klein, she was immediately drawn to the doctor. He was sophisticated, with grey speckled hair. He was also charming and kind, with a smile that could get him anything he wanted. She remembered her first day at work, she asked him why he chose to specialize in fertility. So he could give people the greatest gift of all, he said holding Sydney's gaze as though daring her to blink. The next moment his wife had walked in the door with their two children. Both ran to hug their dad. Sydney looked at his wife. I bet she was president of her sorority, was Sydney's first thought.

Sydney wanted what Mrs. Klein had. Where Sydney went to school, there were no sororities. Even if there were, it wasn't like she had time for that kind of thing. She studied at LaGuardia Community College, just a short train ride from her house in the Bronx. After high school, when most of her friends—the few who did graduate—were getting jobs around the neighborhood, she applied for nursing school. Mostly, she was rejected. She expected that, and told herself that if she wasn't accepted anywhere she would forget about nursing. But then the letter came from LCC. It would be expensive, she would need to work after classes and get a loan from the bank, but she could do it.

When she started nursing school, her friends made fun of her. Asked her why she thought she was better than them. Eventually the teasing stopped being fun for Sydney. She stopped calling those people her friends. And she started taking more night shifts at her restaurant job so she could save enough to get out of the Bronx. She got her associate degree and then found her job at the clinic.

With Mark, it started with just a little flirting. A gaze that lasted an extra moment, a pat on the back, a shared laugh. Then when Sydney had been working for a year, Dr. Klein told her he wanted to celebrate her anniversary. He said he took Rachel out too when she had been working with him for a year. Now it was her turn. Pick any restaurant you want, he said.

Sydney picked a steakhouse she had been wanting to try. She rarely went to restaurants. Being a nurse paid well, but after rent in Manhattan, groceries, and her student loans, there wasn't much left. So she was excited for a free meal at a place she would never have been able to afford. After work she went home, showered, put on a nice dress, did her hair and makeup and took a cab—what a splurge!—to the restaurant. When she got there, Dr. Klein was already there, an open bottle of wine on the table. "Happy anniversary," he said, pouring her a glass. Somewhere during the second bottle he told her she was the most beautiful lab technician he had ever known. Her bronzed skin, mocha eyes, plush lips. "Thank you Dr. Klein," she blushed, twirling her finger in one of her dark curls. "Call me Mark," he corrected her.

At the end of the evening, Dr. Klein insisted on walking her home. It was late, they were in New York City. Girls like her shouldn't walk home alone in the dark. She agreed; how chivalrous, she thought. When they got to her apartment, he said he was a little dizzy. Could he come up and sit down for a moment? Of course, Sydney agreed. She grabbed two bottles of water when he sat on her couch. She handed him one, and he pulled her down, kissing her as the bottles dropped to the floor. An hour later, he left, saying he had to get home.

The next day at the clinic, the flirting became more exaggerated. He squeezed her shoulder, smelled her hair when no one was looking. Sydney enjoyed the thrill, their secret, and happily agreed when he offered to come over again that evening.

For a year, Dr. Klein had been coming over in the evenings. Sometimes it was a few times a week, sometimes once a week. Sometimes a couple weeks went by between visits. It depended on him, when he could get away. Sydney often suggested they go out, have another steak dinner. But Dr. Klein—Mark—was always tired. Just wanted to relax. Sydney understood. Work at the clinic was exhausting. They were always on their feet, always putting on smiling faces with patients.

Lying in bed together, they would talk about vacations they wanted to take. "You'd love Rome," he had said to her once. Sydney fantasized about what it would be like going to Rome with him. But it would never happen as long as he was married. She knew it was just a fantasy. But maybe he wouldn't stay married. He must be unhappy with his wife if he is with me, she thought often. But she never asked about his marriage.

Then, suddenly, after a year, he ended it. Just like that. As though Sydney was nothing more to him than a nice dessert. Something you crave, you enjoy, and then you move on. And now, she was late. After missing her period, she waited two weeks before taking a test. She finally got the courage to take a test after convincing herself that there was no way she could be pregnant. Fate wouldn't allow that; it would be too ironic. A lab technician in a fertility clinic getting accidently knocked up—that would be too cruel. But there were the two pink lines on the test. Both clear, unmistakable.

She had to tell Dr. Klein. She knew immediately that she would keep the baby. She couldn't imagine giving it up and then working on the embryos of women desperate for a child. It would be so wrong. She would keep the baby, love it, and figure it out. She knew a few girls from her high school who were single moms. If they could do it, why couldn't she? Funny, she thought nursing school would make sure she didn't end up like them. But instead, it led her to exactly the same place.

She arrived at the clinic a little later than usual. She was just finishing up her morning routine when Dr. Klein popped in. "Good morning," he said, looking around—anywhere but at Sydney. "Where's Rachel?"

"Still with the patients," Sydney answered. This was it, she had to tell him. She couldn't hold it in.

"Alright," he said, walking out of the lab to his office.

"Wait, Dr. Klein, we need to talk."

"Sydney, it's better we don't." He gave her a nod, like he was trying to convince her, and left the lab, heading to his office.

Sydney felt anger start to boil inside her. How could he brush her off like that! Especially when she was pregnant with his baby! She stood up from her station and stomped into his office closing the door behind her.

"Mark, I'm pregnant!" she yelled, her hands on her hips. Dr. Klein was still hanging up his coat on the rack next to his desk.

"Are you sure it's mine?" he asked calmly.

"What!" That was not the response Sydney expected. She didn't know what she expected, but definitely not that. "Of course it's yours!"

"I'm just asking, calm down," Dr. Klein responded. "We'll take care of it."

"What does that mean? You make babies for a living; don't even tell me you want to kill this one."

Chapter 26

October 14, 2013

The chair was cold and forced Avery to sit up with her back completely straight. It was like the chair was built specifically to make her uncomfortable. To make her do anything just to get out of it. She rested her hands in her lap, afraid of touching the glass table in front of her. Leave a fingerprint. Break it. Everything felt so fragile. She was sitting quietly next to Graham in that lawyer's office. The one they met when they went to Dr. Klein's office the week before. What was his name again? Chad? Chip?

The office was dark despite having a large window on the far wall. The walls were mostly bare besides a gold clock that ticked as the seconds went by. The glass table— a desk, Avery presumed—was almost as bare as the walls. It had a small writing pad and one pen, standing up in a granite penholder. Everything looked so sterile.

"Sorry to keep you waiting," the lawyer said as he entered the room. Only thirty minutes, Avery wanted to say, but instead she just gave him a closed-mouth smile. They didn't have a lot of time before they needed to leave; they only had the babysitter for another two hours.

"How are you doing?" the lawyer said. It was more an opening statement than a question. He sat down across from them at the other side of the glass desk in a big navy-blue chair. Avery watched him closely. Chase. That was his name, she suddenly remembered. "Anyways, I am so glad you could come in so quickly; Dr. Klein wants to settle this as soon as possible. And I'm sure you do too."

"No problem," Graham said, but the lawyer didn't pause for the response. He continued talking.

"We're prepared to offer you two hundred thousand dollars for this inconvenience," Chase said. "We think that's fair, seeing as you weren't really injured by this whole situation. You have a lovely daughter and the rest of your embryos are safe in the lab. We can continue storing them for free as long as you like."

"Is that a normal amount for a medical malpractice settlement?" Graham asked.

"Well it depends on the situation, of course," the lawyer said. "In your case, when there was no harm done to anyone and you won't have any future medical bills because of what happened, it is quite a lot."

Avery looked at Graham, whose forefinger and thumb were wrapped around his chin. He was nodding as the lawyer spoke.

"I think we should think about it for a little bit," Graham said. "May we get back to you?"

"Of course," the lawyer responded. "But you should decide quickly, this is a large settlement; I really had to fight to get you that much. The insurance company could change their mind or if anything comes out that changes things, the deal could be off the table. I would highly recommend you accept this offer before it's gone."

Avery looked back and forth between the lawyer and Graham, who was still nodding.

"Oh, one more thing," the lawyer continued. "I also need you to sign NDAs with the settlement. It's no big deal, totally standard. It just says you won't discuss what happened with anyone."

"Thank you, as I said, we need to think about it," Graham said.

"Sure, but remember the clock is ticking," the lawyer said.

"Is this the same offer you gave to the other couple?" Avery asked.

"We haven't started discussing with them, but this is standard," the lawyer smiled, leaning back in his chair.

Avery nodded and looked back at Graham. "I think we better go," she said. "We'll think about it and get back to you." She stood up, followed by Graham, and shook the lawyer's hand. He led them out of the office toward the elevators and waited with them until the doors opened. Avery felt like he was afraid to leave them alone with the settlement offer.

"Waiting for your call," the lawyer said as the elevator doors closed with the couple inside.

"What do you think?" Avery said when the elevator started going down.

"I do not know, I do not have anything to compare it to," Graham responded. "Maybe we should ask Brad, the lawyer. He may have a better idea of whether this is a good deal."

Avery nodded. The elevator doors opened to the lobby and the couple walked out toward their car. As they were walking, Graham's phone rang. He pulled it out of his pocket and chuckled. "Speak of the devil," he said. "Hi Brad," he said into the phone. "I'm so glad you called; we actually want to consult with you about something."

"Put him on speaker!" Avery said, giving Graham's arm a slight tug. Graham complied.

"Sure, but first we need to talk," Brad said. "We have a hearing in court tomorrow, it's just an initial case conference, but we need to discuss strategy."

"Tomorrow?" Graham blurted. "You said the trial would start after we filed our response? Did we not have a month?"

"That's usually how things go," Brad responded. "But they have some fancy lawyer who somehow got this pushed up, she's trying to catch us with our pants down. But don't worry, we're prepared. We'll even try to use this against them."

"What do you need from us?" Graham asked.

"You guys just need to show up in the downtown civil court tomorrow at 11:00 am," Brad said.

"And what is going to happen in court?" Graham asked.

"We'll discuss the case, they will probably try to get the judge to grant a summary judgment in their favor, but that's not likely, even though it's Judge Baxter. He's a reasonable guy. What I want to hear from you two is that we're fighting this to the end, right? The judge will ask us to go to mediation, but our play is that we are keeping the baby no matter what, right?"

"Yes, sir," Graham responded. "No matter what."

"Got it," Brad said. "So I'll see you in court tomorrow."

"Wait!" Avery said. "We have a question."

"Oh, right, you wanted to ask me something," Brad said.

"We got a settlement offer from the doctor's malpractice insurance," Avery said. "They offered us two hundred thousand dollars. And they want us to sign an NDA. Should we accept it?"

"Well that really isn't my area of expertise," Brad responded. "But I can refer you to another lawyer who specializes in malpractice suits."

Avery sighed. The last thing she wanted was another lawyer. "Can you just tell us what you think?" she pleaded.

"I'd have to read the NDA," Brad responded. "I'll talk to a few colleagues and get back to you." Brad hung up the phone.

"Maybe we should just take it," Avery said, thinking about what they could do with two hundred thousand dollars. It could close their mortgage. Be saved for Amelia to buy a house one day.

"Let's think about it," Graham said.

"But what if they change their minds?" Avery said. "It's a lot of money."

Graham raised his eyebrows and tilted his head slightly. "I do not think the offer is going away," Graham said.

Avery pursed her lips. She felt like she was being ambushed from all sides, needing to make decisions that she was incapable of making. Couldn't everything just go away?

Chapter 27

October 15, 2013

Cameron put on a dark pant suit and her pearl necklace that once belonged to her grandmother. Look wholesome, motherly, their lawyer Alicia said. It was the first time Cameron had put on clothes other than pajamas since the baby was born. The baby—they hadn't given her a name; they couldn't name someone else's baby—had exhausted her. She breastfed her so her milk supply wouldn't go down before she could breastfeed her own baby and dressed her in all the outfits she bought—someone should wear them before they would be too small. She stayed up full nights sometimes when the baby just wouldn't sleep. She swayed side to side, did squats, any movement she could think of when trying to put the baby to sleep. She danced around the living room with the baby in arms when she wouldn't stop fussing. But Cameron felt a distance, like she was a nanny, not a mom.

Cameron looked at herself in the mirror. She didn't recognize who she saw. Dark circles under her eyes, zits, her hair greasy even after a shower. Her cheeks a little puffy, her breasts large and full and her waist a little rounder than she'd ever remembered it. Who was this person she had become?

For the last ten days, she had been swinging between crying and operating on automatic pilot. Sometimes she felt like she was being crushed by the world and other times she felt like she was spinning so fast she would pass out. She hadn't slept more than two hours at a time since the baby came, every night she was getting up multiple times to feed the baby or rock her to sleep. Andy watched her bitterly, unable to sleep but also unable to get close to the baby. It was like there was an invisible glass case around him.

A faint cry came from the bassinet, causing Cameron's heart to sink. She had just put the baby down, she thought she would have at least thirty minutes to get ready. She pulled herself away from the mirror and walked over to the baby who was squirming in her swaddle. Cameron picked her up, hushing her a moment.

"Cam, are you almost ready?" Andy yelled from the living room. "We're going to be late."

"Can you help me out?" she yelled back. Andy immediately appeared in the doorway. "Can you just hold her a minute? She's fussy, and I need to finish getting ready."

"Just leave her in the bassinet," he said. "She'll be fine."

"Hold her," Cameron said sternly and placed the baby in Andy's arms. "Five minutes." She walked to the bathroom, her eyes still on Andy. He held the baby in front of him, like he was afraid to touch her. His eyes looking right through her to the floor. She continued to cry.

"Cam, I can't," he said, placing her down in the bassinet. There was a knock on the door. "The babysitter is here." He left to go open the door. A moment later he returned, followed by Selma, a nanny they had hired from a reputable agency. At first, Cameron was against hiring a nanny, but that was before the mix-up, back when she thought she'd be raising her own child. Now, with a schedule full of lawyer meetings and soon court hearings, she knew they needed help. Just until they got their own baby back.

Selma picked up the crying baby and hugged her to her chest. "We'll be fine," Selma said. "Don't worry about us." The baby slowly quieted down. Cameron patted the baby's head as she and Andy walked out their apartment.

"It's just not fair," Cameron whined after they got in a cab. "Out of everyone who does IVF, why us? What did we do to deserve this?"

"It's not about deserving this," Andy said. "It's about a shitty doctor who fucked up."

All Cameron wanted was to wake up and realize this was all a nightmare. Instead, she was shuffling between taking care of the baby and participating in so many lawyer conversations it made her head spin.

"What I don't understand is why the other couple is trying to drag this out," Andy continued talking. "Why they're making this an even bigger mess."

A week ago they had received—through Dr. Klein who passed it to their lawyer—a letter from the other couple asking to be left alone. The letter enraged Andy who started spouting out all different types of threats. It's basically kidnapping, he said, stealing. "We should put their kid in foster care!" Andy had yelled. "See how they feel about that!" Cameron thought that was a little harsh, but she agreed the couple was wrong. How could they think it was just for them to keep something that wasn't theirs?

After the letter, Alicia filed a complaint against the couple in court. A summons was served, requiring the couple to respond. At the same time, Alicia filed another motion with the court seeking a summary judgment on the complaint. It was the fastest way to get the case resolved, she advised them. It meant one hearing in front of a judge who would decide the matter according to the law. And this was a matter of law, Alicia told them. Their genetic material was their property and needed to be returned. There was no need for a long drawn out trial, which could take months or even years.

The other couple hadn't filed their response to the initial complaint yet, they had time—the summons gave them twenty days from the date they were served. But Alicia pulled a few strings, called in a couple favors and got them an initial case management conference in front of a judge. It was just four days after the other couple was served so they may or may not have retained counsel and may or may not show up to court. If they didn't show up to court, it would immediately sway the judge against them, Alicia told them with a wink. Hopefully they were scrambling.

Cameron's breathing was labored even though she was sitting down. She was afraid of the other couple showing up in court. On one hand, she wanted to see them—she knew one look would be enough to know whether her baby was safe—but on the other hand, she didn't want to put a face to the 'kidnappers' of her baby. What if they looked normal? Like nice people? But that was impossible. Nice people wouldn't do what they did.

They arrived at the courthouse in downtown Manhattan where Alicia was waiting outside for them. When she saw them step out of the cab, she ran over to them. She greeted them with a 'good morning' and a handshake each and led them into the courthouse and into one of the courtrooms. Cameron had never been in a real courtroom before. It was smaller than she imagined. A podium for the judge to sit on, a stand for witnesses, a box on the side for a jury, and two tables sitting side-by-side. They walked in from the back, passing three rows of benches for any spectators before sitting down at one of the tables. The room was empty except for them and a bailiff standing near a closed door at the front of the room. He stood tall, staring at the back of the room, like a British guard.

"When the judge comes in, we all stand," Alicia said quietly to the couple. "We have Judge Baxter, he's very conservative, family values type. That's good for us. Anyway, when he sits, you sit. I'll explain the case and why we want a summary judgment. If the defense shows up, they will probably fight it. Then the judge will make a ruling. He'll decide whether to grant a summary judgment or not. If so, he will decide the matter as soon as the defense submits their response to the complaint."

"And if he doesn't grant the request for a summary judgment?" Andy asked.

"We'll file a motion to expedite a trial," Alicia said. "I have that motion ready here just in case."

Cameron and Andy nodded, as Alicia continued. "You just need to sit here quietly. Don't say anything, don't smile. Also, hold hands, it will look good to the judge."

Suddenly they heard footsteps come in through the back of the courtroom. All three of them turned to see a bald man in a dark grey suit enter. Behind him was a couple—the woman had fluffy blond hair pulled back in a ponytail and was wearing a simple navy-blue dress. She was a little plump, Cameron thought, carrying a few extra pounds around her waist and thighs. The man was tall with glasses and unruly hair that looked like it could not be tamed. The other couple, Cameron knew immediately. The threesome walked through the courtroom, taking their seats at the table next to Cameron, Andy and Alicia. The two lawyers nodded heads at each other, and then both turned to their clients.

Cameron held her breath. She wanted to keep staring at them. She wanted to read them, to hear everything they were saying to each other. She wanted to know where they left her baby while they were here in the courthouse. A small part of her had hoped they would bring the baby, but she knew they wouldn't.

"Stay calm," Alicia said, placing her hand on Cameron's. "Don't stare at them, it makes you look angry, less sympathetic."

Cameron nodded and looked down at the table. A few moments later, the bailiff spoke.

"All rise for the honorable Judge Baxter."

Alicia nudged Cameron, who scrambled to her feet, feeling less graceful than she ever had before.

"You may be seated," Judge Baxter said. Judge Baxter was an older man, probably in his sixties, Cameron guessed. He had thick white hair and rosy cheeks. "What do we have today?" Andy grabbed Cameron's hand and placed their fists on top of their table.

"Your honor, Alicia Black for the prosecution," Alicia started. "We're here to discuss my clients' complaint for declaratory judgment declaring that my clients are the legal and biological parents of the baby born to Avery and Graham Stephens on September 1, 2013. We are also requesting summary judgment on the complaint, as this is a simple issue over returning a child to its biological and legal family."

"Thank you, Ms. Black," Judge Baxter said. "From the defense? I don't see your response to the complaint, have you filed it yet?"

"Hi, your honor, Brad Sandfeld here," the other lawyer said. "My clients only received the summons four days ago and just recently retained me as counsel. We are working on the response and will file it before the deadline. We would be happy with a summary judgment, as we also think this is a simple issue. The child is already with her family and should stay with the parents that birthed her and have cared for her for the last six weeks."

"Interesting," Judge Baxter said with a chuckle. "We agree on a motion. But for different reasons. Let's hear your arguments in the case and I'll decide on summary judgment. Mr. Sandfeld, are you ready to argue or do you need more time since you haven't filed your response yet?"

"We'd like more time, your honor," Brad said. "This hearing today was scheduled with complete disregard to regular court procedures. We were quite surprised that we were summoned for a case management conference before our deadline to respond to the complaint."

"Yes, it is peculiar how this hearing made it on to the docket," the judge said.

Cameron's heard skipped a beat. Was Alicia's plan backfiring? Was the judge angry that they were wasting his time? Andy's grip tightened on her hand. She could feel her hand drenched in sweat—whether it was hers or Andy's, she couldn't tell.

"Agreed, your honor," Brad said. He gave a quick smile to Alicia. So quick, that if Cameron blinked, she would have missed it.

"Very well," Judge Baxter said. "We'll have a hearing on the summary judgment motion on the deadline for the response to be filed, which is..." the judge looked up to the ceiling as though counting the days in his head. "October 31." He banged his gavel.

Andy let go of Cameron's hand. "That's so far away!" she whispered to him. "What are we supposed to do until then?" Andy looked up to Alicia, who was texting on her phone.

"Alicia," he said, getting her attention. "I thought you said we could get this sorted out today. We can't wait until October 31."

"You're going to have to," she said without looking up from her phone. "This is how the judicial system works. I'll do what I can. We can try to settle with the defendants beforehand, but if they refuse, we have to wait for the hearing."

Cameron wanted to cry, to scream. This morning, she thought she was so close to holding her baby. She thought everything was about to be resolved. That this would be the last day of her nightmare. But now she was realizing, that the nightmare had just begun.

Chapter 28

October 31, 2013

The courtroom was cold, but Avery was sweating. She could feel little beads of water on the back of her neck and on her lower back. She was breathing, trying to stay calm. Next to her at the defense table Graham and Brad were deep in conversation about the weather. The weather, like it mattered. At the defense table, that's what mattered. Like they were criminals who needed to prove their innocence. Like they did something wrong. Since when was loving and wanting to protect your baby a crime? It's not a criminal case, Graham kept reminding her, they weren't criminals. It was a civil case, a dispute to be resolved.

Graham kept telling Avery about the judgment of King Solomon in the Old Testament. Two women came to the king claiming to be the mother of a baby. To settle the dispute, Solomon pulled his sword from its sheath and suggested cutting the baby in half. One woman accepted this proposal, while the other begged the king to sheath his sword and give the baby to her rival. From this, the king understood who the real mother was, the one who prioritized the baby's wellbeing overall. That was Avery, Graham said, the real mother, the one who wanted what was best for the baby.

The last two weeks had been hell for Avery. Avery was sure she spent more time in the lawyer's office than at her home. They discussed strategy, their response to the complaint and had discussed whether there was any acceptable settlement. The other couple's lawyer, Alicia Black, had reached out with a few offers, giving Avery and

Graham visitation rights in return for handing over Amelia. Avery had scoffed at the offers—the first offer gave them biannual visitation rights, the second monthly—why should she agree to visitation rights with her own daughter? The only way she'd accept a settlement was if Amelia stayed with them, Avery told Brad. Give the other couple visitation rights, she didn't care how often they wanted to see the baby, they could visit weekly, but they were not getting custody.

Poor Amelia spent most of the last two weeks with them in the lawyer's office, strapped into a stroller instead of being cuddled and read to like she should have been. The last couple days she had been coughing a lot, poor thing. Avery hoped she wasn't getting sick.

Now, again they were in the courthouse, in the courtroom, at the defense table ready to start. The other couple—the plaintiffs—were at their table with their lawyer. Avery couldn't stop herself from looking at them. Did Amelia have any resemblance? If so, Avery didn't see it. The woman was young with shoulder-length perfectly straight brown hair. She was thin, especially so for someone who just had a baby. Very pretty, Avery thought. Her husband looked like he came out of an Abercrombie and Fitch catalogue. Perfect freckles, wide shoulders and thick hair. She wanted to feel sorry for them, but she also hated them for what they were doing to her.

"All rise for the honorable Judge Baxter," the bailiff said. Avery jumped. She wasn't ready to start. Once court proceedings started it meant there was a chance she could lose her baby. Until now, no one could take Amelia away from her. Avery stood up. She felt wobbly, like she could faint.

The judge came in and sat down at his podium. He signaled with his hands that they could sit. "Hi counselors," he started. "Are we ready today to discuss whether we can close this case with a summary judgment?"

"We are, your honor," the plaintiff's lawyer said, standing up. She was a tall woman with dark smooth blow-dried hair. She wore a suit, a pencil skirt to her knees, a white blouse to her neck and a blazer buttoned in the front. Her lips were a dark maroon and curved up in a smile.

"And the defense?" the judge asked.

"Yes, your honor," Brad responded.

"Wonderful," Judge Baxter said. "Let's settle this today then. Ms. Black, please proceed."

"Thank you, your honor," Alicia said. "As you know this complaint deals with declaring my clients the legal and biological parents of the baby born to the defendants. The genetic materials from which this baby grew are wholly connected to my clients, whose embryo was implanted in the defendants by a mistake at their fertility clinic. If we look back at similar cases of this sort, such as Perry-Rogers vs. Fasano which was decided here in New York, we see that the court decided that biology and genetics takes precedent over the gestational carrier in deciding custody disputes.

"Similarly, in California, in Johnson vs. Calvert, it was decided that whoever intended to procreate a child, that is, who intended to birth and raise the child is the legal and natural mother. Through completing the IVF process to create this baby, it is clear that my clients intended to birth and raise her, and therefore they are the natural parents."

"Your honor," Brad began speaking the moment Alicia stopped. "My clients have also proved their intent to birth and raise the child. They completed the same IVF process in order to conceive. We would like to bring McDonald vs. McDonald to the court's attention. In this case, the gestational mother—who was not genetically connected to the baby—was deemed the natural mother due to the fact that she had birthed and cared for the baby—"

"In McDonald vs. McDonald the egg came from an anonymous donor," Alicia cut in. "In this case, the egg came from my client, so this precedent is not relevant here."

"Ms. Black I am not finished," Brad said calmly. "I simply bring up that case because the court stipulated that a bond is created between a mother and an infant before birth and that the bond is strengthened during the birth and after. Additionally, in the case widely referred to as the Matter of Baby M, which was litigated in New Jersey, the surrogate was named the natural mother even though a contract between the surrogate, Mrs. Whitehead, and the couple that intended to raise the baby, Mr. and Mrs. Stern, stated that the baby would be handed over to the Sterns upon birth."

"Again, in that case the egg came from the surrogate—" Alicia raise her voice as she again cut Brad off.

"Please let me finish," Brad said, also raising his voice. "I bring up that case only to say that intent is not the most important thing here. Additionally, I would like to bring up Pope vs. Moore and Twiggs vs. May. Two cases when babies were accidently switched at the hospital at birth. When the couples found out and embarked on a custody battle such as this one, the court ruled that the babies would stay with the families that raised them. In both cases. If you look at all of these precedents together, it is clear that the court should grant summary judgment declaring that Amelia stay with her natural parents."

"Your honor," Alicia jumped in again. "All of these cases are unique and none of the precedents brought up by the defense are relevant in this case. We are talking about stolen genetic materials. Yes, the defendants are not the ones who stole the genetic materials, but the materials are not theirs to keep."

"If the plaintiffs see the baby simply as 'genetic materials' then I think we would be doing the baby a severe disservice by handing her over to them," Brad said.

"Your honor—"

"Alright, enough," Judge Baxter said, banging his gavel. "I see this matter is much more complex than expected and that the law can go either way. Both sides have brought up very valuable points and very applicable precedents. I'm ready to rule on the motion for summary judgment and I must deny the motion. This case will proceed to trial."

"Your honor," Alicia said. "If you could just reconsider, this matter is extremely timely, as the life and care of a baby is at stake. A trial could take years, leaving this poor baby as well as the families in limbo for a long time."

"I understand, but we must ensure that the right decision is reached in this case," the judge said. "The right decision is more important than timeliness."

"In that case I would like to file a motion to expedite a trial on this complaint," Alicia said. "As discussed, every day this case continues a baby is further separated from her parents and the longer it goes on, the more detrimental it is to her psychology and her mental health."

"Your honor, we oppose the motion to expedite the trial," Brad said. "As Ms. Black mentioned, this case deals with a very serious issue and the trial will significantly change the course of this child's life. Therefore we believe this case should be given ample time to be fully and thoroughly researched and developed to ensure the court has all the relevant information for the trial."

"Your honor, this is a stall tactic," Alicia said, her voice growing louder and more shrill. "The defense wants to delay the trial so they can keep the baby with them as long as possible. Then in the trial they will argue that the baby has already bonded with the defendants and that it would be detrimental to remove her from their home."

"Thanks for arguing my case for me, Ms. Black," Brad said. "But this is not a stall tactic. As I said, we want to make sure all the evidence is discovered and we think both sides would benefit from having adequate time to prepare."

"Your honor, the longer it takes for this trial to proceed the more severe and harmful its consequences will be," Alicia argued. "It is in everyone's best interest to complete it as soon as possible."

"Your honor—" Brad started but was cut off by the bang of a gavel.

"Thank you, counselors," Judge Baxter said, banging the gavel two more times. "I hear your arguments and I am going to expedite the trial. This case deals with the life of a child and we need to settle it as soon as possible so this child can start living its life." Another bang of the gavel. "The trial will commence a week from today in this courtroom. See you then counselors." The judge stood up, his black gown flowing, and stepped off the podium toward the door at the front of the room.

"We're off to a great start," Brad said quietly to Graham and Avery. "The longer this takes the longer Amelia is with you and the harder it will be to take her away. A jury won't rip a baby away from her mother."

Chapter 29

March 28, 2019

Finally my hour of torture is over. I leave Dr. Moore's office and step out into the sunshine. It's bright and I pull my sunglasses out of my purse, accidentally pulling my keys and a few loose pieces of paper out with them. The keys fall to the ground with a clank and the papers flutter slowly in the wind. I bend down to grab the runaway contents, slipping the keys back into the purse. The papers I catch as they reach the ground. One is an old receipt from McDonalds. A Big Mac and an ice cream sundae. What junk. I can't believe that I allowed myself to eat that last week. But I guess right now I have a pass. No reason to think about my figure right now, it won't matter in a few days.

It's only noon but it feels like I've been awake for days. Every day feels like this. I spend the days just waiting them out, hoping they will end. Counting the hours until I can go back to sleep, and for what? So I can wake up again and do it all over? What's the purpose? At first I thought this feeling of waiting would go away. That eventually I would start living again, experiencing again, but it hasn't happened. I doubt it will, unless my plan works.

My phone rings. I open my purse and pull it out. It's my mom. I silence the phone and put it back in my purse. I don't have any strength to talk to her, but I know I will have to soon. She always calls me on this day. And I never answer. I'll call her back tomorrow, I tell myself. One more day. Just not today.

She knows the significance of today. The day my life was over. The day I crumbled and realized I would never recover. I haven't, recovered that is. But this year, I am making a change. I've been preparing for today for the last three weeks. Everyday preparing myself with my evening ritual in the bathroom. So my husband wouldn't see. I don't want him to know. He would have tried to talk me out of it. But my plan will work. And it will be good for everyone. For me, it will end my suffering. For my husband too, it will end his.

I walk past a Starbucks and decide to go in. Drink yet another cup of coffee. I deserve it. I won't be having coffee again after today, so I may as well drink as much as I can. There's no line inside, just a few people sitting at tables with their laptops out. A barista is making drinks behind the counter. The blenders whirl and I can hear her squirting syrup into cups. I approach the counter and order myself a large latte. Usually I ask for non-fat milk. But not today. Give me all the fat, I think to myself, holding my tongue. Maybe I should get the non-fat, this is a mistake, I think as I hand the cashier my credit card. But I stay silent. I will drink the latte with whole milk and I will enjoy it. One last time.

I stand back waiting for my drink to be ready. My eyes trail around the little tables. Everyone here looks so young. They must still be in college. Probably doing homework or research. The boy sitting at the table closest to me has big headphones on and is slurping a deep red drink from a straw. Then I hear my name and see the latte sitting on the counter. I grab it and take a sip. It's hot. And delicious. I take a deep breath and go over my schedule for the day in my head. I already made the first two stops. There are two more to go.

Chapter 30

November 1, 2013

"She said we'd win the summary judgment," Andy said to Cameron, his tone accusatory and angry. Cameron kept her head down, she was picking at her fingernails as she sat in the conference room waiting for Kevin Conway, their lawyer in the malpractice suit against the clinic. The room had a big wooden oval table and glass walls all around. Cameron felt like a fish in a tank being stared at by everyone who walked by. They must think we're so pathetic, she thought. She also felt—like a fish—that the air in the tank was suffocating her, that she needed something else to breathe.

"She said we had a good chance," Cameron said defending Alicia. "She also said judges can be unpredictable. But at least he didn't grant summary judgment for their side."

"That would have—"

"Can I get you something to drink?" A young woman popped her head into the conference room. "Mr. Conway will be here in a minute."

"Water please," Cameron responded. "For both of us."

The woman nodded and walked out. Andy was pacing.

"How could the judge not get it?" Andy said, resting his hands on the back of his head.

"Sorry for making you wait," Kevin said as he gracefully slipped through the glass door. Cameron wondered how she didn't notice him walk by through the glass walls. "How are we all doing?"

"Horrible," Andy said. "We had a shitty day in court yesterday."

"That's the law, totally unpredictable," Kevin said. "But Alicia is good, don't worry. Did my secretary offer you something to drink?" Just then his secretary returned with a pitcher of water and three glasses. She set them down on the table and stepped out, closing the door behind her. "Great, then let's get started. In a half hour, the clinic's lawyer will be here with their settlement offer. I discussed with him last week what would be acceptable—"

"Nothing would be acceptable!" Andy blurted out. "I want to make sure that Dr. Klein never practices medicine again. I want him to have nothing when this is over."

"Andy," Cameron said quietly, placing her hand on his waist as he paced by her. "Can you sit down? Listen?"

"I understand there is no way the doctor can make this up to you," Kevin said as Andy took a seat next to Cameron. "But we have to figure out some way to compensate you for what was done. Whether that means we settle or go to a trial, it's still up in the air, but we need to decide what we want out of this." He paused. "Realistically."

"When we spoke originally, you said five million dollars was realistic," Cameron said. "We're not going to settle for less. We'd rather go to trial."

"Understood," Kevin said. "Just so we are clear, a trial would take years. Also, we may be able to win bigger in a trial if you would want to team up with the other couple wrapped up in this case."

"Team up with them!?" Andy yelled. "Never."

Just then, Kevin's secretary knocked on the glass door. Kevin nodded to her and she stepped in. "Chase Greenberg is here with his client."

Kevin nodded to her and then turned to Cameron and Andy. "Ready?" Cameron looked at Andy, silently pleading with him to keep calm. He looked back at her, his eyes red, sunken in, unlike she had ever seen him before. He blinked slowly.

"We're ready," Cameron said to Kevin. His secretary then stepped out.

"Stay silent," Kevin said to them. "I do the talking."

A moment later the secretary returned with the lawyer and Dr. Klein. She led them in and placed two more glasses on the table. The doctor and lawyer sat down across from them.

"Kevin," the lawyer said, his greeting familiar and warm. "This is Dr. Mark Klein." The lawyer then turned to Cameron and Andy. "How are you doing today? Chase Greenberg."

Cameron and Andy stayed silent. Cameron was looking at the doctor. Someone she had trusted; put so much hope in. She hadn't seen him since the embryo transfer in January. He looked different than she remembered. She remembered thinking he was tall, fit, a little sexy even for an older man. Now he looked like a villain to her. He was chubbier than she remembered, his face more pockmarked, his hair whiter. He looked down at the table, but Cameron tried to read his expression. Disinterest, boredom, defeat, she couldn't tell.

His lawyer Chase took a large folder and a notebook from his briefcase and set them down on the table in front of him. He leisurely opened the notebook to a blank page and then slid the folder across the table. "This is our offer," he said. "We think it is more than fair and enough that all the parties will be able to move on."

While Cameron was dying to reach across the table and grab the envelope, she held back. Instead, she stared at it, as though she thought that if she looked hard enough, she could see through it. After sitting back for a moment, Kevin leaned forward and picked up the folder. He opened it slowly, the Pandora's box that would never be closed again. He looked inside, reading for a moment. His face expressionless. Cameron grabbed Andy's leg under the table.

"We asked for five million dollars," Kevin said.

"And we think four million more than covers the inconvenience caused by this situation," Chase responded.

Inconvenience, Cameron laughed in her head. Caused by this situation, as though it happened by itself, for no apparent reason, no one's fault. Although she had to admit, four million dollars wasn't such a small number. Maybe they were asking for too much, she thought for a moment.

"And what's this?" Kevin said, pulling a packet out of the folder and laying it on the table.

"It's a non-disclosure agreement," Chase said. "In return for a quick settlement of this case—at a sum of four million dollars, which by the way is one of the largest settlements of its kind—we would like your clients to sign an NDA."

"What for?" Kevin asked.

"It's a standard NDA," Chase said. "It says that your clients are forbidden from discussing this case and settlement with anyone, including the media, their friends, lawyers, et cetera, et cetera. And of course, they cannot file a complaint against my client with the New York State Medical Board and my client and his clinic must remain anonymous in any further proceedings that arise from this situation. It's simple really."

"Does that mean Dr. Klein gets to continue practicing medicine?" Andy spit out.

Cameron immediately looked to Kevin whose eyes were barreling into Andy.

"Of course," Chase said. "This situation was not caused by Dr. Klein. In the last month, we have conducted a full investigation at the clinic and have overhauled all the medical procedures. Something like this can never happen again, and there is no reason for Dr. Klein to stop practicing, especially when he is one of the top fertility doctors in the country. You wouldn't want to deprive other couples of his services, would you?"

"You can shove this settlement—" Andy started before Kevin jumped in.

"My clients and I need to discuss," Kevin said. "Thank you for your time, you can show yourself out."

Andy turned to Kevin. "We are not fucking—"

"Shhh," Kevin hushed him, although he looked like he would have preferred giving him a smack across the face. When the doctor and his lawyer were gone, Kevin spoke.

"You can't burst out like that and show them our cards. Now they know what is important to you and they can use it as leverage."

"Do you think I give a fuck?" Andy said. "They screw up our lives and all he has to do is pay some money and then he can go on with his life like this never happened?"

"Actually, his medical malpractice insurance will pay," Kevin responded.

"So this whole thing doesn't even affect him?"

"Well, I'm sure his insurance premium will go up. They will also have to report this to the Medical Board, so the board may investigate."

"What a joke," Andy said. "We're not signing that NDA. No matter what."

"Then this case will probably take years to settle," Kevin said. "This type of case, when it goes to the courts will be sent to the back of the line. We'll be lucky to get a court date in the next year. Then, the judge will ask us to go to mediation. By the time we go to trial, your baby will be in kindergarten. Do you want to wait that long to see the money?"

"It's not about the money," Andy said. "Do we look like that's what we care about?"

Cameron sat quietly watching Andy and Kevin volley back and forth. She wanted to agree with Andy, to support him wholeheartedly, but could she stand dragging this on for years? Wouldn't it be better to settle and move on?

"It's your choice," Kevin said. "I'm just giving advice. If you want to take it to court, that's exactly what we'll do."

"Great," Andy responded.

Chapter 31

November 6, 2013

Cameron took her hand off the door handle. Then she put it back on, turned the handle slightly. No, she thought, pulling her hand off again. I shouldn't go, she told herself. It would be too weird. But maybe it would be good for me, she debated with herself.

She was standing in her living room, the baby already in the stroller, the diaper bag packed and draped over the handle. Months ago she had signed up for a mommy-and-me group. It was for moms with due dates in September and the first meeting was beginning in thirty minutes. What would she say when someone asked her the baby's name? What would happen when she got her own baby back and went to the group? Would they notice she switched babies?

Earlier that morning, she had asked Andy what he thought she should do. Should she go? He scrunched his eyebrows at her. "Don't you think you'll be uncomfortable?" he asked. "Do whatever you want, but it seems too weird for me." That ended the conversation and then he left for work.

For the next two hours she continued the debate in her head. The group was recommended to her by a colleague who had two children. Sign up ASAP, her colleague told her the minute she found out Cameron was pregnant. Apparently these groups fill up and have long waiting lists. "The group will help you enjoy your baby," her colleague said. "It will really help with the baby's development and it will be fun for you to meet other moms in the same boat."

Cameron took her advice and called that evening to sign up. To her surprise, she was told she got the last spot. That was in April.

Cameron remembered how excited she was for the group. To meet mom-friends, have people to talk to about what she was going through, share advice with. But now, it seemed strange. How could she bond with other moms when her experience was so different? How would they look at her if she told them? What would they think of her? Would they think she was making a mistake, trying to get her own baby back?

On the other hand, maybe it would be fun. She could pretend to be this baby's mom, try it on like a shoe and see if it fit. Maybe it would be good practice. She could always drop out of the group later if she felt uncomfortable. Or maybe no one would notice if she came with a different baby after a few weeks—after all babies change so much each week.

Cameron put her hand back on the handle. With a deep breath, she turned it and pulled the door open. She held the door with her foot while she grabbed the stroller and wheeled it out, accidently knocking the front wheel on the door frame. Why was it so difficult to navigate that thing?

She went down the elevator and out into the street. The sun was bright above her and shone right into the baby's eyes. A soft whimper came out of her mouth. Cameron unzipped the diaper bag and pulled out a receiving blanket which she draped over the top of the stroller to shield the sun. The baby calmed. Cameron smiled at herself for a moment, she did something right. Then a soft gust of wind blew the blanket off to the ground. Cameron's heart stopped, and she launched forward to try to grab it, but she missed. The wind continued to push the blanket, which was now off the sidewalk and fluttering into the street.

What should she do? The baby started whimpering again, the sun's evil rays getting to her. Cameron watched the blanket. What if she ran out to grab it? And leave the stroller on the sidewalk? No way. But she needed the blanket, she had only packed one. What if the baby spit up or drooled at the mommy group? She would look so unprepared without a receiving blanket. Cameron felt frozen, unable to move. Her dilemma only lasted a minute though; a stranger coming out of a cab caught the floating blanket and walked over to her.

"Lose something?" he said, handing her the blanket. Cameron wanted to cry. She wanted to hug this stranger, who saved her.

"Thank you," she responded, trying desperately to dam the tears in her eyes. She grabbed the blanket, looked to the ground and started walking, constantly repositioning herself to try to cast a shadow over the stroller. Her eyes were full of tears, but she still had a few blocks before she would arrive.

Ten minutes later, she stood outside the community center where the meeting was supposed to start. She was frustrated with herself; she was still fighting the tears. Her eyes would look red and puffy, she wouldn't be able to hide.

"Are you coming to the mommy group?"

Cameron heard someone say from behind her. She turned around to see a woman also pushing a stroller. She had a receiving blanket clipped on the top to block the sun. Clips, Cameron thought, I'll buy those.

"First one?" the woman asked, giving Cameron a warm smile. Cameron nodded. "I went to this group with my first too, it really helps. Let's go inside." The woman motioned to Cameron to go inside and then followed her in, passing her to lead the way. Cameron followed her through the building to a classroom where several other mothers were already sitting on a bright colored mat with their babies lying in front of them.

Cameron watched the woman wheel her stroller inside and park it in a row of strollers on one side of the room. Then the woman lifted the baby—a boy based on his blue overalls—to her face. She cooed at him, brushing her nose against his and then carried him over to the mat and gently placed him down. Then she looked up at Cameron and placed her hand down on the mat next to her. Cameron was still in the doorway, stuck. It's not too late to run away, she thought. But then she pushed the stroller in and parked it in the row. She lifted the baby and carried her to the mat, placing her down next to the baby boy. Cameron looked around the circle of babies, all lying on their backs. Some sleeping, others whimpering softly.

"What a sweetheart," the woman next to her said. "What's her name?"

Cameron felt panic start to sprout inside her. Her heart started to bang against her chest. "Eleanor," she said suddenly, surprising herself. "But we just call her El."

"Beautiful name," the woman said, reaching a finger over to lightly tickle the baby's cheek. "Aw, she is so cute. She has your eyes."

Cameron let out a soft laugh. My eyes, right, she thought. "Thank you," she responded. "And your baby? What's his name?"

"This is Addison," the woman said. "And I'm Julie. Last time I went to this group, I knew all the babies' names, but none of the moms'."

"Cameron," Cameron introduced herself. Her heart rate had started to go down.

"Good morning everyone!" A tall woman said as she entered the room and made her way to the circle. "I'm

Sandra, I am a baby sleep and development consultant and I will be leading our group for the next three months. I also have three kids of my own, ages twelve, ten, and six, all boys. You can ask me any questions about your babies or what's going on with yourselves, and I'll do my best to answer.

"Each week we will start by everyone sharing a little bit about a specific topic, we'll talk about birth, breastfeeding, sleep—if you have something specific you'd like to discuss, just let me know—and then we will do some developmental exercises with the babies, some dancing and then all the babies will go to sleep! These meetings really tire them out!

"Since this is our first meeting, let's have everyone introduce themselves and their little bundles of joy. Let's start over here," the woman said pointing to one of the moms sitting a few over from Cameron.

The mom smiled and wiggled a little to get comfortable. "I'm Naomi, and this is Jonathan. He is seven weeks old. And, I guess that's it."

"Thank you, Naomi," Sandra said and motioned to the next mom to go. Each mom introduced themselves and their babies and then the circle came around to Cameron. Sandra nodded to her when it was her turn.

"Hi," Cameron's voice crackled a little and she cleared her throat. "I'm Cameron and this is Eleanor. She's almost five weeks old...she came a little late." Cameron realized her baby was the youngest.

"That's OK, it's probably because you made such a nice home for her inside your tummy," Sandra said.

Cameron blushed and looked down at the baby in front of her. She was squirming a little and holding on to Cameron's forefingers. The spotlight then went to the next mom in the circle, until all the moms had introduced themselves.

"Great, let's get started," Sandra said, taking out her phone to play some music. "For our warmup, just pat your baby's chest, this helps them loosen up their muscles. Babies are used to being curled up, their arms and legs pulled in tight to their body. We want to help them open up."

Cameron started patting the baby's chest while looking around at the other moms. All of them were smiling at their babies, making faces, talking to them, singing along to the song *The Wheels on the Bus*. Then she looked down at her baby—Eleanor—and smiled down at her. The baby was staring right at her with her mouth open. Then, her lips curled slightly. A smile? Cameron's heart jumped. The baby's first smile! Cameron felt a moment of pride.

"Now let's massage their arms and legs," Sandra said. "Make sure to rub each finger and toe. Touch is really important to babies at this age, it helps them understand their boundaries. They are still learning about their own bodies."

Cameron started massaging the baby's arms and legs, careful to rub each tiny little finger and toe. Next, Sandra had them flip the babies onto their stomachs—using their legs—and pat their backs. Most of the babies started crying softly after a few seconds of tummy time. When Eleanor cried, Cameron lifted her up to comfort her.

When the hour was over, all the moms placed their babies in their strollers and walked out. Cameron walked out quietly with them, as they all talked about the meeting. She waved goodbye to the other mothers and then headed on her way home. That was fun, she thought. A nice break. But now, back to reality. Her heart sank as she got back to her apartment. The baby was sleeping, so she left her in the stroller while she fidgeted with her phone.

That evening, Andy came home late. He arrived with Chinese takeout and kissed Cameron on the cheek.

"How was your day?" Cameron asked him.

"Fine, nothing special," he said. "How about you?"

"Same," Cameron responded. "Nothing special."

Chapter 32

November 7, 2013

Breathe in, breathe out, Avery reminded herself. How was it always so hot in the courthouse? Were they trying to bake everyone here? As if she didn't have enough going on, now she had to feel herself sweating as she sat through the trial. The night before, she barely slept. Amelia's cough wasn't going away and the poor thing kept waking herself up. Avery spent most of the night holding her, rocking her. She felt horrible leaving her with a babysitter again. But she had no other choice. She made a note to herself to make a doctor's appointment when they had a break.

The day before was spent on jury selection. Brad told Avery and Graham they didn't need to come to the courthouse, but they did anyway. Sat outside the courtroom while the lawyers volleyed questions to potential jurors and argued over who was acceptable. They were looking for younger people, maybe parents of adopted kids, or people who were adopted themselves or grew up in foster care. Liberals, people with unconventional homelives. At the end of voir dire, Brad came out of the courtroom smiling. "The jury will like you," he said with a wink. Graham tried to get the specifics of each juror from Brad, but he told them not to worry, the majority would be on their side.

Avery turned around to look at the rows of benches behind them. There were a few people scattered about. A couple women sat behind the plaintiffs talking to the couple. A few men in suits. Avery wondered if any of them were reporters. Please don't make this a media frenzy, she prayed.

"All rise for the honorable Judge Baxter," the bailiff said. Avery bit her tongue at the sound of his voice. She pushed her chair back to stand up next to Graham and Brad.

"Thank you, you may sit," Judge Baxter said as he sat himself down behind his podium. "Can we bring in the jury?" The bailiff nodded, opening yet another door into the courtroom. This door was next to the jury box on the side of the room. When he opened it, the jury members started filing in. The first was an older man, a round pink face, wearing a sweater vest. The next, an African American woman with glasses and big hair pulled up above her head. Then a young boy entered, wearing a Columbia sweatshirt. Avery tried to study each juror, but they were coming in too fast. Before she was done, they were all sitting down in their box. She tried to continue her examination, she wanted them to feel her pain, connect with her, but Brad had told her not to stare. It could make them feel uncomfortable.

"Alright ladies and gentlemen," the judge started. "Let's get started. We're discussing the plaintiff's complaint for declaratory judgment against the defendant. Jurors, please listen carefully, you will be charged with coming up with a verdict." The judge paused, looking carefully at the jury. Then he turned to the plaintiff's table. "Counselor, you may begin with your opening statement."

The plaintiff's lawyer stood up.

"Hi, I'm Alicia Black," she started, facing the jury. "I'm here today to talk to you about justice. About righting a wrong. This is something that you don't always have the opportunity to do, but today, you do. My clients, Cameron and Andy, have been trying to become parents for quite a while. Years of disappointment led them to IVF—in vitro fertilization. It's a process in which the woman injects herself with hormones for two weeks, making her body produce multiple eggs at one time. The eggs are then retrieved and combined with the man's sperm. Once the egg and sperm combine and begin to grow, the embryo is then inserted back into the woman's body, where, if she is lucky, it will implant and she will become pregnant. It's not an easy process for the woman to go through. So you can imagine how happy Cameron and Andy were to learn that their IVF treatment succeeded. After years of month after month disappointment, they finally did it, their dream was coming true.

"The next nine months were spent preparing for the baby's arrival. Cameron took extra care of herself, watching everything she did, everything she ate. They also set up a nursery, took classes to learn about caring for babies. They were so excited that finally, they were getting everything they wanted.

"Now try to imagine how they felt in the hospital when they realized the baby Cameron birthed was not theirs. The blood type was incompatible with theirs, and there was only one explanation. The IVF clinic messed up. Transferred the wrong embryo. This was difficult enough for Cameron and Andy to accept. But then, they found out that their baby, the one made from their egg and sperm, was being raised by another couple. A couple that, as it turned out, is the genetic parents of the baby birthed by Cameron. This gave them hope, maybe everything they went through, wasn't for nothing. That their baby would come to them after all. But it seems, it's not that easy.

"Now, this other couple, the defendants, it's not their fault about what happened. It's not the babies' faults. It's the fault of the clinic, which will pay for its mistake. But the defendants are the ones with the power to fix this. And they have refused to. They think, Cameron and Andy have a baby, who cares that she's not genetically related?

"Some of you are parents. Do you remember the first time you looked at your child and saw yourself looking back at you? That moment changes you. Not just emotionally, or mentally, but also physically. It releases oxytocin into your blood, the hormone that causes you to love, to bond. Now, I'm not saying that you cannot bond with a baby who is not genetically connected to you, not at all, I laud parents who do this. But adoption is a choice. My clients did not make that choice. They chose to create a baby from their own genetic material, which was stolen from them. This moment—of seeing yourself in your child—was stolen from them. And now, it is time to return what was stolen. Only you, the jury, can do that.

"Cameron and Andy are asking for something very simple. They want to switch babies with the defendants so that each couple can raise their genetic daughter and both couples can enjoy the emotional and physical bond of raising their own child. Cameron and Andy are very grateful to the defendants for taking care of their daughter since she was born, and they of course are providing the defendants' daughter the best possible care in the meantime. But now, it's time that both girls go back to their families. The defense is stalling, trying to keep my clients' baby and the longer they do this, the more damage is being caused—to both girls. It's time for the defense to take responsibility for their daughter and to return Cameron and Andy's daughter to her rightful parents.

"During this trial, I am going to show you just how important it is that both children be returned to their respective families. Their real parents, the ones that have been planning for them, the ones who have dared to imagine taking them to ballet or soccer practice. The parents who intended to raise them.

"Over the next week you will hear from medical and psychological experts about why it would be in each baby's own best interest—physically and mentally—for her to be raised by her genetic parents. You will also hear from character witnesses who will attest to how much Cameron and Andy have put in to ensuring that their baby has the best life possible.

"The defense will try to dispute these facts, try to make you sympathize with them. But you as the jury, you must think about what is fair. What is just. And most importantly, what is best for the babies. And that, is to be raised by each of their real parents. Thank you."

Alicia stood for a moment in front of the jury, watching their faces as her words sunk in. During her opening statement, her hands had been opening and closing, gesticulating smoothly, but now they were clasped together in front of her chest. After a few moments, Alicia turned around and sat back down at the plaintiff's table.

Wow, Avery thought, she was good. Scary good. Avery felt herself getting hotter as she continued staring at the jury. They were entranced, all twenty-four eyes stuck on her as she sat down. Breathe, she told herself. Don't look nervous. Avery looked at the other couple. Their hands were clasped together above the table. Their faces blank.

Avery felt Graham's hand on her shoulder. He rubbed her back as though wanting to tell her to relax but it only made her feel sweatier. She wriggled in her chair. Then Brad stood up and approached the jury.

"Hi, I'm Brad Sandfeld for the defendants, Avery, Graham, and their new baby girl, Amelia who is the subject of this case," he started out. "Now, birth is a very traumatic experience. I'm not talking about for the mother.

Imagine, your entire life, since the moment you existed, you were in a warm, dark place. Held tight, fed all the nutrients you need. Now, suddenly, you get too big for that comfortable place and through hours of violent contractions, you are pushed out into a world that is cold, bright, loud. You're naked. You need air, you need food, and you're no longer getting it without effort. You need to learn to breathe, to eat on your own. It's hard, but more than that, it's scary.

"Through all this, there is only one thing you recognize. It's a smell, a sound. It's your mother. It's the voice that sang to you while you were still in your mother's stomach. It's the beating heart that calmed you from the womb. Your mother is the only thing that helps you cope with the trauma you just experienced coming into the world.

"Now, the plaintiffs want to rip Amelia away from her mother. Her mother who breastfeeds her and holds her as she cries. They want to rip her away from her father who built her crib and sings her to sleep. From her two older brothers who play with her and promise to be her protectors. Taking her away would be traumatic for Amelia. It would be detrimental to her psychology, having the same effects children experience when their parents die and they are forced to be raised by strangers.

"I understand the plaintiffs feel that because Amelia came from their egg and sperm, she is their baby. But Avery's womb isn't just an oven where a bun was baked. Avery created this baby. Her body nurtured Amelia throughout the pregnancy, helping her grow into the beautiful baby she is today. Without Avery, the embryo could not have turned into a person.

"And what a person she has become. Amelia is healthy and developing ahead of her time thanks to her family's commitment to her growth. Her mother, a stay-at-home-mom, dedicates her days to providing Amelia with the love and attention she needs. Her father, a renowned literature professor at NYU, works hard to ensure his family has everything they need financially and intellectually. What better place than that can a girl grow up?

"The plaintiffs want to swap babies, like they have absolutely no emotional bond with the baby that Mrs. Cameron Stephens carried for nine months. The baby they are supposedly providing the best care for. Doesn't that seem strange to you? That these people say how badly they wanted to be parents, yet when given the opportunity, are cold and emotionless. If they have so much trouble bonding with the baby that has been with them for all this time, how could they possibly provide a loving home for Amelia, a baby they have never met?

"My clients, Avery and Graham, have created a very warm and loving home environment. In fact, they are happy to open their home and raise both babies, so that both girls can grow up feeling loved by their parents. They've offered this to the plaintiffs, but the plaintiffs have decided to use their baby as a bargaining chip to try to get custody of Amelia. Does that sound like something good parents would do?

"During this trial I will show you why it is so important for Amelia to continue living with her family. We have child psychologists who will testify to this matter and will tell you that ripping her away will have long term, inerasable effects. We have witnesses who will tell you about the home Amelia is being brought up in and what a wonderful job her parents Avery and Graham have done with their two older boys.

"Now, the plaintiffs will tell you this case is a simple custody battle, or like a broken surrogacy contract, but those outlooks would be wrong. This situation is unique and unlike any cases that have come before it. That's why, you as the jury, must go with your gut. What do your instincts tell you about what's best for Amelia? The decision made in this trial will have a colossal effect on her life, as well as on many other lives as well. You must ensure that Amelia stays with her family. Thank you."

Brad nodded to the jury, pausing a moment before turning back to their table. Avery let out her breath. She just realized she had been holding it during Brad's statement. Then she looked at the jury, her fate in their hands.

Chapter 33

February 4, 2013

Free time is a dangerous thing for someone about to embark on the unknown and Sydney had a lot of free time. After telling Dr. Klein about her pregnancy, she quit. There was no way she could continue working at the clinic. No way she could continue helping women who desperately wanted to get pregnant when she did it on accident. And there was definitely no way she could continue working with Dr. Klein.

When she quit, she told him she expected a severance package. Something to keep her on her feet until she found a new job. She also expected child support. Enough that her child could attend private school. She wasn't sending her baby to public school in New York City. That's where she went, where few students graduate. But her baby's father was a rich doctor. He could figure out how to explain that extra expense to his wife.

"Let's think this through," Dr. Klein said to her after she explained her terms. He told her she didn't know the first thing about raising a baby, how difficult it was, especially for single moms. He asked her if she was ready to give up her career—which was so promising—she was talented and she could excel in the field. Maybe even go to medical school one day, she was still so young, just twenty-four. Was she ready to kiss her youth goodbye?

Maybe Dr. Klein was right, she thought. Maybe she should get an abortion. It as a simple procedure and then she could continue with her life. She'd have kids one day, when she was older, married. After she found the right man—someone unattached and who would appreciate her for who she was. She'd probably be less likely to find that man if she was raising a baby on her own.

She didn't have any religious objections to an abortion. After all, the embryo was just a few cells containing her and Dr. Klein's DNA. Much like the skin cells that fall off your arm every day. Or like the embryos she cultures at the clinic. Cultured, she reminded herself. Past tense.

It was her first day not going to work. She woke up at the usual time, 7:00 a.m. and took a shower. Brushed her teeth. Her hair. Then she slipped out of the apartment—at the same time she always did—and stood on the street. Where to go? She usually turned right. Walked the couple blocks toward the subway, down the stairs to the station, and on the train for a few stops. Today, she turned left. She didn't know where she was going, but walking seemed like a good idea. Keep moving.

Her East Village neighborhood was still asleep, aside from a few people making their way to work. Even the homeless people were sleeping, too early for them to beg for a dollar. She walked past the bars, the restaurants, all asleep, boarded up without any remnants of the customers who spilled out of them the night before. The street smelled like trash and spilled beer. She usually didn't notice the smell, but today her senses were heightened. Maybe it was the pregnancy already affecting her, or maybe she was just being more observant. This was no place to raise a child.

A few more steps and she smelled coffee. Beans roasting. The smell came from a small coffee shop up ahead. When she reached it, she walked in. Sacks of coffee beans lined the walls, while a grinder hummed slowly in the back. She looked at the sacks, one labeled Ethiopia, another Tanzania, and Kenya. She weaved through the sacks to the counter near the grinder in the back. A young man was there, bagging the grinds that came out of the grinder. When he saw her, he stopped. "Get you anything?" he asked.

"A small coffee."

"What kind?"

"Doesn't matter," she responded. The man nodded and turned around. She studied his back. It looked strong. Her eyes went down, his butt was tight, round. He probably worked out, she thought. When he turned around again, he handed her a small cup.

"$1.50," he said. "Milk and sugar are over there." She gave him a coy smile and lightly brushed his hand when passing him the money. He flinched but then smiled back at her, holding her gaze as she slowly blinked her eyes.

"Do you live around here?" he asked, putting the money into the register. "I've never seen you before. Usually it's the same regulars coming in all the time."

"Just down the block," she responded. "I'll see you around." She winked and turned around to walk out of the store. She stood straight, slightly swaying her hips. At the doorway, she turned back slightly to see the cashier still looking at her. She shot him a smile and stepped out. I've still got it, she thought to herself.

She took a sip of her coffee. So bitter. She forgot to add milk and sugar in her attempt to flirt with the cashier. Oh well, she thought. She continued walking, the coffee warming her.

She reached one hand down into her coat pocket and fingered the piece of paper in there. The paper that Dr. Klein had given her. When he handed it to her, she crumpled it up. She was going to throw it away when she got to a trash can, but it slipped her mind. By the time she got home, she forgot about the paper. Now she pulled it out of her pocket. On it was a phone number and a name. "I told him that I am friends with your father," Dr. Klein said when he gave it to her. "He's expecting your call."

Maybe she should call, just to learn about all her options. She stopped walking for a moment to pull her cellphone out of her bag. She looked at the note and dialed the number, taking a deep breath before she pressed the green button. It rang once. Twice.

"Hello?"

The response startled her. She expected to reach a receptionist, a greeting mentioning the doctor's office. But it seemed, she was calling the doctor's cell phone. "Is this Dr. Swanson?"

"It is, how can I help you?"

"My name is Sydney. Dr. Klein gave me your number."

"Oh yes, hi Sydney," Dr. Swanson said. "Do you want to come into my clinic today? I can squeeze you in."

"Sure," she said, barely audibly. But he heard her. He told her the address and said to come in around noon. She agreed. She'd go, she told herself. Just to talk. It would help her make her own decision. Because this was her own decision. Not Dr. Klein's or anyone else's. She finished her coffee and threw the cup in an overflowing trash can on the sidewalk.

Chapter 34

November 8, 2013

"Please just be quiet," Cameron pleaded with the baby. The baby was screaming. She wasn't hungry, she had a clean diaper, she didn't need to sleep. Cameron held the baby to her shoulder and was bouncing around her bedroom. Cameron's heart was pounding and she could feel herself starting to sweat. "Please calm down," she whispered into the baby's ear. She had been trying to comfort the baby for an hour, but nothing seemed to work. Whatever she did, the screams continued. Echoing through their apartment that had never felt so small. They were going to be late. Andy was waiting for her in the kitchen. They had to be in court at 9:00 a.m. and before then they needed to drop the baby off with the babysitter. Their normal babysitter, Selma, was out of town, but had recommended a friend who agreed to watch the baby while Cameron and Andy were in court.

Helen's apartment was just a short walk away, but Cameron was afraid to leave when the baby was crying. People would look at them, judge them. They'll know I'm not her mother, Cameron thought. She'd look like a fraud. She made Andy agree to wait while she tried to calm the baby down. But now they were running out of time. They had to go. They couldn't be late for court, their lawyer told them. It would look bad to the judge and the jury and worse, it could delay their case.

"We have to go," Andy said from the doorway, startling Cameron. "The babysitter will calm her down." Cameron nodded, not knowing what else to do. She wrapped the baby up in a warm blanket, placed a small hat on her head, and set her gently in the stroller. The baby continued to cry. Andy took the stroller handle and pushed it out the door. Cameron walked behind him, her head down, willing the baby to stop crying. But she didn't. The entire walk to Helen's apartment.

When they arrived, Helen immediately picked up the baby, hummed something in her ear, and within seconds, the baby was asleep. Looking so calm, like she had never cried in her short life. "Don't worry, all new moms have a hard time," Helen said to Cameron as she placed the baby down in one of three bassinets in her living room. Cameron smiled at her and peeked in the other two bassinets. Both had sleeping babies inside. Maybe if it were my baby, I'd be better at this, she thought.

Cameron and Andy then hurried into a cab downtown to the courthouse. The day before, both sides had given their opening statements. After hearing Alicia's statement, Cameron was sure they would win the case. But then she heard the other side. And she looked at the jury, all the members listening intently to the other lawyer speak. He was convincing, so much so that it scared Cameron. How could people on the outside make the right decision when the lawyer on the wrong side was so good?

They arrived at the courthouse just in time, sitting down at the plaintiff's table just moments before being asked to rise for the judge. Judge Baxter came in, wearing his usual black gown. He motioned to everyone to sit down and asked the bailiff to bring in the jury. Cameron watched the jurors file into the jury box. Their faces were blank, unreadable. She didn't even recognize them from the day before.

"Let's get started," the judge said, not wasting any time. "Plaintiff's counselor, the floor is yours."

"Thank you, your honor," Alicia said as she stood back up. "We'd like to call our first witness, Jim Hanson."

Cameron turned around to the benches behind them. The rows were almost full of men and women in suits. A lot more people than had attended yesterday, she thought. A middle-aged man stood up and approached the front of the courtroom. He looked lost, like he wasn't sure how he ended up there. Alicia guided him to the witness stand, where he sat down, wiggling around a little bit before he cleared his throat.

"Do you solemnly swear that you will tell the truth, the whole truth and nothing but the truth under pains and penalties of perjury?" the bailiff questioned the witness.

"Uh, I do, yes," the witness said, his voice cracking.

"Thank you," Alicia said to the bailiff and then approached the witness, standing close enough to him, but with her body turned slightly to the jury. "Can you please state your name and occupation?"

"Jim Hanson," the witness said. "I am a lab technician at a DNA testing center in Manhattan."

"Can you tell us how DNA testing is done?"

"We receive DNA samples that are taken from a subject's mouth by rubbing a swab against the inside of their cheek," Jim said. "We use a method called polymerase chain reaction to isolate the DNA from the cells. We then split the DNA into chunks that are used to define a DNA fingerprint for the subject. This fingerprint can be analyzed for all sorts of things. To test paternity, match someone's DNA to something found at crime scenes, to determine someone's ancestry, or to test for specific genetic diseases."

"When testing for paternity, or maternity also for that matter, what are you looking for?" Alicia asked.

"We're looking to see how much of the DNA of the child matches the DNA of the father," Jim said. "Or, the mother. We can then predict what is the probability that a subject is a parent of the child."

"Thank you," Alicia said. "Were you the one who conducted the DNA testing on the babies who are the subject of this case? For simplicity, we can call one Baby Cameron, after her mother, and the second Baby Avery." Alicia smiled at the jury, a few of the members seemed to chuckle back at her.

"Objection!" the defendant's lawyer yelled. "Who is the mother is the subject of the trial."

"Sustained," the judge said. "Ms. Black, please refrain from stating who is the mother of the babies."

"Sure," Alicia said. "Let's just call them baby one and baby two. Baby one being the one who was born first." Then she turned to Jim. "Did you conduct the DNA test on baby one, born to Avery and Graham Stephens?"

"Yes," Jim responded.

"And did you conduct a DNA test on Avery and Graham Stephens?"

"Yes."

"Did you also conduct the DNA testing on the baby that my client birthed? We can call her baby two, since she was born second."

"Yes."

"And on my clients, Cameron and Andy Stevens?"

"Yes."

Alicia walked back to the plaintiff's table and picked up a packet of papers. "I have here the DNA test results of the two babies as well as the paternity and maternity tests conducted. Can you please tell me what are the results for baby one?" Alicia handed Jim the papers.

Jim took the papers from Alicia's hand and read the first one over. "For baby one, there is a zero percent chance that Avery and Graham Stephens are the parents."

"Can you please move on to the second page you have there, Mr. Hanson," Alicia said. "And can you please tell me what is the percentage match of Cameron and Andy Stevens to baby one?"

Jim flipped to the next page and scanned it quickly. "There is a 99.9% match between baby one's DNA and Cameron and Andy Stevens."

"Thank you, and now on to the next page," Alicia continued. "What is the percent match between baby two and Cameron and Andy Stevens?"

Again the witness flipped the page and quickly read the results. "Zero percent match."

"What about between baby two and Avery and Graham? The results are on the next page."

Again Jim flipped the page. "There is a 99.9% match."

"Thank you," Alicia said and then turned to the jury. "So to summarize, and clear up any confusion between baby one and baby two, the baby born to the defendants is a zero percent match to their DNA and a 99.9% match to Cameron and Andy. Baby two, on the other hand, is a 99.9% match to the defendants and a zero percent match to my clients."

Alicia then turned to the judge and gave him a quick nod before returning to the plaintiff's table. She sat down gracefully and gave a quick wink to Cameron.

"Mr. Sandfeld, your witness," the judge said to the defense lawyer.

"Thank you, your honor," the lawyer said as he stood up from the defense table and approached the witness stand. "Mr. Hanson, thank you for your testimony today.

You said there is a 99.9% chance that the plaintiffs are genetically related to Amelia Stephens, the baby called baby one by the plaintiff's lawyer, is that correct?"

"Objection!" Alicia said. "The witness has already answered that."

"I'm just trying to make sure everything is clear," the defense lawyer said to the judge. "It gets confusing, baby one, baby two, defendants, plaintiffs."

"I'll allow, but please move on counselor," the judge said.

"Mr. Hanson, is that correct?"

"Yes," the witness responded.

"So that would mean there is a 0.1% chance that the plaintiffs are not genetically related to baby one, as we are calling her?"

"I guess so."

"That's a pretty big margin of error, I would say," the defense lawyer said.

"Objection!" Alicia blurted out again. "That's not a question."

Judge Baxter breathed in deeply. "Sustained. Mr. Sandfeld, please question the witness."

"Of course. Mr. Hanson, would you say that is a large margin of error? Especially when we are dealing with removing a child from her home?"

"I wouldn't say it's a big margin of error, it's standard in DNA testing."

"Yes, but 0.1% means that one out of 1,000 times, you would be wrong. I wouldn't like those odds if I were a parent. And if the plaintiffs are not the genetic parents, as they very well may not be due to such carelessness at the IVF clinic, do they have any rights to this baby at all?"

"Objection!" Alicia jumped in again. "This is out of the witness' expertise."

"Sustained," Judge Baxter responded. "Mr. Sandfeld, please stick to the witness' expertise."

"Mr. Hanson, are there ever mistakes in DNA testing?"

"Rarely."

"But mistakes can happen?"

"Yes."

"What are some reasons for mistakes?"

"The most common mistake is a false positive in a paternity test. It can happen if the subject of the paternity test is related to the real father."

"Are there other reasons mistakes happen?"

"Sometimes there are mutations in the DNA, or miscalculations in the analysis."

"Let's talk about mutations. How could mutations occur?"

"If the DNA sample is left in direct sunlight, or if the cells were tampered with in a laboratory, or something like that."

"Could that have happened in the laboratory at the IVF clinic used by the plaintiffs and the defendants? We already know how careless they were with these embryos."

"Objection!" Alicia yelled. "Speculation. Mr. Hanson is unfamiliar with the IVF clinic's laboratory."

"Sustained."

"I'll rephrase," the defense lawyer said. "Is it possible that if the embryo of the baby, when it was only one or two cells, was left out in a laboratory, the DNA could have mutations and that DNA would have been replicated in each cell as the embryo grew into a baby?"

"It's possible."

"No further questions," the defense lawyer said. He looked over at the jury for a moment before turning back to his table. Cameron was also looking at the jury. Most were still looking at the defense lawyer. Some were looking down, taking notes. Others were still looking at the witness. Her heart was pounding. One grain of doubt. That's all it takes.

Chapter 35

November 8, 2013

Brad winked at Avery when he walked back to their defense table. He has just cross-examined the DNA lab technician who had run their DNA tests. Avery thought he was doing a good job, he sounded convincing, powerful. But that other lawyer kept interrupting all the time.

"That was really good," Brad whispered as he sat down.

"But she kept objecting," Graham whispered back.

"Juries don't like women who object all the time. It makes them look bitchy," Brad responded, still whispering. "She did us a favor."

"Thank you, Mr. Hanson," Judge Baxter said. "You are free to go."

The witness nodded, carefully stood up and exited the witness stand. He then walked hurriedly between the defense and plaintiff tables and through to the exit of the courtroom. Avery watched him disappear.

"Ms. Black, your next witness," the judge said. Avery looked at the lawyer. Wearing a dark suit and high heels, she looked professional, ambitious, Avery thought. Maybe a little bitchy.

"Thank you, your honor," Alicia said. "I'd like to call Dr. Cheryl Green to the stand."

Avery turned to the benches behind her to see who would stand up. A middle-aged woman with straight black hair and glasses stood up. The woman, wearing a dark green turtleneck and black slacks, made her way to the front of the courtroom, to the witness stand and sat down.

She looked like she was sitting on the edge of the chair, her back straight and her chin lifted.

"Do you solemnly swear that your will tell the truth, the whole truth and nothing but the truth under pains and penalties of perjury?" the bailiff questioned the witness.

"Yes," the woman said.

"Thank you," the plaintiff's lawyer approached the witness stand. "Dr. Green, can you please state your occupation?"

"I am a clinical psychologist at Columbia University."

"Thank you. And can you tell us about your area of research?"

"Yes, I research family structure and its effects on child psychology."

The plaintiff's lawyer picked up a large book from their table and held it up, waving it in front of the jury, then the witness, and lastly the judge. "Can you tell me what this publication is?"

"That is the Journal of Child Psychology."

"And what is it?"

"It's a quarterly publication that publishes the latest research in the field."

"Can you tell me about your article that appeared in this issue of the journal? Issue 54, from Spring 2012."

"Yes, I wrote an article about the research I am conducting that compares children raised by biological parents versus children raised by non-biological parents."

"Can you tell me about the conclusions of your research?"

"Children raised by two biological parents are more likely to thrive as adults," the witness said. "They are more likely to get college degrees and less likely to get involved in crime or drugs."

"How did you come to this conclusion?"

"My team has spent ten years observing a pool of more than one thousand subjects who come from all different family structures. We conduct annual interviews with the parents and children and we also test the children for their IQ, emotional intelligence and cognitive abilities. All of the data is then analyzed and we derive conclusions."

"So children raised by their biological parents are more likely to thrive, you say," the lawyer said.

"That's correct."

"Would you then say that it is better for the two girls who are the subject of this case to be raised by their biological parents?"

"Objection!" Brad shouted. "This is a leading question."

"Sustained," the judge said. "Ms. Black, please rephrase."

"Sure. Would both girls' likelihood to thrive be increased by being raised by their biological parents?"

"There are other factors at play of course, but yes."

"No further questions." The plaintiff's lawyer said as she walked back to her table and sat down. Avery could hear her heart pounding through her dress. Was this doctor right? Was it possible they were hurting Amelia's chances to thrive by raising her? Above all, Avery wanted what was best for Amelia, no matter what that was. But it didn't make sense. Then Brad stood up and approached the witness.

"Dr. Green," he said. "When you say non-biological parents, what do you mean? Do you mean adoptive parents, stepparents, foster parents? There are so many different kinds of parents these days."

"Any of the above, but most commonly in our study, we dealt with step-parents."

"Great, and in the beginning, you mentioned children raised by two biological parents. What about children raised by one biological parent?"

"Children raised by one biological parent were less likely to thrive."

"Less likely than those with two biological parents?"

"Correct."

"Children raised with one biological parent. Can you elaborate on what that means exactly?"

"Usually it is children with a single parent or with a stepparent."

"Did your study examine whether there was a causation or just a correlation between a child's likelihood to thrive and being raised by biological parents?"

"A correlation."

"So is it possible that there are other factors at play here? For example, single parents may be more likely to be in a lower socio-economic state and have a harder time supporting their children. Or maybe step-parents are less likely to invest in a child's wellbeing?"

"It's possible."

"So as you mention, your study mostly dealt with step-parents as the non-biological parent. We've all heard about the evil step-mother who treats her own daughters very differently than she treats poor Cinderella, so is it possible that children raised by a step-parent are less likely to thrive because the parent doesn't treat the child as their own?"

"Sure, it's possible. As I mention, our studies deal with data, not with the cause of the data."

"So that is a very different case than what we have here. You're comparing parents who *don't* want a child to parents who *do* want a child."

"Objection," the plaintiff's lawyer said. "Counselor is testifying. He should be addressing the witness."

The judge breathed in. "Counselor please question the witness," the judge said to Brad.

"Dr. Green, do you think a child's likelihood to thrive has to do with the biology of the parents or whether or not the parents are willing and able to invest in helping their child thrive?"

"That is outside my study, so I could not answer categorically."

"Could you answer based on your opinion?"

"Objection!" the plaintiff's lawyer jumped in. "The witness' opinion on this is irrelevant, we're discussing a quantitative study on this matter."

"I'll allow, counselors," the judge said. He then turned to the jury. "But, jury members, remember this is the witness' opinion, it should not be confused as part of her study."

"Dr. Green, in your opinion, could a child's likelihood to thrive have anything to do with whether or not the parents are willing and able to invest in their child's wellbeing?"

"It's possible."

"If that is the case, then my clients—who want this baby so much that they are willing to fight for her here in court—provide the same likelihood to thrive as the biological parents."

"Objection! Counselor is testifying."

"Sustained."

"Nothing further, your honor," Brad said as he walked back to the defense table. He held his fist in front of his chest holding a thumbs up that only Avery and Graham could see.

"Alright, Ms. Black, who's next?"

"We have Bethany Anderson."

Avery looked back to see who would approach. A young girl, probably in her late twenties, stood up. She had straight blonde hair—definitely blonde from a salon—that was pulled back into a ponytail at the top of her neck. It was the kind of ponytail that looked simple, but was carefully styled for that purpose exactly, to look effortless. The girl wore a black dress that hugged her figure and black tights that went down to black leather boots. She approached the witness stand and the bailiff swore her in.

"Bethany Anderson, can you please tell me how you know my clients?" the plaintiff's lawyer asked.

"Just Beth please. I was Cameron's roommate in college and I've known Andy for basically as long as Cameron has."

"Can you tell everyone how long you have known Cameron and Andy?"

"Sure, Cameron and I met when we were freshman, so I guess that was eleven, twelve years ago. Cameron met Andy when we were sophomores, and she introduced him to her friends pretty fast. So I've known him probably ten or eleven years."

"Can you tell us about Cameron's and Andy's journey to get pregnant?"

"Well, when they got married, I knew Cameron wanted to have a big family, she's Southern, you know. All her friends from growing up had babies when they were like twenty-two. Cameron was like the old maid of her group at twenty-five. At first, she wasn't in a hurry, but then, when it wasn't happening, she started making all kinds of life changes. She was super healthy—well she was always healthy, but she became even more healthy. And she was trying all these different things, like she started taking Fenugreek supplements. Do you know what those are? It's some herb that's supposed to increase fertility. And she tried acupuncture, but nothing worked. So they went to doctors. And none of the doctors knew what was wrong. Then they tried hormone treatments, and insemination, and eventually IVF. So it was a pretty long journey."

Avery placed her hand on her heart. Poor Cameron. She understood exactly what Cameron had probably felt like all those years trying to get pregnant. The disappointment, the frustration, the will to do anything if it would just work.

"And how did Cameron and Andy prepare for the baby?" the plaintiff's lawyer asked.

"Wow! I don't think there has ever been a couple who did more!" the witness said. "They took classes, birthing classes and baby first-aid and CPR, and how to take care of babies. And they bought literally everything. They were so prepared. They already baby-proofed their apartment! Which I was so glad they did because I was afraid they were going to leave Manhattan for the suburbs."

"So you would say that Cameron and Andy really wanted this baby?"

"Objection!" Brad jumped in. "This is a leading question."

"I'll rephrase," the plaintiff's lawyer said before the judge could respond. "How much, in your opinion, did Cameron and Andy want this baby?"

"More than anything."

"And was it important to them that the baby be their biological baby?"

"Really important," the witness said. "They wouldn't even discuss adoption. They agreed they would do whatever it took to have their own."

"Why was this important to them?"

"Well, they are Jewish," the witness said. "And according to their religion, the baby is only Jewish if the biological mom is. So, if they adopted, they would have to convert the baby."

"So would that suggest that the baby birthed to the defendants is Jewish?"

"Yes, she is."

"And is it important to Cameron and Andy that their baby be raised Jewish?"

"Very important, at their wedding they both vowed to keep a Jewish home and pass on their traditions to their children. I was a bridesmaid, by the way."

"If their baby is being raised by someone else, how could they pass on their traditions?"

"I guess they couldn't."

"Thank you, Ms. Anderson," the lawyer said. "No further questions."

"Ms. Anderson," Brad said as he jumped out of his seat at the defense table. He didn't even wait for the judge to invite him. "Can you tell me what is this picture?" He held up a picture in front of the witness.

"Um, that's me and Cameron in college."

"What are you two doing in this picture?" Brad then passed the picture to a jury member who took a look and then passed it along.

"Well, it was during pledge week for our sorority."

"Please answer the question."

"We were at a party, just drinking, nothing unusual."

"What were you wearing?"

"Trash bags, it was an ABC party, anything but clothes."

"This was pledge week?"

"Uh huh."

"So when you were pledges? During your freshman year?"

"Yes."

"So underage drinking?"

"Everybody drinks in college, it's not a big deal."

"Not everybody drinks in college. And breaking the law is a big deal."

"Objection!" the plaintiff's lawyer said. "Counselor is antagonizing the witness and I fail to see how this is relevant."

"Oh, it is very relevant," Brad said. "The plaintiffs are showing reckless and illegal behavior. I think this is something the jury should know if they are thinking of handing over a baby to them."

"Overruled," the judge said. "But Mr. Sandfeld, please ask a question."

"No more questions." Brad took the picture from one of the jury members and walked back to their table. When he set the picture down, Avery peeked. Three girls with black trash bags duck taped to their bodies were holding shot glasses and a big bottle of what Avery assumed was vodka. She recognized Cameron as the girl in the middle, her hair flowing long around her shoulders, her tongue sticking out. It was strange getting to know someone this way, Avery thought. A day ago, she knew nothing about Cameron. But today, she felt close to her.

Chapter 36

November 8, 2013

"It was a mistake to ask Beth to testify," Andy said angrily. "She comes off as a joke."

Cameron and Andy were sitting in the conference room in Alicia's office after a long day in court. Her office was almost empty, all the secretaries, and most of the lawyers had gone home already. There were just a few left over, mostly those working on their case, burning the midnight oil.

"She was the only friend who could come on such short notice," Cameron said with a sigh. "And she's the person I've known the longest."

"Yeah, but we should have chosen someone serious," Andy said. "Now everyone thinks you're some dumb sorority girl."

"I'm sure some of the jury members were in Greek life," Cameron said. She was tired. Her breasts were hurting. Engorged after a full day in court and probably leaking into the pads she had stuffed into her bra. She just wanted to go home already. Pick up the baby. Feed her. Go to sleep. Was that too much to ask for?

"Sorry to keep you waiting," Alicia said as she glided into the conference room. "Pizza is on the way."

"Did Beth screw our chances of winning?" Andy questioned before Alicia could sit down.

"No, she was fine," Alicia said. "She gave a good picture to the jury about you two."

"Yeah, a great picture," Andy replied sarcastically. "The cross examination from the other lawyer, it made us look like idiots."

"What he talked about what ten years ago, when you were in college, do you really think the jury will take that seriously?" Alicia looked at Andy for a few moments, waiting for a reply. When he didn't, she continued. "Anyway, we had a good day in court today. The jury likes you; the witnesses were convincing; I think we have nothing to worry about. In fact, you can go home, you don't need to be here."

"No we want to be here," Andy said. "We want to be involved."

A few other lawyers came in the conference room and sat down. Associates, investigators, the team that stood behind Alicia and gave her what she needed to succeed in court.

"We're just preparing for tomorrow's cross-exams," Alicia said. They had finished their case today in court and tomorrow the defense would begin. Cameron thought it would take longer for Alicia to make their case. To convince the jury, but Alicia told them it was better to keep it short. Keep the jury's attention. Ensure a speedy trial. Leave less room for error. Their case was succinct and to-the-point, she said.

"Andy, let's go," Cameron said, putting her hand on Andy's arm. "We're not any use here."

Andy stared at her; his bottom lip slightly open like he had something he wanted to say. But he stopped himself.

"Please," Cameron pleaded. She wanted to go home. Pick up the baby. Poor Helen had been taking care of her all day. They paid her extra for it, but Cameron felt they were already pushing the limit.

"Fine, let's go," Andy said, getting up quickly. Cameron followed him out, rushing to keep up. Andy was silent as they took the elevator down to the ground floor. Neither did he say anything as he swept through the lobby and stepped out to the street. Cameron trailed a little behind him. It was like he was in his own world, she thought. He didn't seem to notice anything around him.

"Wait," Cameron yelled up ahead to him when he missed the turn. "We have to get the baby."

Andy turned back, his eyes darted up and he sighed. "I just want to go home. Can you get her? I'll pick up something for dinner."

Cameron hesitated. What she wanted was for Andy to hold her, kiss her forehead, tell her they were in this together. She had never had to ask Andy for support before, she didn't even know if she knew how to do it. "Fine," she said. "I'll see you at home." She watched as Andy continued walking in the direction of their apartment. His back a little slouched; his gait a little uneven. It was dark out and after a few paces she could only see his outline. A few more paces, and she couldn't recognize his back at all. Then she turned toward Helen's apartment. When she arrived, she knocked softly on the door. A few moments later Helen answered.

"Sorry I'm so late," Cameron said. She spoke almost in a whisper.

"Don't worry," Helen said with a knowing smile. She motioned Cameron inside and put her arm on Cameron's shoulder. "She was a doll. Such a sweet little girl."

Cameron looked over to the three bassinets in the middle of the room. Two were empty. In the third, the baby slept. She was on her back, her head slightly turned to the side. Her eyes were shut tight and her lips curved up as though she were smiling.

"I don't want to wake her," Cameron whispered. Helen nodded and gently lifted the baby from the bassinet, one hand under her head and the other around her body. She pulled the baby into her chest as she walked over to the stroller parked in the corner of the room. In one swift motion, she placed the sleeping baby down. Cameron looked down into the stroller at the baby who had been undisturbed by the move. She had the same expression, but her chin dipped slightly to the other side. "Thank you," Cameron whispered as she rolled the stroller through the door.

"Wrap the blanket around her, it's cold out," Helen said, motioning to the pink fuzzy blanket in the compartment under the stroller. Cameron nodded, gently placing the blanket on top of the baby, careful not to touch her and risk waking her up.

It wasn't a long walk back home, but Cameron went slow. She gently pushed the stroller over every crack in the sidewalk, praying that each one wouldn't be the one to disturb her. Poor girl, Cameron thought. She did nothing wrong, she deserved to be loved. She deserved a mother who knew how to love her. But through a cruel twist of fate she ended up with the wrong parents.

She walked by the restaurants, bars and shops that lined the street. Inside she saw couples dining, girlfriends talking. Everyone looked so happy, Cameron thought. They were all just enjoying themselves, like nothing else mattered. When would she do that again? Soon she arrived home and slipped her key in the lock. She opened the door to a dark apartment. Gently pushing the stroller in, she navigated through the living room to the bedroom, careful not to knock into anything. Still afraid of waking the baby, she left her in the stroller, next to the bassinet in their bedroom. With a quick motion, she silently closed the bedroom door and sat down in the kitchen to wait for Andy. The kitchen was dark except the shadows cast in from the streetlights outside. The shadows stretched and flowed on the floor in front of the windows. She could hear the rumble of cars from the street outside, every so often a horn honked, disturbing the rhythm. She realized she'd never really heard the cars outside before; she'd never noticed them, but now they seemed louder than ever, the rumble growing into a roar. Just don't wake the baby, she prayed.

It was a while before she heard Andy's footsteps outside the door. Then she heard the key in the lock and the click as the door slid open. He was carrying a bag from the deli on the corner, the one right next to the bar they used to frequent on late nights on their way home. Just for one last drink, they always said as they stepped into the dive. It was never just one, but they always helped each other stumble home. It was a while since their last drink together. Before the baby, the pregnancy, before the IVF treatment. Probably a year ago, Cameron thought.

"There was a long wait," Andy said as he placed the bag on the counter. He pulled out a roast beef sandwich for himself, pickles on the side, and a chicken salad for her. Their usual order. Andy looked down as he slowly unwrapped his sandwich.

"You OK?" Cameron asked. She smelled the beer on his breathe. The sweat on his back. His shirt was crumpled from the long day in court.

"Just tired. Are you not hungry?" He said between chews. Cameron reached for her salad. She wasn't hungry. But she needed to eat. "Maybe we should take the offer of putting the baby in social services during the trial. This is just too much for us right now. Everything going on and taking care of that baby."

"No," Cameron responded. "What if they did that to our baby?"

"They wouldn't, they want to keep her."

"But what if? We wouldn't want that. We can't do that."

"Maybe it would motivate them to stop all the bullshit."

They continued eating in silence. Andy finished his sandwich; Cameron closed her salad after a few bites. Maybe things would be better in the morning. They had a long weekend ahead of them. Veteran's Day. Maybe they could find the time to relax and remember who they were before this all started.

Chapter 37

November 11, 2013

Usually Avery loved long weekends. They would always do something fun together as a family. Drive out to Long Island, have a picnic in the botanical gardens, but not this weekend. This weekend was torture. The Friday before, the other couple's lawyer had finished their side of the case, arguing why Avery and Graham should give up their daughter to strangers. The lawyer was convincing. So convincing, that Avery wasn't sure what she would decide if she were on the jury instead of at the defendant's table. But they'd only heard one side so far. Their side, the defense, would start today. And hopefully prove to the jury that Amelia should stay with them. So instead of enjoying the long weekend, Avery kept praying it would be over soon. The sooner they would start the defense, and the sooner the trial would end.

Avery hadn't slept all weekend. Friday night, she was too wound up from the day in court. Saturday night, her brain was thinking of what she would do if they lost the case. A desperate plea to the other couple? Could they run away? Sunday night, she was tired enough that she would have slept, but Amelia had other plans. She couldn't sleep, she cried and screamed unless Avery was holding her. Avery spent the night sitting in bed with the baby in her arms, trying not to nod off. At one point in the night, she thought she'd be relieved if they lost the case. Maybe the other baby would sleep through the night, but then she felt guilty. How could she think that? As Monday morning approached, Avery was starting to feel the anxiety and lack of sleep creep up on her.

The plan was to do a little hike in Marine Park. Avery needed to get up, make lunches to pack in a picnic basket, organize everything they needed for Amelia during the trip. She kept running through the list of things to bring—a blanket, baby sunscreen, a hat, change of clothes, diapers, wipes, the list went on. As she repeated it to herself, her heart started pounding faster. She needed to try to enjoy the day—for her boys—all the while knowing in the back of her head that she was way behind with her Etsy store.

Before Amelia was born, she had accumulated a lot of inventory ready for shipments. She had multiples of each of her items ready, so when orders came in, she just needed to pack and ship them out. But that was two months ago. Now, her inventory was almost gone, except for a few of her less popular pieces. And the orders kept coming in. On Friday she had gotten a big order from a girl in California who wanted matching necklaces for her seven bridesmaids. The girl wrote a long note with her order, pleading that the pieces come on time, which meant Avery needed to send them this week. But when would she have time to make them and get to the post office? She would have to work at night and probably need to overnight the package, which would eat into her profits. But as she had learned, happy customers were as important as profit, if not more. Happy customers meant recommendations, reviews, future orders. Late shipments led to bad reviews, complaints, and sometimes even requests for refunds.

She had hoped to spend Saturday and Sunday working on that order, and a few others that she was behind on from the previous week, but the days started and ended before Avery had time to enter her studio. Amelia had been fussier than normal, needing constant attention. Graham wanted to help out, but he was also behind on his work and was receiving constant phone calls about a bitter dispute between two of the professors in his department—one had helped edit a paper for the other and wasn't given credit in the publication. He wanted that professor fired, while the other professor said the editor had done a poor job and didn't deserve credit. Avery tried to sympathize when Graham complained about the dispute, but all she could think about was how behind she was.

At least the boys hadn't given her too much trouble. She made the breakfast—homemade waffles on Saturday and eggs on Sunday—but after that they went out with friends. She just had a load of dishes to clean and put away.

They had been planning to hike together on Veteran's Day for the last week. They hadn't had much family time lately, and Graham and Avery both thought it would be good for them to clear their minds and take a break. That was, of course, when Avery thought she would have had the weekend to work on her orders.

As the light shone through the bedroom window on Monday morning, Avery decided to get up. Amelia was sleeping in her arms, as she had been all night. Every time Avery tried to put her down in her bassinet she would start screaming, so somewhere around 2:00 a.m. Avery gave in and just decided to hold her for the rest of the night. Amelia needed to sleep—that was more important than Avery getting her sleep.

Avery dragged herself out of bed and to the living room. She placed Amelia down on the couch for a second as she carefully wrapped her baby carrier around her body. Amelia woke and started whimpering, leading Avery to try to hurry as she tied the carrier closed and slip Amelia into it. Amelia let out a shriek and then fell back asleep wrapped into Avery's chest. Avery carefully pulled the fabric of the carrier over Amelia's face and then went into her studio. She would try to work for a little before the boys got up. First, she checked her computer. Three new orders. But they were all small—one for just a pair of earrings that she actually did have in her inventory, and the other two for necklaces she would need to make. She also had a message from a customer who had ordered something a week ago and was wondering when she would get the tracking number for the shipment. Avery made a note to herself to make sure to send that order out tomorrow.

She closed her computer and went to her cabinet to grab the materials she needed to make the necklaces for the bridesmaids. Once everything was setup on the table, there was a knock on the door. She looked up and there was Aiden and Maddox. Her heart sunk a moment, but then she felt guilty. It wasn't their fault, she reminded herself.

"What do you boys want for breakfast?" she asked with a smile, trying not to look disappointed that she wouldn't have any time to work on her orders.

"Dad's making toast," Aiden said. "We just wanted to know if you wanted any."

Avery smiled. "Sure, with cream cheese," she responded. How sweet of them, she thought.

"We also wanted to know if you wanted help," Maddox said. "We don't have to go hiking today. We can do family time here. We can pack up the jewelry."

Avery wanted to cry. The lack of sleep, her anxiety about her work and the trial, the sweetness of her boys, it was overwhelming. She couldn't stop herself when the tears came out. "That would be really nice," she responded with a sniffle. "After we can go out for ice cream."

"Only when we finish," Maddox said, a smile beaming on his lips. "We'll be back with your toast." Then the boys left her in her studio. Twenty minutes later, they came back. Aiden was carrying a plate with her toast, followed by Maddox and Graham, all of whom were ready to get to work. Avery showed Aiden how to connect and close the clasps on the necklaces she was making. Then, she showed Maddox how to address the envelopes and efficiently wrap the pieces in bubble paper before stuffing them inside. Graham was in charge of quality control.

By the end of the day, Avery had all her outstanding orders ready to ship. Aiden even offered to take them to the post office after school the next day. It was early evening, already getting dark and they hadn't eaten anything since the toast in the morning. Instead of going out for ice cream, Avery recommended dinner at the nearby diner. They rarely ate out as a family, it was an expense they tried to avoid, but Avery felt like splurging. They deserved it. All of them.

Chapter 38

March 28, 2019

I've been walking for an hour and I find myself in front of the courthouse. The place that completely changed the trajectory of my life. The building looks ominous, a huge cinder block in the middle of a lively neighborhood. I sit down on a bench outside and look around. The sidewalk is empty, but I still see the ghosts all around. The bright flashes, the arms grabbing at me, the screams trying to get my attention. My heart starts racing as I see the ghosts start to become opaquer. They are real. They are coming for me. I close my eyes. I have to remind myself these are just shadows haunting my memories. They aren't really there. I'm alone, no one can get to me now.

I often replay everything that happened in my head. The trial, where we all fought to be the biggest losers. How stupid we were. We thought that if we won everything would be better. That winning would solve our problems. Looking back, I can't believe I ever thought that. The trial was just the beginning of our suffering. The real suffering came later.

I still have an hour before I need to get to my third stop of the day. I like to be there at the same time every year. So she knows when to expect me. I get up from the bench and start walking. I need to pick up a few things on my way.

I stop in a flower shop. It's surrounded with little buckets full of water with bouquets growing out of them. I need to find the perfect one. One that she would like. Something gentle and fragile, like her. I first look at the roses. There are red, yellow, and purple ones. But these aren't fitting. Roses have thorns. They are beautiful but dangerous. Too bold.

Then I stop in front of the carnations. White, pink or orange. But these are too ordinary. Then I look at the lilies. The great flowers with white and pink spotted petals. They are majestic, grand, mystical even. They are perfect for her. I pick a small bouquet, examining each flower to make sure it is perfect. One flower has a petal that's a little bent, so I choose a different bouquet. This one is fine. Each flower is perfect. I pay and start going to my next stop.

Chapter 39

November 12, 2013

Tuesday morning Avery got up early and made lunches for the boys. Breakfast was cereal. She didn't have the time or energy for anything else. The boys didn't complain. They made their own bowls and even rinsed them out in the sink when they finished. Avery reminded Aiden about taking the packages to the post office when they got home from school. The money would be on the counter and he needed to make sure to get tracking numbers for everything.

When she finished with the boys, she went to get Amelia, who was still sleeping soundly in Graham's arms. Graham had helped hold her for part of the night, after watching Avery struggle to stay awake. Now, he was sitting in the bed, slouched forward, his head falling down. He piped up immediately when Avery entered the room, smiling sheepishly as though caught in the act. Avery carefully took the baby from his arms and held her close. A few moments later, she fluttered her eyes open. She had grown so much in the last two months. Her face and body were now coated in cute little baby fat. Her hair—straight and brown—was starting to grow. Her eyes were blue, not blue like every newborns', but an ocean blue that Avery knew didn't come from her or Graham's genes. Her lips were thin, always looking like a pout, like she was thinking hard about something. She was beautiful. Like Cameron, Avery thought.

Avery lifted her shirt to feed the baby, cradling her gently in front of her chest. She loved the feel of Amelia's hand on her side. As Amelia drank from Avery's breast, she rubbed her hand up and down on Avery's skin. Never forget this feeling, Avery told herself. It made her sad, thinking this feeling would be gone soon. These little moments, they never stay with you long term.

When Amelia finished nursing, Avery placed her down in her bassinet and got dressed. A dark dress, something maternal, that didn't hug her body they way most of her dresses used to. When she still had a body that called for tight dresses. Amelia whimpered softly as Avery got dressed. She was going through a phase when she didn't like to be put down; she wanted to be held all the time.

Soon there was a knock on the bedroom door. Avery's mother. She had arrived over the weekend to help out when Avery and Graham were in court. Avery was so thankful. The babysitter was getting expensive, and she didn't want to put her baby in daycare already, where she wouldn't get the love and attention she deserved. Avery had complained to her mother when they last spoke about the situation. "I'm getting on the next plane," was her mom's response. She'd stay as long as needed, she said.

"You ready to go? Graham is waiting for you downstairs," Sophie said, lifting the baby from the bassinet. Amelia quieted immediately. Avery thanked her mother, kissed her baby and went downstairs, where Graham was sitting with two cups of coffee. Avery grabbed one and took a sip. It was lukewarm, but good enough. Then they got in their car to drive to the courthouse. Even with the traffic, it was more convenient than the subway.

When they arrived, Graham parked in an overpriced lot and they went into the courthouse, navigating the halls to their courtroom. Brad was already at their table, reading some files. The plaintiffs were also already there, whispering quietly to each other. Avery looked at Cameron, her straight brown hair pulled back into a ponytail at the nape of neck. She was wearing a light pink long-sleeved dress and a pearl necklace. Her eyes were focused on her hands, which were fidgeting in her lap.

"All rise for the honorable Judge Baxter," the bailiff said. Avery's heart stopped. Here we go, she thought as she stood up with the rest of the courtroom. Avery looked back at the rows behind them. They were full. Beyond full. Men and women in suits sat squished together in each one. Who are all these people here, she thought. The judge walked in and motioned the room to sit. He ruffled the papers he had in his hand and asked the bailiff to bring in the jury. Avery watched them file in, careful not to stare too hard. Brad said it could freak them out.

"Alright, I hope everyone had a nice Veteran's Day," Judge Baxter started. "When we left off the plaintiffs had just finished their case, am I right? Ms. Black, anything else?"

"No, your honor," the plaintiff's lawyer said.

"Great, so on to you Mr. Sandfeld."

"Thank you, your honor," Brad said as he stood up. "We'd like to call Dr. Amir Dunbar to the stand."

A short man stood up from the third row in the courtroom. He was wearing a white button-down shirt—no tie or jacket—and big, thick glasses. The man walked to the front of the room, his head held high, and sat down at the witness stand in one graceful movement, as though he had done it many times before.

"Dr. Dunbar," Brad said as he approached the witness. "Could you please tell me your occupation?"

"I am a law professor at Harvard. I focus on law and bioscience," the witness responded.

"Thank you. I want to ask you about a recent lecture of yours, about how the Moore vs. Regents case is relevant in today's world. Do you know which lecture I am talking about?"

"Yes."

"Could you summarize?"

"Yes, in Moore vs. Regents, John Moore was treated for leukemia at the UCLA Medical Center. The cancer cells removed from Mr. Moore were used for research that led to a patent granted to the doctor at UCLA. Upon learning about the patent, Mr. Moore sued the hospital for a share of all profits derived from their research using his cancer cells. The California Supreme Court ruled that Mr. Moore's cancer cells belonged solely to the hospital, and that Mr. Moore had no property rights to the cells."

"So the court ruled that genetic materials removed from the patient no longer belonged to the patient, rather the materials belonged to the hospital?"

"Correct."

"What was the reason for this?"

"Well, the reasoning was based on John Locke's property theory," Amir said. "You know, John Locke, the English philosopher and physician." Amir paused while Brad nodded his head. "Locke's theory is that the labor of a person's body makes something his property. He uses the examples of someone picking oranges or acorns in a forest. The person's labor of picking the oranges or acorns makes the oranges or acorns their property."

"Labor is what makes something someone's property then?"

"According to John Locke, and several courts, including the California Supreme Court, which have made rulings this way in similar lawsuits."

"Right, so let's apply this to today's case. If Mr. Moore's tumor belonged to the hospital due to the labor the hospital invested in turning it into something patentable, then what does that say about the plaintiffs' genetic material? Does it too belong to those who invested the labor into making the genetic material into a baby? Say, Avery and Graham? Avery who carried the baby for nine months, and Graham who has helped raise her for the last two months?"

"Objection, your honor," the plaintiff's lawyer said. "Counselor is testifying. And you cannot compare a tumor to a baby. In the court case cited by Mr. Sandfeld, Mr. Moore did not intend to keep his tumor after it was removed, unlike in our case, where my clients intended to keep their genetic materials after they were removed."

"I'm not comparing a tumor to a baby," Brad shot back before the judge could say anything. "I think Ms. Black misunderstood my point. It's genetic materials. Cells. Microscopic DNA. The baby, in this case, is more like the patent. Something that took time and effort to create. The genetic materials on the other hand, take no effort to create, they just are."

"Counselors," the judge raised his arms. "Overruled. Mr. Sandfeld you may continue your questioning. Ms. Black you can make your arguments in your cross-examination."

"Thank you, your honor," Brad said, clicking his heels. "Mr. Dunbar, should I repeat the question?"

"No," Amir said. "According to this philosophy, whoever invested the labor to turn the genetic materials into a baby would be the rightful owners."

"So, the defendants? Avery and Graham?"

"Correct."

"Thank you. No more questions." Brad turned around and walked back to the defense table, giving a little wink to Avery.

"Ms. Black, your witness," the judge said.

The plaintiff's lawyer stood up and approached the witness stand. "Mr. Dunbar, do you believe in John Locke's theory?"

"I believe it has merit."

"So in the example you give, someone picking oranges or acorns, what if they were picking them from a private orchard? An orchard that belonged to someone? Would the person picking the oranges or acorns still be the owner of them?"

"Well, we have to adapt the theories to today," Amir said. "John Locke created this theory in the 1600s."

"So in the 1600s, if someone picked an orange from a private orchard it wouldn't be considered stealing?"

"Objection!" Brad yelled. "Counselor is badgering the witness."

"Overruled," the judge said. "Mr. Dunbar, please answer."

"Yes, I suppose," the witness said hesitantly.

"So who owns the orange?"

"Well, the orchard owner."

"So the person who planted the seeds, the tiny, microscopic cells that turned into the orange?"

"Objection!" Brad yelled.

"On what cause?"

Brad cleared his throat. "Orange seeds are not microscopic."

"Counselor, be reasonable," the judge said. "Mr. Dunbar, you may answer."

"I guess so."

"No further questions." The plaintiff's lawyer pivoted on her heels and turned back to the plaintiff's table. Avery looked at the couple, sitting there with their hands clasped together. They sat close to each other, even leaning in a bit so their shoulders touched. Avery noticed Andy's firm grasp on Cameron's hands. Cameron and Andy looked at each other as their lawyer sat down. The look was brief. A shared smile, an understanding of the eyes, a glimpse and then it was over.

Chapter 40

November 12, 2013

Cameron sat still at the plaintiff's table. She felt stiff—her legs crossed, her back straight, her hands clenched inside Andy's on top of the table. She was afraid to move, that she may just fall apart. She hadn't slept more than a three-hour stretch in more than a month. The lack of sleep, the crying of the baby, and the anxiety of the trial were starting to get to her. She didn't feel like herself anymore. She always felt like she was on the edge, teetering between keeping it together and completely falling into oblivion. Every day, she felt her balance was getting worse, and soon she would fall.

Now that the defense had started their side, Cameron was more nervous than before. Before, she knew more or less what was going to happen, she was prepared. But she was not prepared for this. And she hated being unprepared. Her heart thumped; her ears shook. Remain calm, she told herself over and over. Don't fall apart.

Alicia sashayed back to their table after finishing her cross examination of the defense's first witness. She destroyed the witness, Cameron thought as she gave a quick glance to Andy, wondering if he thought the same thing. But it didn't matter what Andy thought, only what the jury thought.

"Your next witness, Mr. Sandfeld," the judge said as the previous one was excused from the stand.

"I'd like to call Dr. Harriett Sharon to the stand," the defense's lawyer said. Cameron looked up to see a tall woman approach the witness stand. She was wearing a black suit, glasses, and her hair was pulled back in a tight bun. She sat back in the chair comfortably as the bailiff swore her in.

"Dr. Sharon, could you tell the court your occupation?"

"I am a child psychologist," she said. "I research trauma in newborns and infants."

"Do newborns experience trauma?" the lawyer asked.

"They do," the witness said. "Contrary to what most people believe, trauma can have a very serious effect on newborns and it can seriously disrupt the child's development."

"What are some of the effects of trauma on newborns?"

"There are many," the witness said. "For one, newborns may have trouble bonding with parents or siblings after a traumatic event. They also have delayed development in the areas of language, mobility, social skills, and emotional intelligence."

"Could you give us an example of what that could mean for the child?"

"Yes, it could mean that the child doesn't learn to speak until age four or five even. Or that they will be unable to make friends in the future. Or they will have trouble learning to crawl or walk."

"What could constitute a traumatic event for a newborn?"

"Anything that could cause trauma for an adult could cause trauma for a newborn, such as a car accident, an illness, a death in the family, et cetera," the witness said. "But most commonly for newborns, trauma is caused by issues with the primary caregivers."

"What sort of issues?"

"Well, if a mother is suffering from postpartum depression that could cause trauma for a newborn. Or if a newborn is suddenly separated from their primary caregiver, this is also a serious cause of trauma."

"So if a baby is separated from their primary caregiver, it could cause the baby to have delayed development?"

"Yes, that is correct."

"Would giving Avery's and Graham's daughter Amelia over to the plaintiff's cause the baby to experience trauma?"

"Objection!" Alicia shouted. "This is speculative. The witness has no way of knowing what could happen."

"Sustained," the judge said. "Mr. Sandfeld, please rephrase."

"Do you believe that Amelia could experience trauma if she is removed from her home and given to the plaintiffs?"

"I believe so, yes," the witness responded.

"And this could cause Amelia's development to be significantly delayed?"

"Objection, your honor, this is repetitive," Alicia said.

"Overruled, I will allow for clarification purposes," the judge responded.

"Dr. Sharon?" the lawyer questioned.

"Yes, I believe it could cause serious developmental issues for the baby," the witness said.

"Based on your expertise as a child psychologist, what do you think is in the baby's best interest in our case? Should she stay with the parents who are raising her or be removed from her home and given to the plaintiffs?"

"I believe it would be best for the baby to remain with her current family, so long as that is a stable environment," the witness said.

"Thank you. No further questions," the lawyer said. The lawyer nodded to the jury and almost skipped back to the defendants table.

Cameron's ears were ringing. Would they traumatize their baby by bringing her home? Are they making a huge mistake? She started to feel the anxiety bubbling up from her stomach to her ears. It was getting hot, too hot. She stayed still; she couldn't move. One move, and she may end up on the floor.

"Your witness, Ms. Black," the judge said just as Alicia stood up from their table and approached the stand.

"Dr. Sharon, you work with older children as well as newborns, correct?" Alicia asked.

"That's correct. My research of trauma extends up to age seven," the witness responded.

"Seven," Alicia repeated. "So at age seven, how much do children understand about family relationships?"

"Well, they are very aware of their family cell," the witness said. "They understand who their parents and close relatives are."

"What if a child at age seven, finds out that their parents, are not their real parents?" Alicia said. "You know, like children who are adopted. When they find out they are adopted, could that be traumatic?"

"Yes, that is a very traumatic experience for a seven-year-old," the witness responded.

"Their whole world is turned upside down, right?"

"Objection!" the defense lawyer yelled. "Counselor is testifying."

"Sustained," the judge said. "Ms. Black, please ask a question."

"Dr. Sharon, how would this type of trauma affect a child?" Alicia asked.

"Often times when a child finds out they are adopted, they experience feelings of loss and uncertainty. They feel lied to and it sometimes leads to identity crises." The witness said.

"I see," Alicia responded. "And what are some of the characteristics of children who may experience this type of trauma?"

"Similar to those of an infant," the witness said. "They may have delayed development, have trouble making friends."

"Are there additional effects for older children? Let's say, could they become more violent, become sexually involved at an earlier age?"

"Yes, those are definite possibilities," the witness said. "Children often need an outlet for their anxiety caused by trauma. So violence and sexual activities often become those outlets."

"I see," Alicia said. "So let's say this child we are dealing with, the one who is biologically related to my clients, let's say she stays with the defendants, and in five or seven years from now, she finds out that the defendants are not her real parents. And let's be honest, she will find out, just look at all the reporters in the room today." Alicia motioned to the rows of benches in the courtroom where men and women in suits were sitting shoulder to shoulder, each furiously writing in notebooks. "How would this child feel? Could she experience trauma?"

"I suppose so," the witness said.

"And this trauma, is it any less serious than the trauma you discussed earlier about infants?"

"No, it would not be less serious."

"Would it be more serious? Now that the child is older and has a greater understanding of the family cell, as you mentioned?"

"It's impossible to compare what sort of trauma would be worse. Every child experiences trauma differently. But children definitely have a better understanding of what is causing the trauma when they are older."

"No further questions, thank you." Alicia smiled at the witness and returned to their table. Cameron tried to look up at her, but she felt the muscles in her back constricting her. She continued looking down, at her and Andy's hands clasped together. She could hear the scribble of the reporters behind her, making a spectacle of her life. Like she was there for their entertainment, an elephant in the ring at the circus, suffering for the enjoyment of others.

"Mr. Sandfeld, another witness?" the judge asked.

"Yes, your honor," the defense lawyer said as he stood up. "We'd like to call Mr. James Turner to the stand."

A man stood up from the benches and approached the stand. He was wearing khaki pants and a plaid button-down shirt. He looked uncomfortable on the stand, like he didn't know how he ended up there. The bailiff swore him in and the defense lawyer approached.

"Mr. Turner, could you tell us how you know the defendants, Avery and Graham Stephens?" the defense lawyer said.

"Yes, I am a guidance counselor at their older son's school," the witness said.

"Their son Aiden? How old is he?" the lawyer asked.

"Yes, Aiden is thirteen, in eighth grade."

"How long have you known Aiden?"

"Three years, I've been his guidance counselor all throughout middle school. I can't believe he's going to high school next year."

"Tell us a little about Aiden."

"Objection!" Alicia yelled. "I don't see the relevance of this."

"It's very relevant," the defense lawyer said. "We're discussing my client's ability to raise a child, so we're looking at a child they have already raised."

"No one is questioning their ability to raise a child," Alicia said. "The question is about them raising someone else's child."

"I just want to show that they have created a stable environment that has been great for a child's development," the lawyer responded. "Your honor?"

"You may proceed, but make sure it is relevant," the judge said.

"Of course," the defense lawyer said. "Mr. Turner, please tell us about Aiden."

"Aiden is a very special kid," the witness said. "He is very smart, has a lot of energy and likes to look out for others. Especially his little brother, but also kids in his own class."

"What do you mean by that? That he likes to look out for others?"

"About a month ago, one of his classmates was being bullied, and Aiden stood up to the bullies. Made them leave the kid alone. It takes a very special kid to do that."

"So that isn't something you see very often?"

"No, usually only with kids who have younger siblings who they are protective over. Maybe their younger siblings were bullied, or they just see it as their responsibility to look out for them."

"So Aiden is a good big brother?"

"Objection!" Alicia yelled. "This is speculative and irrelevant."

"Counselor, please don't veer too far off course," the judge said.

"No problem, please bear with me," the lawyer said to the judge. Then he turned to the witness. "Mr. Turner, could you tell us about Aiden's family?"

"Yes, I've met his parents several times over the last three years," the witness said. "They are very loving and very involved in his school. His mother is on the PTA and participates in every fundraiser and event. I believe she organized the book fair last year. Aiden is also very close with his little brother Maddox; he talks about him a lot. I also know he was very excited for his little sister."

"That's wonderful," the lawyer said. "Would you say that Avery and Graham have provided a stable home environment for Aiden? One that allows him to thrive?"

"Very stable," the witness said. "Especially compared to many of his classmates, you can see the difference between him and others. Aiden comes to school every day with a homemade lunch—which says a lot about how much parents care about their kids' health—and he always comes to school with finished homework—another thing that only happens if parents encourage their children."

"So Avery and Graham are good parents?"

"Objection!" Alicia yelled. "Also speculative and good parenting can differ from child to child."

"Sustained. Counselor, please be more specific," the judge said.

"Mr. Turner, are Avery and Graham good parents to Aiden?"

"I would say so."

"Wonderful. You also mentioned that Aiden was excited about his little sister. Could you please elaborate?"

"Yes, he talks about her a lot," the witness said. "I know also in his English class he wrote an essay about her. About how important she is to him."

"Oh yes, I have that essay here," the lawyer said as he shuffled back to his table and pulled up a piece of lined paper. "Could you read us the essay?" He handed the paper to the witness.

The witness took the paper and focused his eyes on the scribbled pencil. *"A few weeks ago my baby sister was born. Amelia May Stephens is her name. When mom and dad brought her home from the hospital they let me hold her. I sat down on the couch and mom put her in my lap. She looked at me and I told her how lucky she is to be a Stephens. Because Stephenses look out for each other. They take care of each other. Just like dad and mom take care of each other, me and Maddox take care of each other. And now it is all of our jobs to take care of you.*

"She didn't understand what I was saying to her, but she looked at me. She is so small, I can't wait until she grows up into a person and we will be able to talk to her and play with her. I am going to teach her to play ball, even though she is a girl. I won't let her be one of those girls who can't catch. I'm going to be the best big brother there is!"

The witness looked up. His eyes glimmered and his mouth curved up into a half smile.

"So it seems big brother Aiden is already very attached to his little sister," the lawyer said.

"Objection!" Alicia yelled. "Counselor is testifying."

"Sustained," the judge responded. "Mr. Sandfeld, please ask a question."

"Sure, yes," the lawyer said and then turned to the witness. "Mr. Turner, would you say that Aiden is very attached to his sister?"

"Very much so."

"In your opinion, would removing her from their household also be traumatic for Aiden?"

"Definitely."

"Nothing further, your honor," the lawyer said and trotted back to his table. The judge motioned to Alicia who stood up for her cross examination.

"Mr. Turner, you testified that Avery and Graham are great parents to Aiden, but what about to their second child, Maddox?" Alicia asked.

"I don't know Maddox personally, but from what Aiden says about him and his parents, I'm sure everything is fine."

"How are you sure? Are you just assuming?"

"I guess so."

"Is it possible for parents to treat each child differently? Maybe they favor one child, or treat one differently than the other?"

"I don't think Avery and Graham treat Maddox differently."

"That's not what I asked," Alicia said. "I asked if it was possible for parents to treat each of their children differently?"

"I guess, sure, it is possible," the witness said slowly.

"So if it is possible, then you don't know if they treat Maddox the same as they treat Aiden, and you don't know if they treat this new baby differently either?"

"I guess I don't know," the witness said, emphasizing the last word.

"Are you aware that Maddox was in detention last week?"

"Like I said, I work for Aiden's school, not Maddox's, so I don't know those things," the witness responded.

"So, you also don't know why Maddox was in detention, do you?"

"No."

"For skipping school."

"Objection!" the defense lawyer yelled. "How is this relevant? Additionally, the witness has said this is outside of his ability to testify."

"Sustained," the judge said. "Counselor please make your point."

"Mr. Turner, what do you think about parents whose children are skipping school without permission?"

"Well, I guess, usually those parents don't know their kid is skipping."

"Parents who don't know where their children are. Is that problematic to you?"

"Objection! Counselor is badgering the witness!"

"Sustained."

"No further questions, your honor," Alicia said as she turned back to their table.

"Alright," the judge said. "Mr. Sandfeld, do you have another witness?"

"No, your honor, the defense rests."

"Great," the judge responded. "We'll continue tomorrow with the closing statements." The judge banged his gavel, got up from his bench, and left the courtroom through the large door at the front of the courtroom. Cameron still didn't move, even as the courtroom started to come alive with a low murmur that spread from the back of the room to the jury.

"Cam?" Andy said, already standing up. Alicia was packing her bag, also standing up. "Ready to go?"

"Oh, sure," she said as she stood up and rubbed her hands down her skirt. They turned around, the benches were already almost empty, so empty that Cameron wondered if she had imagined the crowd that had been sitting behind them during the testimonies.

"I'll walk out with you," Alicia said as they started toward the back of the room. "Stay close to me."

Cameron didn't think about what Alicia said. It seemed so ordinary, so logical that they should walk out together. But when they exited the courtroom and then the courthouse, she understood Alicia's comment. Suddenly flashes of light ignited in her face. There was yelling. People shoving things in her face.

"Cameron, did you feel that something was wrong when you were pregnant?" "Cameron, how did you find out about the switch?" "Andy, what are you going to do with the other baby if you lose the case?" "Cameron, are you breastfeeding?" "Andy, where is the other baby now?" "Cameron, is there something you want to say to the other couple?" The questions overlapped and continued to shoot out from the crowd. It was so loud; she couldn't have answered if she wanted to. Instinctively, she looked down at the ground, placing one hand on her forehead and with the other she tried to hold Andy's hand. She grabbed for it, but couldn't find it until she felt his strong grip on her forearm, pulling her through the crowd.

"My clients will not be answering any questions," Alicia said in her commanding voice. "We'll release a statement when the trial is over. Thank you and please stop harassing Mr. and Mrs. Stevens." Alicia guided them toward the street and into a black Lincoln that was waiting for them. "Don't talk to the press. Keep quiet and this will all boil over soon," she said as she closed the door of the car. The car pulled away, leaving the flashes of the cameras behind.

Chapter 41

February 14, 2013

The sun shone through the window of Sydney's bedroom, waking her up. It felt strange waking up after the sun. Usually in winter, she was on her way out when the sun rose. But, with nowhere to be, she stayed in bed longer. For some reason, she didn't stop her alarm clock from going off every morning at 6:30. Now, she just turned it off every day and went back to sleep. It was like a reminder of what her life used to be. A life she wasn't sure she was ready to say goodbye to just yet.

She rolled over on her back and stretched out, kicking the covers off her legs. Then she rolled over away from the window and pulled her pillow above her head. Valentine's Day, she thought to herself with a sigh. Valentine's Day and she was alone. Last year on Valentine's Day she woke up to a bouquet of roses from Mark. It was so romantic she thought. He promised her a special Valentine's treat, but he had ended up spending the evening with his wife. He was sorry, he said, when he came over the next night, but it would be too suspicious if he left her on Valentine's day. She understood, happily sharing an expensive bottle of Pinot Noir with him on her couch.

Well, this year she wasn't totally alone. There was a little baby growing inside her. She still hadn't decided what she wanted to do, but she knew she had to make a decision quick. Last week she had met with Dr. Swanson, the doctor Mark had recommended. He did an ultrasound to measure the fetus. According to its measurements, she was ten weeks pregnant. In New York, abortions are legal up to twenty-four weeks, the doctor said, but if she wanted to abort, better sooner rather than later. She didn't want to start showing and then have to answer questions.

She sighed, not wanting to pull herself out of bed. Maybe she could just stay there and sleep through the day. But no, she wouldn't let herself become like that. Lazy. Someone who wasted the days away. She needed to start figuring out what she wanted to do. She needed a new job—something not fertility related—maybe a new apartment—one that didn't remind her of Mark. Then, at that moment, the real reason she needed to get out of bed was that she needed to throw up. For the last week, she had felt sick all the time. Why the hell did they call it morning sickness if it plagued her all day long, she thought to herself as she rushed to the bathroom and lurched over the toilet seat. Why did women go through so much trouble to get pregnant when this was what it felt like? She didn't understand how the human race just didn't go extinct. Why would anyone want to go through this, she thought, realizing that this was probably the easy part. Labor, well, that was something she didn't even want to start imagining.

After hugging the toilet bowl for twenty minutes, Sydney pulled herself up and turned on the shower. She stripped off her clothes and stepped under the stream. It burned her skin, but in a good way. The steam filled her nose, calming her nausea, and the water washed away the sweat and stink on her skin. When she felt clean, she turned off the water and dried herself off. She looked at herself in the mirror. She didn't look pregnant, she thought. She even looked a little thinner than before. Probably because she was too nauseous to eat and spent her days throwing up stomach acid. She put her hands on her stomach, and gently touched the silver ring in her belly button. Then she blow-dried her hair, brushed on a little make up and put on her clothes. First stop of the day, the coffee shop. She had been going every morning since she first walked in ten days ago. The barista—Tom was his name—was nice and sometimes she stayed a while to talk to him in between customers. He was a PhD candidate at NYU. Studying ancient Roman philosophy or something like that. She laughed when he first told her. What was the point of studying that, she asked. It's not like there were many jobs for philosophers. He had smiled at her and joked that maybe that was the reason he worked at a coffee shop.

She left her apartment, pulling her hat over her ears. There was snow on the ground, ice on the sidewalks, a chill in the air. Be careful not to slip, she told herself as she turned toward the coffee shop. She walked slowly, trying not to step on any patches of ice on the ground. Soon she smelled the beans roasting from the shop. She breathed in the smell, one of the few that didn't make her sick to her stomach. She walked in the store and made her way through the bags of beans to the back. Tom was behind the counter mixing a drink together for a customer waiting at the counter. He looked up and smiled when he saw her, giving her a quick wink. Once he finished and the customer had left with her drink, Tom brought over a dark cup of coffee to Sydney and handed her a small brown paper bag.

"What's this?" she asked.

"Open it," he said. She gently pulled open the bag, releasing the vile smell of eggs and cheese. She suddenly felt like she was about to turn inside out, that she couldn't breathe or she may pass out. "You always just drink black coffee," Tom said. "I thought I'd get you a nice bagel to go with it. Happy Valentine's Day."

Sydney swallowed and closed her eyes for a second. She wanted to run away, get as far away as she could from the poisonous smell coming from the bag. On the other hand, she couldn't stop thinking how thoughtful this was, how it was sort of romantic.

"You don't like bagels," Tom said slowly. Sydney could hear the disappointment in his voice.

"No, I love them, really," she responded. She didn't know how to act, she couldn't tell him she felt sick, he would think she was weird. She definitely couldn't tell him she was pregnant. Then she could never show her face in that coffee shop again. "I just remembered; I have a meeting. I'll eat this on the way." She scrunched the bag closed, weakening the smell that still lingered in the air. "Thank you."

"Sure," Tom said as though trying to figure out what he had done wrong. Sydney started walking out of the shop. She had to leave. She needed to get far enough away so she could barf whatever was left in her stomach. She quickly waved at him, carrying the bag and coffee out the door.

"Wait," Tom called, following her out. "Are you doing anything tonight?"

Sydney stopped in the doorway. Fresh air. It calmed her senses. "No, actually," she said.

"Would you want to grab a drink?" he asked. "There is a really nice bar I like a few blocks from here. I think you'd like it; they have all these great cocktails and stuff." He had one hand on the back of his neck.

Sydney smiled. A drink. She would really like that. One drink wouldn't hurt, she thought to herself. Don't pregnant women in France still drink wine? "Sure," she said with a nod.

"Great," he responded, a smile growing on his face. "Let me get your number. I'll text you where it is and then you can tell me if you're running late or anything. Meet at eight?" He handed her his phone.

Sydney nodded again and typed her phone number in, calling herself so she could save his. She stood still in front of him, looking at his face.

"Don't you have a meeting to get to?" he said.

"Oh, right," she said. "I'll see you tonight!" She waved and started walking quickly away from the coffeeshop. She waited until she had walked a few blocks before she dropped the brown bag in front of a homeless man sleeping on the snow. At least someone could enjoy the bagel.

Chapter 42

November 13, 2013

"Graham!" Avery yelled from the bedroom. "We can't go to court today! Call Brad!"

Avery was holding Amelia in her arms; the poor baby was burning up. She had been fine earlier. She had been coughing—Avery reprimanded herself for not taking Amelia to the doctor for her cough yet—but besides that she had seemed fine. Then, Amelia woke up with a shriek, her hair was wet and her face was red. Avery grabbed her immediately, feeling the heat radiating from her tiny body. She tried to comfort her daughter as she threw on a pair of sweats with one hand and ran down the stairs.

"Graham, get in the car, we have to go to the hospital now," Avery shouted. The strength of her voice even shocked herself. Graham jumped up from the table and followed Avery outside to the car where Avery had already buckled Amelia into her car seat. He slipped into the driver's seat and turned on the car, dialing Brad's number—number two on speed dial—as he started driving toward the hospital. Avery was in the back, sitting next to the baby, who was still crying, her eyes squeezed shut and her mouth drooping open.

"Brad," Graham said. "We cannot make it to court today. We have an emergency, the baby has a fever, we are going to the hospital." Graham paused. "Thank you. Bye."

"What'd he say?" Avery asked.

"He said he will ask the judge for a continuance. He will say it was an emergency."

Avery started to imagine what would run through Cameron's head when they heard that court was postponed for an emergency. But that wasn't important. What was important was taking care of Amelia. Fifteen minutes later Graham pulled up in front of the emergency room at the hospital. Before he stopped the car Avery was already getting Amelia out of her seat and ready to go. In seconds, she was out the door, carrying Amelia in her arms. She ran up to the reception window, passing a long line of people.

"I'm sorry to cut in like this, but my baby has a fever," Avery said desperately to the receptionist who was compiling paperwork for the person at the front of the line. The woman didn't look up when she told Avery to go to the children's emergency room on the third floor. Without thanking her, Avery ran toward the elevators and pressed the button frantically until the doors opened. Amelia was still whimpering, nuzzling her head into Avery's shoulder. Avery rode up to the third floor where the doors opened to another reception, this one with cartoon animals on the walls. Avery ran to the receptionist, careful not to step on any of the children playing on floor.

"Hi, my daughter has a fever, she's two months old," Avery said. The woman handed her a clipboard and asked her to fill out the form and bring it back up to her. Avery took the clipboard and sat down in one of the plastic chairs. Balancing Amelia on her lap she scribbled down Amelia's and her information as fast as she could and brought it back to the receptionist, who read over the form slowly. Then she motioned Avery to come in through the doors at the side of the room. A nurse greeted Avery and brought her into a room with multiple beds separated by curtains. Avery sat on the bed, holding Amelia in her arms.

"Please undress her and place her down here," the nurse asked. Avery did as she was told and placed the naked baby on the bed, while keeping a hand on her. The nurse took a thermometer, which she covered in a clear cream, and gently slid in Amelia's bottom. Amelia squirmed, but she didn't seem more uncomfortable than she already was. A moment later, the thermometer beeped, and the nurse pulled it out.

"101.8," the nurse said. "I'll get the doctor immediately." The nurse then disappeared, leaving Avery with her baby. She realized she left the diaper bag at home and didn't have a clean diaper for her, so she tried to put the old one back on. Just then a doctor came in through the curtain.

"Avery Stephens?"

"Yes," Avery responded. "And this is Amelia, she has a fever of 101.8."

"You don't have to dress her," the doctor said, motioning Avery to lay the baby back down. He walked over to her and started to feel her body from her head to her stomach. He checked the fontanelles, the soft spots on her skull that had yet to harden, her lymph nodes under her chin, her chest and then her stomach. "I'm going to do a blood test if that's all right with you."

"Sure, of course," Avery responded. "What are you looking for?"

"Just to see if everything is normal," the doctor said, as he walked to a small chest of plastic drawers near the bed and pulled out a needle and a few tubes. Avery's heart sank. She wasn't sure she would be able to watch him sink a needle in her baby. The doctor pulled gloves onto his hands and grabbed a cotton ball that he wet with alcohol. "Please try to hold her still." He grabbed Amelia's right hand and in one fluid motion, pricked the top of it. Immediately, she started wailing. Avery held her tight, at the same time trying not to start wailing herself. The doctor gently pressed on Amelia's hand, squeezing the blood through the needle to the tube. Avery watched, wondering how it was possible for the doctor to be taking so much blood. How many tests was he going to run? The doctor filled one tube and switched to a second. *He's going to take all her blood*, Avery thought right as the doctor stopped squeezing Amelia's hand. Amelia's wails began to weaken and turned back into a soft whimper. The doctor didn't take out the needle. Instead, he replaced the vial of blood with a small tube and taped the needle and tube to Amelia's arm.

"The tests are going to take a couple hours," the doctor said. "In the meantime, I want to give her something for her fever."

"Something for babies?" Avery confirmed.

"Of course," the doctor said. "I'll be right back." A moment later he returned with a small bag of liquid that he attached to the IV in Amelia's hand. "A nurse will come check on you every half hour. If you need anything in the meantime, just press that button." The doctor motioned to a red button on the side of the bed.

"Is Amelia sick? Is she OK?" Avery asked.

"Babies often get fevers," the doctor said. "Usually it's nothing, but we want to be sure." Then he left. Avery wanted to dress the baby, but she wasn't sure how with the IV in, so she just held Amelia close. She wished she had a blanket or something. She forgot her phone in the car, and she started to wonder if Graham would find her. As though he heard her thoughts, Graham pushed the curtain open a moment later. He was carrying the diaper bag and Avery's phone.

"I thought I left the bag at home!" Avery said.

"I grabbed it," he said as he handed it to her. Avery opened it and pulled out a new diaper and a blanket for

Amelia. She changed her and wrapped her, careful not to touch the IV. She told Graham about the blood test and what the doctor said.

"What do you think it is?" Avery asked Graham. Neither Aiden nor Maddox had been sick in their first few months of life. In fact, Avery could barely remember dealing with fevers with either of them as infants.

"It is November, so maybe the flu?" Graham said. "We have been taking her out a lot. She has been in the cold."

"And she's been coughing for the last week," Avery said. The flu. Something that seems so trivial, but to an infant, it could be the end.

"I'm sure she will be fine," Graham said, resting his hand on her head. "She already seems cooler than before."

Avery touched Amelia's forehead. Her temperature had gone down and she had fallen asleep in Avery's arms. Avery hadn't even noticed that the baby stopped whimpering. The curtains opened again, this time a nurse came in. The nurse checked the needle in the baby's hand and the bag that was slowly emptying through the tube. Then she touched the baby's forehead and asked Avery and Graham is they needed anything. Both Avery and Graham shook their heads and thanked the nurse before she slipped out through the curtains.

They sat silently until Graham's phone rang. "It is Brad," Graham said before picking up. "Hi…OK…thanks…Yeah…Monday…Sure…Bye." He hung up. "Brad said the judge postponed the closing arguments until Monday. He said not to worry. And he gives his best to you and Amelia." Avery nodded and continued to sit silently until the nurse came back to check on them. She did the same check of the IV and the baby's forehead and slipped out again. Avery guessed they had been waiting an hour. They continued to wait. The nurse came by for two more checks before the doctor returned.

"We got the blood test results," the doctor said. "And I want to do another test if you don't mind."

"Why, is something wrong?" Avery spit out. "What's wrong?"

"That's why I want to do another test," the doctor responded. "Has she been coughing? Any unusual rashes? Is she eating normally?"

"No rashes, and she eats fine," Avery responded. "She's been coughing for the last week. Why do you ask? What do you suspect it is? What did the test say?"

"She had a high white blood cell count and a low red blood count," the doctor said. "It's probably nothing, but we have to be sure."

"What does the cell count mean? What could it be?" Avery continued questioning the doctor.

"I wouldn't want to worry you for nothing," the doctor said. "We'll know more after we do more tests. I want to do a bone marrow aspiration. The test is a little more serious than a blood test, we will need to use anesthesia to put her to sleep for it."

"What's a bone marrow aspiration?" Avery could feel fear building up inside her.

"We insert a needle into her hip and suck out a little bone marrow," the doctor said. "We can test the bone marrow for a lot of different things, diseases, maybe lack of nutrition. It can tell us why her blood count came back abnormal."

"What kind of diseases?" Avery asked.

"Like I said, I prefer not to put scary ideas in your mind unless we know something for sure," the doctor said. "To do the test, I need you to sign these papers. They say you agree to the anesthesia and to the test being done, and that you understand the risks."

"The risks? What are the risks?"

"There are always risks with anesthesia, but it's rare that anything happens. There's a risk she won't wake up, that she could have an adverse reaction to the anesthesia, or that the needle could hit her spine. It's all very unlikely though."

"Do we need to do this test?"

"I highly recommend it," the doctor said. "I want to know what caused the fever, instead of just medicating to resolve it."

Avery looked at Graham. He looked back at her and tilted his head, as though to say, 'it is up to you.'

"OK," Avery said as she took the forms from the doctor. She glanced over them quickly and held her breath as she signed at the bottom.

"Thanks," the doctor said as he took the forms from Avery. "We'll do the test in an operating room. You two can be in there, but you need to be dressed in scrubs. A nurse will come set you up." The doctor left them for a moment and came back with three nurses. One was wheeling a small bassinet, which she asked Avery to place the baby in. Avery set Amelia down and the nurse started to wheel her down the hall, while one of the other nurses escorted Graham and Avery to a clean room to prepare for the test.

Everything was happening so fast; Avery didn't have time to think. She quickly put on the scrubs and followed the nurse into the operating room, where the doctor, two nurses and an anesthesiologist were waiting. The doctor asked if they were ready and when Avery nodded her head, the anesthesiologist switched a new bag into the IV. Amelia's eyes started to flutter close until she looked completely peaceful. Then, the doctor started to screw a giant needle into Amelia's hip. Avery cringed as she watched the needle slowly turn, burrowing deeper and deeper into her daughter's tiny hip bone. Avery felt faint, she felt a sudden pain in her own hip as her panic started to rise. How deep were they screwing that thing in? She wanted to ask the doctor if he was sure he knew what he was doing, but Graham held her shoulders tight, reminding her not to interrupt. After a few minutes, the doctor pulled a tube from the needle, extracting the bone marrow from Amelia's hip bone. Then, he gently dragged the needle out and bandaged the open wound. The nurse took Amelia and led Avery and Graham to a private room where they would wait until further notice. Amelia should wake up in fifteen minutes, they said. If she wasn't awake in half an hour, press the red button, the nurse told them.

Avery let out her breath. She couldn't stop looking at Amelia, sleeping silently in her bassinet, breathing in and out. Avery concentrated on her chest, afraid to look away for a moment and miss the gentle rhythm of her breath. She grabbed Graham's arm, unsure of what to do with her hands. Her poor baby, being poked and stabbed by all these doctors, and for what? Because she may have the flu? No, it couldn't be the flu, Avery thought. They wouldn't go through all this for the flu.

Amelia soon started to stir. She moved her head side to side and then her eyes opened. They opened wide, her expression one of shock and wonder. Poor girl, Avery thought, she's probably so confused. Avery held on to Amelia's hands as she hovered over the bassinet. Soon, the doctor came into the room. He put a stethoscope to Amelia's chest, shone a light in her mouth and eyes, checked her reflexes.

"She seems to have recovered from the operation just fine," he said. "But I'd like to keep her here overnight for observation. You're welcome to stay here as well." Avery looked at the one small cushioned chair next to the bassinet.

"What about the test results? When will we get those?" she asked.

"It takes three business days, so either Friday or Monday," he said. "We'll call you with the results." The doctor gave them a quick nod before exiting the room, leaving Avery and Graham alone with the baby and a feeling of dread that would haunt them.

Chapter 43

November 13, 2013

THE TRIAL OF SOLOMON RIGHT HERE IN MANHATTAN read the top headline of the New York Post that morning. Cameron didn't usually read tabloids, but it was everywhere. The lobby of their building, the sidewalk, inside the subway station. Everyone in New York saw a picture of Cameron walking out of the courthouse, one hand over her forehead, the other down by her side. Cameron hated how she looked in the picture. Her body looked round, disproportional. She looked tired, washed out. The front page also had a picture of the other mother, Avery, with a sad smile on her face, looking directly at the camera. *She looks more like a real mother than I do,* Cameron thought, *more sympathetic. No one would think I am the mother after seeing this.*

She knew she shouldn't read it, she should try to ignore it, but she couldn't. She grabbed a copy in the subway station on their way to the courthouse. She was staring at the front page with the huge headline and pictures of her and Avery. Then she turned open to the page with the article.

Two mothers fight over baby, the top of the page said. *That's not even fair,* Cameron thought. *That makes them sound so pathetic.* Cameron kept reading.

A trial that requires the wisdom of King Solomon is in full swing in the downtown civil court. Two women are fighting over who is the real mother of a baby—the genetic mother or the one who birthed her? After an IVF mix-up, Avery Stephens gave birth to a daughter who is not genetically related to her. Now, the genetic mother, Cameron Stevens, is fighting for her life to get the baby. How will it end? The jury is still out...

Cameron stopped reading. Whoever wrote this must think this is so simple, she thought. They missed all the important details. How could anyone understand the situation from reading this? Cameron looked down, embarrassed that she was reading a story about herself. Then she threw the newspaper to the ground.

"I told you not to read it," Andy said. He was sitting next to her on the subway on their way to court. "It can only make you angry."

"You were right," she said, putting her hands on her cheeks. She wasn't ready for another day in court, but with any luck this would be one of their last. Both sides were supposed to make their closing arguments and then it was up to the jury, a group of strangers that would decide her fate. Cameron wanted to cry. She felt helpless, exhausted, overwhelmed. The night before, Alicia had handed her an article about postpartum depression. She recommended that Cameron read it, she said she could even recommend a few people Cameron could talk to. Cameron had stuffed the article in her purse before Andy could see. Then, she read it late at night after he had already fallen asleep. The article said many women have anxiety after giving birth. That it can be overwhelming. It said hormones were partly to blame, but also the lack of sleep and the difficulties of being a mother. That's not me, Cameron told herself. She was just anxious because of the trial, not because of postpartum depression. She would feel better once everything was over.

When the subway made it to their stop, they got off the train and made their way above ground to the courthouse. Already a crowd of reporters was gathered outside. Once they noticed Cameron and Andy, they ran to them, screaming questions and flashing cameras. Holding Cameron's hand, Andy pushed through them, knocking one cameraman to the ground. "Pigs," he said as they made it into the courthouse. They walked through security and to their courtroom where Alicia was waiting outside talking on the phone. She hung up when Andy and Cameron approached.

"You ready?" Alicia asked as she led them through the room to their table. "We had our jury experts analyzing each jury member last night. There is a very good chance we win this. We also think deliberation will be pretty quick."

The rows of benches in the courtroom were already filled. Even more so than the day before. Cameron scanned the audience as though searching for a familiar face. There weren't any.

"The judge opened an overflow room for observers since there were so many people lined up here this morning," Alicia said. "Your story is really making headlines."

"Can't you tell the judge that we don't want media attention?" Andy said as they sat down. "Don't we have a right to privacy?"

"Unfortunately not in court," Alicia said. "Trials are open to the public and that includes reporters." Alicia looked at her watch. "We should be getting started any moment."

Cameron looked over to the defense table. It was empty, the other couple and their lawyer had yet to arrive.

"All rise for the Honorable Judge Baxter," the bailiff said, causing a roar in the court as everyone stood up. The judge came in through the front door and sat down at his podium, motioning everyone to sit down. As they did, the defense lawyer came running in through the back of the court room.

"Mr. Sandfeld, you're late," the judge said as the lawyer made it to the front of the room. "Where are your clients?"

"Your honor," he said, a little out of breath. "I have to ask for a continuance. My clients are having a slight emergency and cannot make it to court today."

"An emergency?" the judge asked.

"Yes, your honor," the lawyer responded. "They send their regrets and would appreciate it if we could continue tomorrow."

"Your honor," Alicia jumped in. "This is a stall tactic. The defense is trying to delay the end of this trial. They are afraid of losing!"

"No!" the defense lawyer yelled. "There was a family emergency that my clients must attend to. We can continue tomorrow."

"What's the emergency?" Alicia asked.

"My clients request their privacy in this emergency, just know they wouldn't ask for this if it weren't serious," the lawyer said.

"Fine," the judge banged his gavel. "If it is a real emergency, I don't want to make this more difficult for them. If it is not, Mr. Sandfeld, and I find out that this is a stall tactic, then you will be sanctioned by the court."

"I understand, your honor," the lawyer said. "Thank you, we really appreciate it."

"We'll continue on Monday," the judge said. "I hope that gives your clients enough time to sort out this emergency." He emphasized the last word.

"It will, thank you," the lawyer said as the judge banged his gavel again.

Cameron looked from Andy to Alicia. "No need to worry," Alicia said. "These things happen all the time. Most likely the lawyer needs more time to get ready for the closing statements and he is just taking advantage of the judge. This gives us more time to prepare as well, so in the end it is a good thing for all." Cameron nodded. It was only Wednesday, so it meant they now had four more days until the closing arguments. Four days felt like forever to Cameron then, she didn't know if she could wait that long.

"Come on, Cam," Andy said. "Let's try to do something fun. Get our mind off everything." As if that were possible, Cameron thought. But she agreed.

For a moment she thought about her mommy-and-me group that would be meeting today. She could still make it, go pick the baby up and take her there. It was fun to pretend for an hour that everything was normal. Maybe that would get her mind off of everything. But what would she say to Andy? She followed him out of the courthouse, through the reporters and back on to the subway. Instead of going home, he recommended they go to a spa. Get a couple's massage. Cameron could get a mani pedi and a facial. Cameron nodded, she couldn't go to the mommy-and-me group. But she could take this time to have some quality time with Andy. "Let's go all out," Andy said when they got there.

They started with a massage. Cameron and Andy undressed and lay down on the two tables standing side by side in their private massage room. The masseuses came in and started to rub warm oil over their bodies. Cameron tried to relax, to concentrate on the quiet piano music playing in the room, on the feeling of the masseuse's hand over her tense shoulders. But she couldn't. Her mind raced. Was Alicia right that the lawyer just needed more time? Or was there a real emergency? Could the emergency have something to do with their baby? No. If it did, surely someone would tell them. It would be cruel not to. The fifty-minute massage seemed to drag on forever. Cameron wanted to open her eyes, to tell the masseuse just to stop, but she didn't. She held still, squeezing her eyes and trying to slow down her breath. Finally it ended and the masseuses left the couple alone in the room. Cameron stayed still. She was on her back. She felt heavy, tired.

"Man, I needed that," Andy said. Cameron could feel Andy's hands touch her shoulders and gently pull the towel down her body. "How about a happy ending?" He nuzzled her nose and then started to kiss her neck. Slowly he moved on top of her. Cameron still didn't move. She wondered if the table was strong enough for two people. If the spa had cameras in the rooms. If it was normal for people to have sex after a couple's massage. "Don't you miss me, baby?" Andy asked as he slipped inside her.

Chapter 44

October 21, 2013

"Can you describe your exact movements on the morning of January 4, 2013?" the woman in the suit said. Sydney watched the woman as she pinched the side of her glasses and read the question from her clipboard.

"How am I supposed to remember exactly what I did on a specific day ten months ago?" Sydney answered with her arms crossed in front of her chest. But she did remember. Specifically that day, because it was the day after Dr. Klein dumped her. The woman raised her eyebrow. She was sitting across from Sydney at a large wooden table inside a rectangular conference room at some fancy insurance company office.

"Are you saying you don't remember that day at all?" the woman asked.

"Could you be more specific?" Sydney said with an antagonizing tone. "Maybe if you can tell me what you're interested in, I can give you what you are looking for."

The previous week she got a call from some lawyer asking if she could come in and answer a few questions. "What about?" she asked him on the phone, but he declined to answer. He just told her that she needed to come in, otherwise she would get a subpoena and be forced to come in. Better to do it the easy way. Sydney's first thought: it must be Dr. Klein's divorce lawyer. They probably wanted her to tell them about how horrible Dr. Klein's marriage was. She could testify about how unhappy he was, how crazy his wife was. Probably because he was trying to reduce the settlement his wife would be getting. But Sydney wasn't going to help him. He deserved to pay a huge settlement. The bigger the better.

She wondered if the divorce was in any way caused by her decision. When she told him what she was going to do with the baby, he responded solemnly. "I understand," he had said on the phone. "My lawyer will take care of the specifics." That was the last time Sydney spoke with Dr. Klein.

Sydney scheduled a time with the lawyer—not the lawyer who she had dealt with regarding her pregnancy—after one her shifts at the pediatrician's office where she was working. When she arrived at the office, something seemed off. It wasn't a lawyer's office; it was an insurance company. One that specialized in malpractice. Sydney recognized the name of the company, but she wasn't sure from where exactly. Why were they involved in the divorce?

"I think you'd probably be more interested in what happened the night before January 4," Sydney said with a sly smile. "That was the last time it happened." Sydney paused and watched the woman sitting in front of her. The woman again fidgeted with her glasses.

"The last time what happened?" the woman asked.

Sydney leaned forward a little. She could see the woman was captivated, waiting to hear what juicy information she was about to give. "That was the last time Mark—Dr. Klein—and I slept together. Then I dumped him."

Sydney leaned back, waiting for the next question. But the woman remained silent, so she continued talking. "Mark was cheating on his wife for more than a year. He used to come over all the time." Sydney smiled. Cheaters always paid more in divorces.

"Did that affect anything in the clinic the following day?" the woman asked as she scribbled on her yellow notepad.

"Well, I'm sure Dr. Klein was just devastated after I dumped him," Sydney said. "But we were very professional."

"Can you describe that day at the clinic?" the woman asked again. "Was there anything unusual?"

"No, everything was normal," Sydney said. "We had a few transfers, a few retrievals. I did the transfers with Dr. Klein and Rachel, the other nurse, she did the retrievals. Dr. Klein seemed to stay closer to his office between procedures, probably because he didn't want to see me, but everything was normal."

"Do you remember any of the transfers that occurred?" the woman asked.

Sydney thought back to that morning. She did vaguely remember trying to flirt with one husband. He was good looking, like an Abercrombie & Fitch model. She remembered hoping to make Dr. Klein jealous, but the husband only had eyes for his wife. The other transfers were sort of a blur. When you do the same procedure over and over—four times a day for two years—how are you supposed to remember each one? When Sydney was trying to recall the other transfers from that day, a different thought popped into her head.

"Why are the transfers relevant for Dr. Klein's divorce?" she asked the woman.

The woman raised her eyebrows and again touched her glasses. "His divorce?" she asked, clearing her throat.

"That's why I am here, right?" Sydney said. "You're negotiating his divorce settlement?"

"I work for Dr. Klein's malpractice insurance," the woman said.

"Why are you guys involved with his divorce anyways?" Sydney cut in.

"I don't know anything about his divorce," the woman responded. "This is about an incident that happened at the clinic on January 4."

"What happened?" Sydney asked. She suddenly felt silly for telling this stranger about her and Mark's relationship.

"There was a mix-up of two embryos that were transferred that day," the woman responded. "As you mentioned, you did the transfers with Dr. Klein, so we're just trying to figure out exactly how something like that could happen. Does the name Cameron Stevens sound familiar?"

Sydney shook her head. A mix-up? How was that possible? She always checked the labels on everything—the vessels that she took from the freezer, the petri dishes with the fresh embryos, the women's bracelets. It was her job to check those labels and make sure there wasn't a mix-up. She knew she checked. There was no way she could have made a mistake.

"Was it possible you were distracted on January 4?" the woman asked. "Seeing as you and Dr. Klein had just broken up?"

"No," Sydney said firmly. "I always made sure that the labels on the embryos matched the label on the woman."

"On that day, there were two women with similar last names," the woman said. "A Stephens and a Stevens, spelled differently, but sound the same. Is it possible that there was some confusion and that the labels weren't adequately checked?"

The déjà vu. Sydney suddenly remembered having that feeling while she tried to ignite Dr. Klein with her eyes in the operating room. Was it possible she made a mistake? She stayed silent.

"What are the procedures for checking the labels?" the woman asked. "Did you have multiple checks in place? Multiple people checking?"

"Just me..." Sydney said, almost whispering. "But, but I'm sure I didn't make a mistake!"

The woman looked at her and scribbled on her notepad. "Can you tell me how you are so sure that you didn't make a mistake?"

Sydney felt her heart starting to race. She started sweating. "Do I need a lawyer?" she blurted out.

"No," the woman responded. "You are covered by the clinic's malpractice insurance for your time working there. We're just trying to understand how the mistake occurred."

"I have no idea how it could have occurred," Sydney said. "I need to leave." She shot up from her chair and darted out the door, careful not to look at the woman or anyone else she passed. At the elevator, she pressed the down button repeatedly until she heard a ping and the silver doors opened.

"Sydney?"

She looked up to see Rachel stepping out of the elevator in front of her.

"Sydney, are you alright?" Rachel asked.

"Rachel," she said. "I think I made a mistake."

Chapter 45

November 15, 2013

Leukemia. That's what the doctor said on the phone. When her phone rang, Avery jumped to answer. The doctor asked if they could come in to talk, to discuss the test results. Avery panicked. "We won't come in unless you tell me the results right now on the phone," she said to him. He sighed, saying it was better to discuss them in person. But eventually, he relented. And he said that word that no one ever wants to hear. Leukemia. "We need to discuss your options," the doctor said as Avery silently tried to comprehend what she heard. She agreed and promised they would get there as soon as they could.

Since they left the hospital two days ago, Avery noticed that Amelia looked pale. She seemed fatigued, even for a newborn who slept fifteen hours a day. She started to suspect something was wrong. But she never could have suspected this. There was no way. There must have been a mistake.

Avery and Graham took Amelia and went back to the hospital to meet with the doctor. After a short wait, they were escorted into his office where he sat them down and began to talk.

"The bone marrow aspiration test showed that your daughter has acute lymphocytic leukemia," the doctor said. "We can see it is in the early stages, but I would recommend starting treatment right away."

"She's a newborn, how is this even possible?" Avery asked.

"It's rare in infants," the doctor said. "There are only about 150 cases annually of infant leukemia in the US."

"What treatment do you recommend?" Avery questioned. She looked down at Amelia who was lying down in her stroller watching the mobile above her head.

"There are a few options," the doctor responded. "But you should speak with a pediatric oncologist. This isn't my specialty."

"Could you just tell us about what the options may be?"

"The oncologist will probably want to perform more tests," the doctor said. "Then he may recommend chemotherapy, radiation, a bone marrow transplant. The oncologist will come up with a treatment plan based on further testing. We have a great pediatric oncologist here who I am going to refer you to."

Avery nodded. She had so many questions, but she couldn't speak.

"The doctor is just down the hall," the doctor continued. "He will admit Amelia and get started with developing a treatment plan right away."

"Admit her now?" Avery blurted.

"Infant leukemia is very serious," the doctor said. "She needs immediate treatment."

"Can we just take her home and think about it for a couple days?" Avery asked. The shock overwhelmed her.

"Your daughter is really sick," the doctor said. "I cannot advise taking her out of the hospital."

Avery slowly blinked in agreement. Then the doctor picked up his phone to page a nurse, who entered the office so fast she must have been waiting right outside. The nurse led the family down the hall to a small room with a bed and two little chairs inside.

"The rooms are designed for children a little older than yours," the nurse said apologetically looking at the bed. "I need to take your baby's vitals and then the doctor will decide what to do next."

Avery stayed standing, holding Amelia in her arms. She couldn't take her eyes of Amelia. Her pale face, bright eyes. How could she be so sick? The nurse beckoned Avery to lay Amelia down on the bed. Slowly, Avery knelt and placed the baby down, keeping her hands on Amelia's stomach. The nurse then wrapped a band around Amelia's arm and clipped a monitor onto her toe to get her blood pressure. When the machine connected to the band and monitor beeped, the nurse nodded and detached the monitors from Amelia. She wrote the results down on her clipboard and left the room.

"Do you think we did this to her? Like because of the switch?" Avery whispered to Graham.

"No," Graham responded resolutely. "It is not our fault."

"Does this affect the lawsuit?" Avery asked. "Should we tell the other couple?"

"We need to talk to Brad," Graham responded. They called the lawyer and told them they needed to have an emergency meeting. Brad accepted and invited them to his office right away.

"Can we actually have the meeting somewhere else?" Graham asked, inviting Brad to meet them in their hospital room. The lawyer accepted and promised to be there in half an hour. For the first few minutes of the wait, Graham and Avery were silent. But the silence was deafening to Avery. Her head was anything but silent.

"Does this affect our position in the lawsuit?" she said suddenly.

"You tell me."

Avery hesitated. "No. Amelia is still our daughter and we want to keep her. We will do whatever we need to do for her treatment."

"Agreed." Then, they went back to silence, not saying a word until there was a knock on their door. Brad walked in and eyed the couple sitting on the little bed with their baby. He shifted his eyes to the two plastic blue chairs in the room and squatted down on one of them, pulling a notepad out of his briefcase.

"Amelia has leukemia," Avery blurted out. The words seemed to shoot out and explode all over the walls. Like the diagnosis could never be taken back now. Brad's mouth dropped open.

At that moment, Amelia started to whimper. It was time to feed her, Avery suddenly remembered. She was so used to feeding Amelia in public that she could open her bra and put the baby to her breast in one swift movement.

"I, uh, OK, when you said it was an emergency…well, I didn't expect this," Brad said, pausing between every syllable.

"We want to know how this affects the trial," Graham said.

"Well, that's a good question," Brad said.

"How do we tell the other couple?" Avery said. "They should know."

"Well, I would say it isn't really relevant to tell them yet," Brad said. "After all, this shouldn't affect the outcome of the trial. The trial is about whether they should raise their genetic child or the one they birthed. Whether their genetic child is sick, is irrelevant."

"Yes, but wouldn't they want to know?" Avery asked.

"There are a lot of things they may want to know," Brad said. "But my job isn't to think about what they want, it's to think about what's best for you."

"And that is to not tell them?" Avery asked.

"I know you don't want to hear this, but you basically are getting a 'get out of jail free' card," Brad said. "Don't waste it."

"What do you mean?" Avery said. Amelia let go of Avery's breast. In a quick move of her arms, Avery flipped the baby around and placed her on her other breast.

"Having a kid with leukemia is tough, you don't want to go through that," Brad said. "We can throw the closing statement, let them win, and voila, you can start over with a healthy baby."

Avery and Graham looked at each other for a moment. Avery tried to read his face, tried to understand what he thought. What should they do, but his expression was blank, as though he were trying to read the same thing on her face. Then, she looked back to Brad.

"Are you crazy?" Avery yelled. "Leukemia or not, Amelia is our baby! Maybe they will drop the case if we tell them."

"It will just complicate things," Brad said. "As your lawyer, I advise you not to say anything until the trial is over. Only if we lose, of course. Trust me."

"Are we going to lose?" Avery said, her voice still raised. Amelia stopped eating on the second side. She let out a small cry, and Avery lifted her to her shoulder and patted her back gently.

"I think we have a good chance of winning," Brad responded. "If that is what we still want."

Amelia burped. "It is what we want," Avery said angrily, still holding Amelia to her shoulder. "Don't forget that."

"Of course," Brad responded. "Don't worry. Everything will go as planned. Take the weekend to try to relax."

Avery scoffed at that notion. Relax. As if that were possible. Avery was confused. Dazed. It was like the day was all a dream. A nightmare. Too absurd to be true. She needed time to accept everything that she had learned today. To figure out what they should do. To devise a plan. But time was something they didn't have.

Chapter 46

November 16, 2013

The doctor's office was cold. Avery wished she had brought a jacket with her, something to put over her shoulders, but how was she supposed to know they were going to have spent the night in the hospital? A nurse had been caring for Amelia since the day before, connecting her to an IV, taking a blood sample, and making sure she was comfortable until the doctor was able to meet. Avery and Graham had been the opposite of comfortable, but that was of no concern to the nurse.

In the morning, they were escorted into an office at the end of the corridor. Avery sat in the stiff chair in front of a wooden table that looked more fit for dining than for desk work. She had Amelia in her arms and Graham next to her. Avery looked around the office. On the walls hung diplomas, one from Harvard—a bachelor's degree in chemistry—another from Stanford—a Doctor of Medicine—a certificate of residency in pediatrics from Mercy Hospital in New York and a fellowship certification in pediatric oncology. Each award was in an identical gold frame, perfectly spaced one next to the other. Across the diplomas, on the other side of the room, was a tall bookcase, filled with what appeared to be textbooks. Giant books, squeezed side-by-side, filled every shelf. Avery wondered if the doctor ever looked through the books, or if they were more for show.

A sudden click notified Avery that the doctor had arrived. She turned around to see an older man opening and then gently closing the door. He was tall, wearing a white lab coat that covered him to his knees. She noticed his hands, they were big, long fingers with knuckles like pearls. He wore glasses that balanced on his large nose.

"I'm Dr. Mike Saltzman," he said, reaching out his right hand to shake theirs as he made his way around the desk. "How can I help you today?" Graham and Avery took turns shaking his hand and introducing themselves. A strong grip, Avery thought to herself.

"Our daughter has leukemia," Avery said. "We were in the hospital last week because she had a fever. They did a bunch of tests and told us that she had leukemia." Avery felt strange repeating the word so many times. "We were referred to you. For treatment."

"I'm so sorry," the doctor said. "How old is she?" He was looking at the infant in Avery's lap.

"Eleven weeks," Avery responded. "The other doctor said it is really rare at her age. Maybe there was a mistake?"

"It's possible, but unlikely," Mike said. "Can you give me some background on your daughter? How was the pregnancy?"

"Normal," Avery said.

"And the birth? What week was she born?"

"Thirty-seven," Avery said. "But it was fine."

"How has her health been until now?"

"Everything has been fine," Avery said. "She had a little cough for the last few weeks, and then a fever, but nothing major. Are you going to do chemotherapy?"

"Most likely," the doctor said. "But there are a lot of different medications that we can use. Unfortunately, or I guess, fortunately, there aren't a lot of cases of infant leukemia, so there hasn't been a lot of research about what drugs are best at this age. There may be some clinical trials of something new we could enter." The doctor paused, as though waiting for questions. When Avery and Graham were silent, he continued. "She will need a bone marrow transplant as well, that usually increases the likelihood of survival. One of you can be the donors, the closer the donor is to the patient, the higher the chance that the transplant will work. Are you available today? We can take a blood sample from each of you today and start creating our treatment plan."

"Uh, doctor," Avery said. "We're Amelia's parents, but we're not genetically related to her. Does that affect whether we can donate bone marrow?"

"Oh, you adopted? Are you in touch with the birth parents? The transplant has a higher likelihood of success if we get bone marrow from one of them," the doctor said.

"Actually no, it's complicated," Avery said, taking in a deep breath. She hated having to explain the mix-up. It made people look at her differently. Like she wasn't Amelia's real mom. Everyone had an opinion about it. Wanted to share stories that they thought were similar. They never were. "There is a chance that Amelia will go back to her genetic parents. We're in a custody battle right now."

"OK," the doctor said slowly. "I recommend we start doing some testing. If she has leukemia, she needs treatment, it doesn't matter who has custody."

Avery sat quietly. For the first time, it dawned on her that she may not be the one there with Amelia when she goes through chemotherapy. If they lost the case, it would be Cameron taking the baby to hospital visits, caring for her when she would be sick, watching her helplessly. Avery felt something that she couldn't quite explain. Relief? No, couldn't be. Distress? Maybe. She felt like they were making a lot of decisions that maybe weren't theirs to make.

"Doctor, I think we need to think about this," she said. "A couple days."

"Avery," Graham said, placing his hand on her arm.

Avery shot Graham a look like a dart right into the bullseye. She knew they should start treatment, that they should continue on this path as though there would be no interruptions or roadblocks, but Avery was hesitant.

"Doctor, we want to go home for a couple days," Avery said. "We'll bring Amelia back to start treatment. We promise."

"I can't advise that," the doctor said. "Your daughter needs to stay in the hospital."

"No, she can't!" Avery suddenly exclaimed. She even surprised herself with the force by which she was against staying in the hospital. She just needed some time. Enough time to think, to try to wrap her head around the situation. To understand it more clearly. She would feel better about what needed to be done after she could just think.

The doctor looked at the couple, a twinge of disappointment in his eyes. "You need to keep the baby here. For her own good," the doctor said. "She could get sicker in minutes. We need to monitor her. We need to start treatment."

"I want to bring her home for a few days!" Avery felt like a child having a temper tantrum over not getting the ice cream she wanted. She felt silly, petty, but she didn't care. She knew what she wanted.

"Ma'am," the doctor started, but was cut off by a storming Avery.

"You can't force us to leave our daughter here," Avery said frantically. "We'll sign any papers you need from us."

"Avery," Graham said quietly. He was about to continue, but stopped when Avery shot him a look that could kill.

"If that's what you want," the doctor said. "You will need to sign the paperwork saying that you went against the doctor's recommendation and that the hospital bears no responsibility for anything that happens."

"Fine," Avery said, standing up.

Avery and Graham left the doctor's office and signed the paperwork, allowing them to take Amelia home, against the doctor's recommendations. When they got home, Avery fed the baby and put her in her bassinet to sleep. When she came back to the kitchen, Graham was waiting for her.

"Avery, what is going on?"

"I don't know," she responded as she sat down at the table next to him.

"So what do we need to think about? Do you want to meet with another doctor? Research some treatment options?"

"No," she said, unable to look Graham in the eyes. She didn't know how to explain her hesitation. How to express what she was feeling when she didn't understand it herself.

"Maybe you do not want to say this, but are you just hoping that this will not be our problem anymore in a few days?" Graham asked.

"Graham! How could you say something like that?" Avery screamed. "Do you think I love our daughter less because she is sick? What kind of person do you think I am? What kind of mother do you think I am?"

"It would be a perfectly natural feeling, Avery," Graham responded calmly. "No one could judge you for it."

"I would judge me for it!" she yelled back. With that, she stood up, turned around and walked out the front door. A little fresh air. A few minutes to calm herself. She would come to her senses if she could just have a few moments to herself to breathe.

Chapter 47

November 18, 2013

Cameron and Andy were back in court. They had gotten off the subway a stop earlier, walked the last few blocks, and snuck into the courthouse from a side entrance, hoping to avoid the cameras waiting for them. The courtroom was filled with reporters waiting to hear the closing arguments. They were all standing around, talking to each other when Cameron and Andy walked in. She could feel the eyes all on her, studying her clothes, her hair, her makeup. She tried to look simple, plain, tried not to give them anything to judge her about, but now she was afraid she had failed. Was her lipstick too dark? Her dress too tight? Did her hair look messy? She looked to the floor as Andy led her to their table at the front of the courtroom. As she sat down, she took a quick glance to the defense table. It was empty. She wondered if they would be coming in today, or if the emergency would make then ask for another continuance.

Her question was answered a moment later when the couple arrived with their lawyer. They rushed through the courtroom to their table and sat down quickly. Cameron tried to look at them, but she couldn't get a good look. The husband's back faced her, blocking her view.

"All rise for the honorable Judge Baxter," the bailiff said just as the door at the front of the courtroom opened and the judge walked through. The crowd behind suddenly became quiet, so quiet that Cameron could hear the swish of the judge's gown as he strode to his podium. The judge sat down and motioned the court to do the same.

"Are we ready today, Mr. Sandfeld?" Judge Baxter asked.

"Yes, your honor," the defense lawyer said. "We again thank you for the continuance."

"Great, I hope the emergency was resolved," the judge said without waiting for a response. He then turned to the bailiff. "Can we bring in the jury?"

The bailiff opened the third door in the courtroom, allowing the jury members to come in and take their seats in the box. Cameron looked at them, wondering what each of them thought. Did they think she was as pathetic as she felt? Did they want to help her? Give her back her baby? Or did they think she was as crazy as the papers made her look?

"Alright, Ms. Black, the floor is yours," the judge said.

Alicia stood up and approached the jury. "Ladies and gentlemen," she started. "We started this trial talking about justice. About righting a wrong. About bringing a child home to her parents. Her real parents. My clients, Cameron and Andy Stevens, want what every parent wants. To raise their child, the child that they intended to have. I want you to try to imagine what Cameron and Andy have been through. They struggled to get pregnant, and went through the difficult process of IVF, and then a pregnancy, which all women understand is no easy task. Next, the birth, again something all women can agree with, is painful beyond belief. After all that, to find out that the clinic made a dire mistake with their embryos. After all that, all their trials, all they want to do is go home and love the baby that they went through all of this for.

"You heard from Jim Hanson, the lab technician who conducted the DNA testing of the baby. He told you that there is a 99.9% match between the baby and clients. Ninety-nine point nine. That is the highest match possible in DNA testing. His testimony leaves zero doubt that my clients are the genetic and biological parents to the baby in question. And, that the baby that Cameron birthed is, beyond a doubt, the baby of the defendants.

"After establishing beyond a doubt that Cameron and Andy are the parents of this baby, we talked about the importance of being raised by biological parents who want to parent. You heard from Dr. Cheryl Green, a renowned child psychologist who has been studying this realm for years. She told you that children raised by two biological parents are more likely to thrive as adults, to get college degrees and succeed as adults. Isn't that what you want for this baby? Shouldn't that be what the defendants want for her, if they really cared about her? Wouldn't they want her to have the best chances in life to succeed?

"Now, the defense lawyer tried to tell you that the defendants are just as dedicated to the baby's success as Cameron and Andy are. But did they take classes on how to raise a healthy baby? Did they take classes on baby first aid and CPR, as Cameron and Andy did? Did they do any of the things that Cameron's longtime friend Bethany Anderson told you about? Did they buy brand new baby equipment—the best of everything—so that they would be prepared? It would appear they didn't. They already have two kids and we all know that people always invest more in their first. What's that joke about the pacifier? When a pacifier falls on the ground, what do the parents do? With the first child, they sterilize it. With the second child, they wash it with water, maybe soap. With the third child, they stick it right back in the baby's mouth. Now doesn't this baby deserve a sterilized pacifier? Doesn't this baby deserve the dedication and thought of the first-time parents who intended to raise her?

"The defense is trying to confuse you. They compared this baby to a tumor and tried to pretend that the rule of 'finders keepers' applies. Do you think that the rule of finders keepers applies to babies? Think honestly for yourselves.

"The defense wants you to think that this case falls in gray area. But it doesn't. This is black and white. We ask you; no, we beg you to decide to send both babies back to their real families. Give each one the best chance in life in thrive. Do what is best for the babies, and that is for them to be raised by their biological parents. Thank you." Alicia stood still for a few moments in front of the jury, letting her words hang in the air. Soak into the jury members. Then, she pivoted on her heels and went back to their table.

Cameron felt her eyes start to water. Alicia was so right. How could the jury not be convinced, if they weren't already? She started to feel that they could win. That maybe it would be OK in the end.

"Mr. Sandfeld?" the judge said, turning to the defense table. The defense lawyer stood up and walked over to the jury. He cleared his throat.

"Ladies and gentlemen, this case is all about what is best for a little girl. Not any little girl, but what is best for Amelia Stephens, the little girl who was born two and a half months ago to Avery and Graham Stephens. For the last two and half months, this girl has been living with her family in Brooklyn. She's started to recognize people, learned to lift her head up, and she's even begun to smile. She's gotten to know her surroundings, finally able to feel safe in the big world where she is growing up.

"Now, the plaintiffs want to rip her away from her home. They are trying to make you think that is what is best for her, but use your logic. Does that sound reasonable? Does it sound like the plaintiffs are looking out for the best interest of the baby, or simply, their own best interests?

"During this trial, we talked about whether the fact that Amelia came from the plaintiffs' genetic materials is relevant. And we saw that it is not. What is relevant, is what was invested in taking those genetic materials and turning them into a baby. Was it the plaintiffs who did that? No, it was Avery Stephens. Over nine months her body turned a couple of cells into a living, breathing person. Doesn't that require a lot more effort than just shedding some genetic materials? If you have ever known a pregnant person, you know this is true. That pregnancy is no easy task. It is constant discomfort, constant exhaustion, but for the good cause of creating a baby.

"If Avery's exertions for creating this baby are not enough, then think about the lifelong trauma that Amelia will experience if ripped away from her home. The plaintiffs think that because she is a baby, she will forget about this trauma, that it won't stay with her throughout her life, but we all know that's wrong. We know for a fact that what happens in a baby's first few months affects who they are in the future. You heard it from Dr. Harriett Sharon, but you all knew it yourselves. That's why we all spend so much time and effort helping our babies develop, holding them when they cry, playing with them. We do this because we know it will affect the baby. The plaintiffs tried to tell you that the baby will be traumatized no matter what, but don't you think that letting her stay in a loving home will protect her from trauma? She will always know that she is loved and receiving the best care possible.

"Avery and Graham are well equipped to provide her the best care possible. They have raised two wonderful boys who are smart, kind, and ready to be the best big brothers in the world. Amelia is lucky to have them, to have two brothers looking out for her, always there to protect her. Like guardian angels. And as I have mentioned, Avery and Graham are happy to adopt the baby birthed by the plaintiffs and raise her as well. She would also benefit from having two wonderful big brothers.

"You, ladies and gentlemen of the jury, now have a huge responsibility. Amelia's life is in your hands. It is up to you to decide what happens to her, and whatever your decision, it will affect her the rest of her life. So whatever you decide, make sure it is a decision you can live with. For those of you with children of your own, imagine they were taken from you when they were two and half months old. How would you feel? Is there anything that could have convinced you that that is what is best for your child?

"What I am asking of you today is simple. Allow a baby to remain with her family. With the family who loves her and is already giving her the best upbringing possible. Let Amelia Stephens stay with her parents, Avery and Graham. Thank you." The lawyer stood still a moment in front of the jury, scanning each of their faces, then he turned around and walked past Cameron and Andy, giving them a quick look before he sat down at the defense's table.

"Alright, thank you counselors," the judge said and then turned to the jury. "Jurors, you will now be escorted to your chambers to discuss the evidence you were provided here in court and decide the outcome of this case. Please remember, that your decision must be based only on the evidence you saw and heard here in court. That means your decision must not be influenced by anything you read or saw outside of the courtroom. In fact, you shouldn't have read or watched any of the news about this case as you were told at the beginning of the trial. If it is suspected that something or someone from outside the courtroom has influenced your decision, I will have to declare a mistrial and we will have to start over. Understood? The foreman will be in charge of collecting your votes. You need a majority to agree in order to come to a decision, that means seven out of the twelve of you must agree. Good luck."

When the judge finished speaking, the bailiff opened the door to the jury box and led the members out through the door to their chambers. Cameron watched them file out and disappear from the courtroom. She wished she could have talked to them, told them about how important this was to her, but all she could do was hope that somehow, they understood.

Chapter 48

November 18, 2013

Sydney sat quietly in the last row of the courtroom, squished between the edge of the bench and a woman in a wrinkled suit. She came to the closing arguments after reading about the trial in the New York Post. When she saw the article, she immediately knew it was her clinic. Her mistake. She scanned the article quickly at first, looking for any mention of how the mistake happened. When she didn't see an explanation, she breathed a sigh of relief. The investigation must not have been leaked to the papers.

Then she stared at the pictures of the two women on the paper's cover. One, Cameron, looked timid and lost, while the other, Avery, looked shell-shocked but determined. She didn't immediately recognize the women, but she knew who they were. She remembered that day at the clinic, the day after Dr. Klein had broken up with her. How angry she felt, how distracted she was. The déjà vu. A simple mistake that turned into a tornado ripping apart the lives of two families.

After she had met with the investigator at the insurance company, she was afraid. What if they decided to blame everything on her? Could they prove she was at fault? Even if she was the one who made the switch, wasn't Dr. Klein to blame? After all, he was the doctor. And it was his fault she was distracted that day. After meeting the investigator she had waited for Rachel outside the office building. It was an hour before she appeared in the building's lobby.

"What did you tell them?" Sydney bombarded her when she walked out.

"The truth," Rachel said calmly. "That we check and double check all samples. And that I have no idea how this could have happened."

Sydney begged Rachel to sit with her somewhere they could talk. Then, she blurted out everything. About her affair with the doctor. How he broke up with her. How angry she was. How she was pretty sure she caused the switch.

Rachel listened patiently. "You're covered by the clinic's malpractice insurance," Rachel said when Sydney finished talking. "You have no personal liability."

"I won't lose my nursing license?" Sydney asked desperately.

Rachel shook her head. "Professionally, you are sound," Rachel responded. "But, personally, you need to think about how you could let something like this happen. These types of mistakes ruin people's lives. Maybe this isn't the right profession for you."

Sydney nodded bashfully. She thanked Rachel for her advice and said goodbye. A final goodbye. Rachel had tried to call her a few times after that, but Sydney didn't answer. It was just another reminder of her guilt. She also stopped answering calls from the insurance company or any other phone number she didn't recognize. Let them serve me with a subpoena, she thought. The subpoena never came.

It wasn't exactly guilt that she felt about what happened. Guilt would imply it was totally her fault, and Sydney didn't see it that way. If Dr. Klein hadn't started with her, or if he hadn't broken up with her, this never would have happened. So it was Dr. Klein's fault, she reasoned with herself. Sydney was also a victim in her own way. She did feel shame, grief, regret. She wished she could have done something for them, fixed this mess, but that's life, she thought. So unjust, so delicate, that any decision—no matter how small—can completely alter someone's entire being.

In the courtroom, Sydney watched the lawyers give their statements. First, the plaintiff's, who talked about justice. Then, the defense, who talked about family. As if justice and family were opposing forces. Sydney couldn't help herself from watching the jury during the closing statements. They all looked so pensive, listening so intently. What would she have done in their shoes? Who would she choose? She was happy she didn't need to make that decision.

When the lawyers finished and the judge gave the jury their instructions, the courtroom suddenly became alive. The woman in the wrinkled suit next to her shot up, but then looked down at Sydney.

"Who do you work for?" she asked, eyeing her up and down. She had a small notepad in her hands and a pen behind her ears.

"No one," Sydney responded, as though she needed to defend her presence there.

"So why are you here? Are you a friend of Cameron's?"

Sydney shook her head and looked away. She didn't want to speak to any reporters. Then the woman pushed past her toward the door at the back of the room. Sydney watched the woman slip out with the rest of the audience members, leaving the rows almost empty. It was just Sydney and a few people in the front row—probably lawyers, based on the way they were dressed. Sydney sat still. She looked up to the front of the courtroom, where both couples were standing with their lawyers. Graham and

Avery were listening to theirs talk as he fidgeted with his belt. On the other side, Andy and Cameron stood together in front of their lawyer. Andy was nodding his head while Cameron focused on the floor.

Soon Avery and Graham followed their lawyer through the back of the courtroom and out the backdoors. A few minutes later, Andy and Cameron followed. Sydney watched them walk by her, catching Cameron's eye for a moment. Sydney wanted to look away, but her eyes were stuck. She held Cameron's gaze, but it felt to her that Cameron didn't really see her. I'm sorry, Sydney mouthed to her, but it was as though Cameron were somewhere else entirely. When they were gone, the courtroom stood still. Sydney didn't move. She waited in the back row for a moment. For what, she wasn't sure, but she wasn't yet ready to get up.

Suddenly she felt a vibration coming from her purse. She opened it and pulled out her phone. It was Tom. She looked around the courtroom before answering the phone. "Hello?" she said in a whisper.

"Hey, where are you?" he asked. "You haven't responded to any of my texts."

"Sorry, I was distracted," Sydney responded.

"Studying too hard, huh?" he joked. "I can hear you're at the library."

"Yes," she laughed. "I'll be home soon." She hung up the phone, thinking about the last nine months she and Tom had been dating. Their first date—on Valentine's Day—she met him at a trendy cocktail bar in the East Village. She remembered walking there and seeing him through the window sitting down at one of the tiny little tables shoved into the corner of the bar. He was wearing a button-down shirt, different from his usual black t-shirt at the coffee shop. Sydney waited outside for a while before deciding whether to go in. She wasn't sure if she should start dating anyone then, but more than that, she wasn't sure what to do about ordering a drink. Should she have a cocktail? Should she order something without alcohol? If she did, how would she explain that? She couldn't tell him the real reason. Maybe he would think she was a recovering alcoholic, or maybe he would just think she was some boring uptight loser. Either way, it would definitely put an end to the date before it even started.

After watching Tom squirm in his seat for ten minutes, she walked inside. He smiled with relief when he saw her and waved her over like an airman helping a plane come in for landing. She brushed through the tables and sat down across from him. A moment later, a waiter came by, setting down two glasses of pink champagne—a Valentine's Day present, the waiter said. Tom thanked the waiter and raised the glass in order to toast. Sydney looked at the glass in front of her and up at Tom, with his goofy smile and big shining eyes. That was the moment she had made her decision.

She lifted the champagne flute and clinked Tom's glass. Then she brought the glass to her lips and took a sip. It was sweet and bitter at the same time. Delicious and refreshing. She ordered a cocktail and decided to let herself enjoy the evening. The next day, she called Dr. Swanson and made her appointment for the dilation and curettage procedure.

She never told Tom about the procedure. Nor did she tell him about Dr. Klein. She was starting a new chapter in her life, one where she was somebody different, someone who didn't make stupid mistakes with married men, someone responsible who took care of herself. That was who she wanted to be. Who she wanted Tom to see her as.

She then found a new job at a pediatrician's office. It seemed fitting. Like the right next stage after working with embryos. Every once in a while she would recognize one of the moms who came in. They would look at her funny, as though trying to remember how they knew her. She would just smile and tell them that she just had one of those faces, that seemed familiar to everyone, but they had never met before. Usually the moms just nodded and went on to asking questions about their babies.

One day, when she and Tom were out together, he asked if that was what she wanted to do with her life, work in somebody else's office. Sydney shrugged. She hadn't really thought about it ever, except the one time Dr. Klein had mentioned it when he was trying to convince her to get the abortion. She had always thought being a nurse was the best she could be.

Then Tom bought her a big thick book. When he handed it to her, she didn't understand what it was. "A study guide for the MCATs," he told her. The test she would need to take if she ever wanted to go to medical school. At first, she laughed and placed the book on her coffee table. She was afraid of opening it, but it was always there in case she ever wanted to. Tom joked that the book made a great coaster for the time being. Then one day when Sydney was bored at home, she opened it. She started reading and realized that knew a lot of the answers in the practice tests. Maybe it wouldn't be so hard, she thought. She could take the test and then decide whether to apply to medical school. She signed up for a test in early December. A month before applications were due.

The book was in her bag now. She brought it with her everywhere, never knowing when she may have a few minutes to take a practice test or read a chapter. Sometimes, she would go sit in one of the NYU libraries and just study. The book was now dogeared, crinkled, and ripped in some parts, but the information on the pages was still good.

Sydney stood up from the bench in the back of the courtroom. She was the only person left in there now. She left the room and the courthouse and started walking toward her new apartment with Tom. When her lease ended last month, she and Tom agreed to move in together. Yes, it was quick, but also convenient. She wasn't sure she could continue to afford living alone and they were already spending several nights a week together.

It was dark by then. The air was chilly. Sydney couldn't stop thinking about Cameron and Avery. She promised herself she would never forget what happened to them. She would carry it with her through medical school and she would do everything in her power to make sure nothing like that ever happened again on her watch.

Chapter 49

November 20, 2013

Cameron had just dropped the baby off at Helen's apartment when her phone rang. It was Andy. She had just seen him an hour ago, before he left for work. He had taken so much time off because of the trial and everything, he was anxious to get back. As soon as the closing arguments ended, he immediately shot off to his office. The day after he went in early and stayed late—there was just so much to catch up on. Today also he went in early and told Cameron not to wait up, again.

Cameron ignored the call and put her phone on silent as she slipped it back into her purse. She didn't feel like talking to him, what could he have to say, anyway? She wanted a day of quiet, a day to herself. Her maternity leave was also about to be over. She had planned on taking eight weeks off and going back in after Thanksgiving—that gave just a little more than a week left. But she was afraid that her maternity leave would end and she still wouldn't have even met her baby. She spent her entire maternity leave taking care of a baby who belonged to someone else. By the time she got her baby, she'd be back in the office every day, working long hours, pumping milk, and coming home with just enough time to pick up the baby, give her bath and put her to sleep. She wouldn't get to know her, wouldn't get to spend time holding her, bonding with her, doing tummy time—Helen would be doing that. Cameron felt that even when she had her own baby, she would never feel like a real mother. Maybe she shouldn't go back to work. Take a leave of absence. Quit. Focus on trying to be a mom. But she loved her job. And if she wanted to take a longer break, there was no guarantee her job would be waiting for her when she was ready to go back. She had seen too many ambitious and talented women give everything up when they became mothers. She had always pitied them. Thought they were pretending when they said they were happy staying at home with their kids; that their priorities had changed and they no longer strove to advance their careers. Cameron didn't want to be like them. She wanted to do it all. Be a mother and an ambitious career woman. She could have done it too, if the mix-up didn't happen.

After the closing arguments ended, Cameron decided to call the therapist that Alicia recommended. She'd never talked to a therapist before, never felt like she needed one. They were for other people, people with real problems. But now she felt like maybe she was one of those people with real problems. Not just with the baby, and not just with Andy—she was losing him—but with herself. She didn't know who she was anymore. She spent too much time judging herself. Thinking about what had happened. Wishing it could have been different. Willing the past to change. All the 'what-ifs' were swirling around and around in her head all the time, there just wasn't any room for other thoughts.

She was going to meet the therapist now. Not for a real session, just to chat for fifteen minutes and decide if she wanted to set a real appointment. She would see how she felt; if she was comfortable; if talking to someone felt good or awkward. When she arrived at the therapist's office, the door was open. She knocked quietly, peering in at the woman reading something at her desk. The woman looked up and welcomed Cameron inside. Cameron tiptoed in and sat down in one of the large chairs. She waved her hand over the leather armrest, feeling the metal knobs that lined the edge. The therapist glided around the desk to sit down across from her.

"Hi Cameron, I'm Sarah," the therapist said. "How are you doing?"

Cameron's lips peeled up into a smile, an automatic reaction to whenever anyone asked how she was doing. Normally she would just respond 'fine' and ask the other person back. But that wasn't why she came.

"I don't know," she responded. "That's why I am here."

"Why don't you tell me a little about yourself and why you wanted to meet," Sarah said.

"Well, I'm twenty-eight, actually, twenty-nine, I just had a birthday that I completely forgot about. I live on the Upper East Side with my husband Andy. I work in PR," Cameron started listing off the things that defined her. "I'm from Atlanta and went to school in Boston. And…and I…I had a baby about a month and a half ago, but it wasn't mine."

"Who does the baby belong to if it wasn't yours?"

"That's the question really," Cameron said. "Maybe the baby is mine." Cameron paused watching for a reaction from the therapist. She tried to decide if she felt that the therapist was judging her, making assumptions, but her face didn't change with Cameron's statement. She looked sympathetic, pensive, like she was really listening. So Cameron just let it out, she let it all out, about the IVF, the mix-up, the new baby, and the trial.

"How are you handling this?"

"I don't know."

"And your husband? How is he handling it?"

"I don't know," she responded. "He doesn't want to talk about it. He's angry. He won't look at the baby I'm taking care of. He's just waiting for the trial to end and for us to switch."

"How do you feel about that?"

"What if we lose?" Cameron said. "And we're stuck with this baby? He won't want to be her dad."

"Do you want to be her mom?"

"Do I have a choice? I mean, I've been taking care of her for six weeks already, and if we lose, then what? I went through all of this and I'm not a mom? I have to start from scratch again to have a baby?"

"Is that what you want? To be a mom? Or to be a mom to your biological child?"

"I don't know what I want," Cameron responded. "I always thought I wanted to be a mom, that was what I was supposed to want, but…" Cameron's eyes started to tear up as she continued talking. All the 'what-ifs' came spinning out of her mouth, littering the couch, the floor, the entire room. Before she knew it, the therapist put her hand up.

"I'm so sorry, but I have to stop you," she said. "I have another patient coming in. Can we schedule an appointment to continue?"

Cameron peeked at her phone in her purse. Five missed calls from Andy. Six text messages. But she just looked at the time. She had been there for almost an hour already. Way more than the fifteen minutes she had planned. "I'll call you," Cameron said, standing up to leave. She shook the therapist's hand and left the office. She felt embarrassed by how much she had said, how much she whined. She couldn't do that again.

When she was outside, she called Andy back. "Cam, what's going on, where are you?" Andy said when he answered.

"Sorry, my phone was on silent, I didn't hear."

"The jury has made a decision," he said. "We have to get to court. I'm already on my way. Just meet me there." He sounded exasperated.

Cameron's heart started to race. So fast? They had just been deliberating for one and a half days. Was it such an easy decision? Alicia told them it would probably be a few days, by the end of the week, definitely before Thanksgiving. Cameron thought she would have more time. Time to prepare herself for what would happen, whether that meant continuing to raise this baby, or getting a new one. She immediately caught a cab downtown to the courthouse, to the back entrance, where Andy was waiting for her.

"What took you so long?" he said as he rushed her inside. "Alicia is stalling them." Andy had his hand on her shoulder and guided her to their courtroom where Alicia was standing in the front of the room talking to the judge. She sat down when she saw Cameron and Andy approaching.

"Are we ready now?" the judge asked. Cameron nodded. She looked at the defense table, where the other couple was holding hands. "Bring in the jury."

The bailiff opened the door to the jury chambers and led the members into the courtroom. Most were looking down as they walked in. Some looked at the defense, some at Cameron and Andy. But what did that mean?

"Mr. Foreman, do we have a verdict?" the judge asked. The room was silent, so silent that the silence felt like it needed to be cut through with a knife. The jury member at the end of the front row stood up, holding a small piece of paper in his hand. He cleared his throat.

"We have, your honor," he said. "The jury has decided, seven to five, for the plaintiffs."

The lump in Cameron's throat suddenly dropped. Disappeared. Her eyes popped, her chin dropped, her eyes—for the second time that day—welled up with tears. They won! They would be getting back their baby! Everything was going to be all right! She would get to be a real mother. Andy would be the father that Cameron always knew he would be. She didn't need therapy. They could forget everything that had happened over the last few months and continue with their happily ever after.

Chapter 50

November 20, 2013

"Mr. Foreman, do we have a verdict?" the judge asked. Avery's hands were balled up inside of Graham's fists. She was sweating, it was hard to breathe. The foreman stood up and cleared his throat.

"We have, your honor," he said. "The jury has decided, seven to five, for the plaintiffs."

Suddenly it was like a roar erupted in the courtroom. There was a ringing in Avery's ears, the sound pierced her brain and then, she felt dizzy, weak. She tried to continue holding on to Graham's hands but she couldn't. Then, everything went black.

It could have been moments later, minutes, or even days, but when Avery opened her eyes, she didn't know where she was. Her head hurt, it felt cold. Loud. There were so many people yelling. "Avery!" she was suddenly able to pick out Graham's voice. "Avery, are you all right?"

She opened her eyes. She was on the floor. Graham was right above her. Brad was standing next to him, yelling something that was lost in the noise. "Avery, can you hear me?" Graham said. "Are you OK? You just fainted."

"What happened?" Avery asked, trying to lift her head. It was heavy.

"Don't move, you may have hurt something," Graham said. "Paramedics are on the way."

"Don't be ridiculous," Avery said, trying again to lift her head. "What happened?"

"The floor is really hard, you hit your head, just wait a minute," Graham said.

"Graham, what happened?" Avery repeated a third time. "Did we lose?"

Graham looked at her with his big eyes, the edges turned down slightly, the bags underneath hollow. "We lost, Avery. It is over."

"It's not over!" Brad was suddenly bent down next to Graham. "I'm already trying to get the judge to declare a mistrial, the jury should have been sequestered with all the media attention this case was getting but they weren't. If not, we can appeal."

"No," Avery said. "We can't keep going on like this." The next moment Brad was pushed aside by a large man in a navy-blue shirt.

"Ma'am, can you tell me your name?" the man said. He lifted Avery's right arm and put two fingers on her pulse.

"Avery Stephens. I'm fine," she said. "Just let me get up." She pulled her hand from the paramedic and pushed herself up from the ground. As she stood up the room started to spin. She leaned on the table, gripping the edge with both hands. "Graham, get me out of here," she said through gritted teeth. She could feel the reporters staring at her, like vultures eyeing their prey. She kept looking down, afraid to show her face. Graham grabbed her arms and started to pull her through the back of the courtroom and out the doors. Outside a crowd was waiting and started launching questions right at them. "Avery, was that the first time you passed out? Or does that happen often?" "Avery, do you have a medical condition that caused you to faint?" "Graham, what are you going to do now?" "Are you going to appeal?" "Is there something you want to say to the other couple?" "How does it feel that you are going to be losing your daughter?"

Losing your daughter. The words hit her like a cannonball almost knocking her back over. But Graham held her steady, parting the sea of reporters and leading her through. He pulled her all the way outside, to the nearby parking lot and helped her into the car.

"Are you OK?" he asked once he sat down on the driver's side.

"We lost," Avery said. "How did we lose?"

"I do not know."

"But Amelia needs us," Avery said. "Especially now, that she is sick."

"She also needs biological parents for the bone marrow transplant," Graham said. "So…"

"What happens now?"

As if on cue, Graham's phone rang. It was Brad. Graham answered with a weak 'hello' and put the phone on speaker.

"The judge denied my request for a mistrial," Brad said. "He ruled that we need to hand over the baby as soon as possible. A social worker is going to meet you at your home this afternoon to take Amelia and you will get your biological daughter back for now. I tried to stay the order, but the judge ruled that it needs to be done as quickly as possible. I'll file an appeal, and then if we win the appeal, you'll just switch back."

Avery shook her head. "Brad, we can't just keep switching back and forth, we're talking about children. No appeal," she said, feeling defeated. "It is what it is. It will be best for both babies for everyone to just move forward."

"Are you sure? It was such a close case, there is a good chance of winning an appeal," Brad said.

"Brad, is there a way for us to meet the other couple?" Avery said with a big sigh. "Talk to them? Be there when we switch the babies? We need to tell them about Amelia."

"Are you sure? I would advise against that, this is a very sensitive situation," Brad said.

"Brad, can you find out?" Avery pleaded.

"I'll reach out to their lawyer, see if they are interested in that," Brad said. "But remember that I'm saying this is a bad idea."

Graham hung up the phone and looked at Avery. She caught his eyes for a moment, but she couldn't look at him. She looked down at her hands.

"It is going to be all right," he said. "We are still parents to a daughter. We will just have to get to know her. And Amelia, you will always be her mom, even if she does not know it."

"She'll never know who we are," Avery said. "How much we loved her—love her."

"We gave her everything we could for the last eleven weeks," Graham said. "I am sure some of what we did will stay with her."

"We don't even know what our daughter's name is!" she suddenly started crying, thinking about the fact that her baby was going to be switched with a stranger. After spending the last eleven weeks getting to know Amelia, she would have to start all over getting to know this new baby, what made her smile, the way she slept, the sound of her cry. It felt like a daunting undertaking, to mourn a baby while trying to fall in love with a new one. And she would be mourning Amelia, losing the daughter she loved so much. But she believed—she had to believe—that the other couple would be good to her, would be good parents. If not, why would they have fought so hard?

Graham's phone rang again. Again it was Brad.

"The other couple doesn't want to meet," Brad said. "But they asked if you would want to do the switch at the courthouse. Then it could be immediate. We can close two mediation rooms. They said they can be there in an hour."

Avery sighed and nodded to Graham.

"Sure," Graham responded. "We can go bring her now. We just ask for some time to say goodbye before we hand her over."

"That's reasonable," Brad said. "I'll meet you back at the courthouse."

Graham hung up the phone and started the car. Everything was silent except the soft rumble of the engine. Graham weaved out of the parking lot and toward Brooklyn. When they got home, Graham stopped the car, but the two of them sat still.

"We should write them a letter," Avery said. "About how much we love Amelia. And how important it is to us that they take good care of her. And we have to tell them she is sick."

Chapter 51

November 20, 2013

The room was stifling. Hot, like only a room could be in the middle of winter when the heater was on all day. Cameron tried to steady her breath, she blinked slowly, trying to imagine what it would feel like the moment she would hold her daughter. Something would click, she knew it. She would be able to feel it. It would feel something like euphoria, solace, that feeling that mothers always talk about when talking about their newborns. It was just moments away.

The other couple's baby—the one Cameron had birthed—was lying down calmly in the stroller at Cameron's side. Cameron looked down at her, smiled, and put her hand down to touch her hand. The baby instinctively grasped Cameron's index finger, holding it tight with her palm. Eleanor, Cameron said in her head. Those little hands, Cameron thought, she'd miss them. The gray blue eyes, the blonde peach fuzz hair on her head. She'd become fond of the baby over the last month and a half. Fond, was the way she could describe it. Did she love this baby? She didn't know. But she definitely felt something for her. How could she not, after everything they had been through together?

Andy and Alicia were talking quietly in the corner of the small room. It was almost like a classroom. Empty, with a few folding desk chairs and a whiteboard in the front. Cameron looked up at her husband and Alicia, but then looked down again at the baby. Soon there was a knock on the door and a woman walked in. She was short, wearing a gray pencil skirt suit and glasses. Her short hair framed her face.

"Hi, I'm Amy Grant," she said as she slipped inside. "I'm a social worker here in Manhattan, and I am going to help with handing over the baby to her legal guardians." Amy shook hands with Andy and Alicia and then with Cameron. She then took a seat in one of the folding chairs across from Cameron and motioned the others to come around. "In a few moments, I am going to take the baby and bring her to the couple in the next room. At the same time, another social worker will be taking the other baby and bringing her to you. Do you have the baby's birth certificate and immunization records? I need to bring all her paperwork to her new guardians."

Cameron nodded.

"Do you have any questions?" Amy asked, making eye contact with all three of them. "Do you want a few moments to say goodbye?"

Cameron was about to nod again, but stopped herself when she heard Andy's voice. "We're good," Andy said. "We're ready."

Amy smiled at him. "Alright, then let's do this." Cameron handed the baby's birth certificate and immunization records to the social worker and then looked down one last time at the baby. She smiled at her and felt her eyes well up. She blinked back the tears, there was no reason to be sad now. The social worker stood up and walked up to the stroller. "May I?" she asked Cameron. With permission, she gently lifted the baby and held her to her shoulder.

"What a darling little thing," she said patting the baby's head with one hand. "The other social worker will be here in a few minutes. Thank you for your cooperation." Cameron nodded to the social worker, and then watched her slip back out of the room. When she left, it was like she opened a black hole, leaving a void in the room. Cameron suddenly felt heavy, like the gravity in the room got stronger, pulling her down into that black hole.

"You ready?" Andy said enthusiastically. He rubbed his hands together in front of his chest. Cameron put on a smile, a wide one, wide enough to show her teeth. "So, what are we going to name her?" Andy asked. "We said something with an E right?"

"I don't know," Cameron responded, but Andy was already talking to Alicia again, leaving Cameron alone in the chair. She sat, watching them talk. A minute passed, and then another. Ten minutes later, they were still talking and the baby hadn't arrived.

"What's going on?" Andy said, turning toward Cameron. He then looked back at Alicia. "Alicia can you go check?"

Alicia slipped out of the room. A few moments later, she returned. "Just another minute," she said. "The other couple was taking a while to say goodbye."

Then, another knock on the door came. Another woman opened it, carrying a small baby in her arms. Cameron noticed that this baby was bigger than the one she was used to. Makes sense, she was a whole month older. Cameron stood up.

"Hi there," the woman said. "I'm Darcy Jones and here is your little bundle of joy!" The woman approached Cameron and handed her the baby. Cameron took the baby in her arms, surprised a moment by the weight, and held her up so she could look at her. The baby whimpered a moment, then stopped, focusing her eyes on Cameron's face. Cameron stared at her, her deep blue eyes, little button nose, pale puffy cheeks. She had straight brown hair, wild and long for a three-month-old, a double chin and a big round tummy. This is my baby, Cameron told herself, but it felt so hard to believe. She pulled the baby close to her chest to hug her, smell her hair. She had the same, clean smell as the baby Cameron had grown used to. The smell of baby laundry detergent and shampoo.

"Hey little munchkin," Andy came over to her and ruffled the baby's hair. "What a cutie!" Andy looked at the baby with a gleam in his eyes. Then he looked at Cameron, a huge smile on his face. "She looks just like you! What a beautiful family we are!"

Cameron forced herself to look at Andy. So happy, with no trace of all the stress and anger that had been plastered on his face for the last few weeks. She tried to mirror his expression, tried to absorb some of the contentment that he radiated. But she felt nauseous, weak.

"Do you want to hold her?" she asked Andy.

"How do I do it?" he asked back.

"Just make sure to support her head," Cameron responded and gently handed the baby to Andy. He wrapped one arm under her bottom and spread the other hand out on the back of her head and held the baby a few inches from his face.

"I'm your daddy," he said smiling to her. "Say dada."

"It's going to be a little while before she can talk," Cameron said as she sat down. Andy looked down at her and then back at the baby.

"You don't even know how badly your mommy and daddy wanted you," Andy said to the baby. "We went through so much just to get to hold you."

"We should go home," Cameron said.

"Wait," the social worker said. Cameron had forgotten that she was still in the room. "The other couple asked me to give you this." The woman held up a small envelope.

"What is it?" Cameron asked.

"I don't know," the social worker responded, handing the envelope to Cameron. "A message I guess."

Cameron carefully ripped open the top of the envelope, pulling out a small packet of papers folded nicely in three. She unfolded the packet. The top page was a handwritten note, Cameron pulled the page aside and looked at the second page, it looked like blood test results. Was it their immunization records? But they looked so different from the records Cameron had given them. The next page had a name and phone number written on it. She turned back to the handwritten note and began to read quietly.

Dear Cameron and Andy,

First and foremost, we want to tell you that we appreciate you taking care of our biological daughter during this whole ordeal. Now that you are taking our Amelia, we want to tell you that we understand how important this was to you. We are happy for you, that you got what you wanted, even if it comes on our behalf. Over the last eleven weeks we have gotten to know and love Amelia. She is a beautiful and happy baby, who loves to smile and be cuddled. She brought so much joy into our house, we just regret that we were so focused on the trial that we didn't get to enjoy her as her much as we would have liked to. If you are willing, we would love to stay in contact and be a part of Amelia's life in any way you see fit. We would also like to extend the offer for you to continue being a part of our biological daughter's life, if you want.

While we are sure that right now you are celebrating your win and the togetherness of your family, we unfortunately need to be the bearers of bad news. Last week, on the day we were supposed to be in court for the closing arguments, Amelia woke up with a fever. We took her to the emergency room where it was discovered that she is sick. She has acute lymphocytic leukemia and needs chemotherapy and a bone marrow transplant right away.

We've enclosed the test results from our visit to the hospital, a blood test and a bone marrow aspiration, and the name and number of a pediatric oncologist who we met with earlier this week. He would be a great choice to lead Amelia's treatment.

We're so sorry to tell you this, especially when you are probably on top of the world. But maybe your win is a blessing in disguise. The doctor said a genetic relative should be the donor for the bone marrow transplant, so Amelia being with you gives her the best chance of recovery.

We're here for you if you want to talk to us, or if you have any questions about Amelia's first months of life or her disease. We wish you the very best raising her and wish a speedy recovery for her. We will love her always, no matter what happens.

Avery and Graham Stephens

"So, what does it say?" Andy said, still cooing at the baby. Cameron dropped the papers, letting them scatter on the floor. She couldn't speak, her throat was closing up. The room was spinning, the floor turned to flames. She opened her mouth to say something, but there was nothing she could say. She just shook her head and put her hands on her face. The nightmare just wouldn't end.

Chapter 52

March 28, 2019

It's been five years since Amelia died. We kept the name, Amelia May, we just changed the spelling of the last name to Stevens. Every year on the anniversary, I visit her grave. She was less than seven months old. And what a nightmare those months were.

I arrive at her grave—my third stop of the day—and bend down. I place the lilies I bought at the bottom of the headstone.

Amelia May Stevens
September 1, 2013-March 28, 2014
A moment in our arms, forever in our hearts

It really did feel like just a moment that we got to hold her. When the trial ended, and I finally got to hold her, I didn't even have the chance to soak it in, to feel the joy of motherhood, before everything was taken away. It was like a sick joke, I finally got my daughter, but she was being taken away again.

Right after we got her, we started treatment. We visited all the top oncologists in New York—including the one the other couple had seen—learned about the latest treatment options, all the upcoming clinical trials. Andy and I both donated bone marrow to be transplanted to Amelia after her chemotherapy. The doctor said it would help. Maybe it would have. Maybe it would have given her a few more weeks, or just days. Who knows? Maybe it would have done nothing at all. She never got it.

We spent the next months in hospitals, holding a screaming baby who didn't understand what this cruel world was doing to her. First we flipped her world upside down by taking her and then we spent months torturing her with needles and chemicals. And all for what?

I remember when we started the chemo. We were in the hospital, an IV was plugged into her arm. I had just woken up from the anesthesia after donating bone marrow. Amelia was crying, screaming. The shrill sound of torture. I held her in my arms, but there was nothing I could do for her. My comforting meant nothing. I couldn't stop her pain.

After that, she started losing weight. And her beautiful hair. Her face became gaunt, her arms and legs like toothpicks stuck into a round belly. The doctors were optimistic. At first, they said treatment was going well. If that was how she looked when things were going well, I was afraid of what would happen when things weren't going well.

After a week in the hospital, we brought her home. She was tired, all she wanted to do was sleep. But she couldn't. Violent vomiting would wake her up. She didn't want to eat. I couldn't breastfeed her; it was too hard for her. I pumped and tried to drip the milk into her mouth with a syringe. But she would just vomit it out. I prayed that maybe a few drops would stay. Anything so she wouldn't starve. We took her back to the hospital—she was three pounds lighter after two days at home. So they poked another hole in her, a direct line to her stomach to slowly pump in milk. Her weight stabilized and we could go home for another few days before the second injection of treatment.

I wasn't sure I could handle more chemo. Watching the baby waste away like that. I felt horrible, all I could think was that we could have avoided all this. I felt so guilty. But if we had just decided to keep the baby I gave birth to, we wouldn't be there. Instead we would have been home with a healthy child. The absurdity of it all.

The second chemo injection was worse than the first. Amelia was weaker, the drugs were stronger. She lost more weight. She didn't even cry anymore. Like she had accepted everything that was happening. Like she gave up. The doctors were less optimistic. They didn't say as much, but I could tell, when they stopped talking about new ideas for treatment or praising her progress. They knew they were just buying us some time. More time in the hospital, more time watching our baby suffer.

We went in for a third infusion. A third round of vomiting. By then, Amelia's arms and legs were bruised everywhere. The doctors said it was because her blood cell count was so low. And that was when she got a systemic infection. An infection. Maybe it was just a common cold, but it was strong enough to overpower her. The doctors tried to cure it with more drugs. More medicine.

I mostly held her and cried. Not just for her. But for me. And for the baby I gave up. I kept thinking about what my life would be like if we didn't try to fight. Or if we never found out about the mix-up. I could have been doing tummy time as my baby learned to lift her head, I would have reveled when she rolled over or sat up for herself. I would have been making baby food by blending vegetables and fruits and photographing her face with every new food. I would have gone back to the mommy-and-me group, signed up for swimming lessons, took her in the stroller around the park. But I got to do none of that.

I started daydreaming about the baby that grew inside me. Thinking about her all the time. Wondering if she was crawling yet. Whether her hair had gotten long enough to be tied with a bow. What was the sound of her babble. Whether she remembered me or had already gotten used to her new family. I wanted to know everything about her, to hold her one more time. After all, she is the only one who knows my heart from inside.

But we didn't keep in touch with the other couple. Andy wanted to sue them again when it was all over, as if they were to blame. He would curse them, like this was their plan all along, to switch their sick child with a healthy one. I didn't want to remind him that it was us who caused the switch. It was our fault.

The infection was the beginning of the end. I sat with her for two days until she just didn't wake up. Just like that, she took her last breath. On March 28. The funeral was small. Just us and our families. We debated whether to tell the other couple. Eventually we decided to tell their lawyer. He must have passed along the message, as I saw them at the cemetery after the funeral. Waiting in their car for us to leave.

"You would have been in kindergarten now," I say to the grave. "I would have taken you to buy school supplies, like pencils and markers. You'd probably already know how to write your name; you were so smart." They always say it is important to talk to your babies, so I still do it.

I'm sitting on the grass next to the gravestone. I don't care if my clothes get grass stains or dirt on them.

I just want to be close to her. I have to tell her something important today. I lean forward and put my hand on the headstone. A deep breath, and I tell her about my next stop.

Chapter 53

March 28, 2019

I leave the cemetery. It's midafternoon but the sun is still up and shining. I look at my phone. Perfect timing, I think to myself. I have thirty minutes until I need to be at my last stop. I start walking, feeling the cold wind on my face. My eyes start to tear up and I try to swallow them back down.

I still can't believe I am doing this. I knew this would take a lot of courage and I suddenly feel like maybe I don't have it in me. Maybe this is a mistake. That I should just keep going as I have been for the last five years. No, I tell myself. You can do this. It will be worth it.

A few months ago, I remembered something. That Amelia came from one of twelve embryos. There were more embryos that were frozen and packed away to be used at a later time. Before we settled with Dr. Klein, I secretly contacted his lawyer. I didn't tell Andy, because I didn't know how he would react. But I made a deal with his lawyer. I promised I would get Andy to agree to the settlement if he would make sure my embryos were transferred to a different clinic and that Dr. Klein would pay the clinic to store them and provide me any treatment I wanted. The lawyer furrowed his brow at me and accepted my deal. Once I knew my embryos were safe—after multiple checks that they were indeed mine—I convinced Andy that we needed to settle. To move on. We got four million dollars and promised not to disclose the name of the doctor or the clinic. I don't know what happened to him and his clinic. Whether or not he is still doing IVF for hopeful couples. If they made any changes at the clinic to make sure there were no mistakes. It didn't matter to me anymore.

At the time, I didn't know if I would ever use those embryos. If I even wanted to try again. To get pregnant, have a baby. Be a mother. It would be too painful, I thought. Constant reminders of what I lost. But I decided, better not to close that door. Keep the opportunity open.

I forgot about those embryos for a while. Months went by when I never thought about them. Life just carried on. I went back to work, my monotonous job in front of the computer. I continued to go out with friends, until they started to disappear. Had babies and moved to the suburbs. Everyone around me was moving forward. But not me. I was stuck. Still living in our Upper East Side apartment. Still just a couple with no family. Instead of being the girl everyone was jealous of, I was the girl they pitied. Prayed they wouldn't become.

The years just started to pass by. Andy and I got in a comfortable rhythm where every day was the same. Just living to pass the time. Nothing to look forward to, nothing to live for. A few months ago, I decided things had to change. And that's when I remembered those embryos. Frozen in their little test tubes in a drawer at the fertility clinic I chose. I called the clinic, to check in and see if I could start the process to try to get pregnant again. So I set an appointment and met with the doctor. He prescribed me the hormone shots that I would need to give myself every night. Then every other day I would come in to do a blood test to check my hormone levels. Yesterday the doctor called to tell me that it was time. Today would be the transfer.

I'm walking to the clinic. For some reason I am nervous, like I am about to perform, but really all I have to do is lie down and hope for the best. When I get to the building, I take the elevator up. There's a mirror in the elevator and a woman staring back at me. I look at her; there are creases around her lips, crow's feet by her eyes. Even makeup cannot hide them. I put my hands on my cheeks and try to smile. The elevator dings and the doors open. I walk out and into the waiting room at the clinic. There are two couples sitting down. One is filling out forms on a clipboard with their arms interlaced. The other is just waiting quietly with hands clasped together. They all look at me briefly as I sit down. I'm probably the only one who comes for a transfer alone.

Maybe I should have told Andy. He could have been here with me. But no, I want it to be a surprise. When I get the positive pregnancy test, I want to show him that our lives are about to turn around. That I figured out how to fix things. That we will have a reason to be happy again. I know he will be happy. Maybe he doesn't think he wants this, but when it happens, he will.

I check in with the receptionist, and quietly wait for my name to be called.

Epilogue

March 28, 2023

Cameron put her hands on her hips as she walked toward the small path in front of her. She was out of breath and needed to take a break.

"Wait up for me, darling," she called ahead to the brown ponytail in front of her. Ella stopped and turned around. "Be careful with the flowers," Cameron said between breaths. Ella wanted to hold the lilies; she had picked out the bouquet all by herself.

"Don't worry, take your time," Andy said from behind her, putting his hand on the small of her back. "I don't want you to overexert yourself."

Cameron smiled and kissed Andy on the cheek. He knelt down to kiss her stomach and then rushed up ahead to Ella, who had turned again and was skipping her way down the path. When Cameron caught up to them, they were already sitting in front of the headstone. The bouquet was leaning carefully at its base.

"Mommy, I miss her," Ella said.

"I know, dear, we all do," Cameron said, leaning on Andy as she awkwardly folded herself down on the grass next to her daughter. "She would have been a great big sister. Just like you're going to be soon."

"Mommy, can I feel the baby?" Ella put her hands on Cameron's big stomach, rubbing it softly. "Mommy! He kicked me!"

Cameron laughed, her head falling back. When she lifted it, her eyes caught Andy's. This was the third time he had come with her to Amelia's grave. She remembered how uncomfortable he had felt the first time. When they approached the grave, Cameron had knelt down, putting her hands on the headstone. She spoke to Amelia, like she always did. Andy stood behind her, as though afraid to get too close.

It was impossible to imagine how things had changed over the last few years. Four years ago, two weeks after the egg transplant, she found out she was pregnant. When she told Andy, his first reaction was anger. Not because she was pregnant, but because she went behind his back on something so important. She knew he was right. She told him she was afraid of how he would respond. That he would have tried to talk her out of it. He slammed the door in her face when she said that. But a couple hours later he came back. He had been crying. And he was sorry. He said he had just realized how far apart they had grown. After that, they decided to go to couple's therapy together. They chose a new therapist, someone who didn't know their story, someone who would be totally objective. The first session was hard. It was full of accusations and yelling. Whose fault was it that they had grown apart, why the other one didn't make an effort anymore. The second session was all tears. And then came the apologies. From both sides. And after that, they began to rebuild. They talked about what made them fall in love with each other in the first place. Cameron said it was his kind soul and how thoughtful he was. Andy said it was her charm and self-confidence. That made Cameron laugh. She had never thought of herself as confident before.

All the while, her stomach started to grow—which brought excitement and fear at the same time. Were they one hundred percent sure there wasn't another mistake? At twenty weeks they did an amniocentesis to test the fetus' DNA. It came back a 99.9% match.

After that, Cameron went one last time to see the baby she had given up to Avery and Graham. She woke up early and waited outside the school. When the school bus pulled up, Cameron held her breath as the girl jumped down the bus stairs and skipped into the school courtyard. "Goodbye," Cameron whispered to her as she disappeared into the building. That was the last time she saw her.

Then, on December 9, 2019, Ella was born, five days before her due date. In the delivery room, Cameron cried like she had never cried before. It was both a happy and a sad cry. Happiness for the new baby and sadness for the ones she had lost, both of them. When she held the baby on her chest, she felt overwhelmed with love. A feeling she hadn't experienced before. Maybe in the past she wasn't ready for it, but at that moment she was. She felt connected to the baby, that the little baby was an extension of herself. Andy also cried when he first held her. He turned around, hoping Cameron wouldn't see his tears. She saw, but she pretended not to.

They brought the baby home to their Upper East Side apartment filled with a brand-new crib, stroller, and toys. They had donated all their baby things after Amelia died—they couldn't imagine they would use them again. Now, they were happy to have a fresh start.

They were a family, Cameron felt, a perfect family, just the three of them. They were happy. And then, came the surprise. Cameron missed her period one month. Her first thought was that she was going through early menopause. She was thirty-eight years old, and it didn't seem possible that after her battle with infertility in her twenties she would become fertile so much later. But three home pregnancy tests showed otherwise. That their perfect little family of three was becoming a perfect family of four.

"You know, you and Amelia are technically the same age," Andy said to Ella. He was sitting on the grass with his arm around her.

"What do you mean?" she asked curiously.

"Babies come from eggs," Andy explained. "And the eggs that you and Amelia came from were made at the same time."

"Like the eggs we had for breakfast?"

Andy laughed. "Yes, but much smaller. We put you in the freezer so we could have you later."

"So I'm really nine and half years old?"

"I guess you are," Andy said, giving a playful tug on her ponytail.

"Does that mean I can get my ears pierced?"

"Not yet," Cameron said with a laugh.

"I wish she was here to teach me how to be a big sister," Ella said, her tone suddenly changing.

Cameron smiled at her daughter, putting her hand on her shoulder. They hadn't told Ella about the mix-up. Not that it was some big secret, but it was just something she didn't know how to explain. How could she tell her she 'sort of' still had a big sister out there, one she would never know?

"You'll do just fine," Cameron said, giving Ella's shoulder a little rub. "You're already perfect."

What to know what happened with Avery and Graham?

Go to my website www.avivagatauthor.com to get a FREE bonus chapter.

A note from the author

Infertility is something that affects about 15% of couples, yet it is something that is rarely talked about. Women who are unable to get pregnant after a year of trying are often left feeling like there is something wrong with them, or like everyone else around them is suddenly pregnant. But I want to tell all those women out there that you are not alone.

I came up with the idea for this book because it was my biggest fear. I spent more than a year trying to get pregnant. During that year, my husband and I did every test and everything came back fine. But for some reason, my body just didn't want to do what it was biologically programed for. I felt like a failure as a woman.

We then decided to do IVF. The process is emotionally exhausting and physically difficult. You spend weeks pumping yourself with hormones, making you feel bloated, tired, and overly sensitive. The hormones make your body produce multiple eggs at one time. Think, in a normal month, the female body produces one egg. With these hormones, the body can produce about twenty. When the eggs are ready to drop, a doctor retrieves them in an operation using full anesthesia and a vacuum-like device to suck the eggs right out of you. This leaves you feeling aches and cramps for several days while you recover and wait for the transfer.

In the meantime, the eggs are taken to a lab and examined. Not all will be viable, but the ones that are will be introduced to sperm in hopes that they will become fertilized. The ones that do fertilize are then watched to see their growth. The strongest ones are used for immediate transfers, while other strong candidates are frozen for later use.

When we did IVF, we had sixteen eggs retrieved. Twelve of them were deemed viable and of those, nine became fertilized. However, in the end, just three were good enough to use. We transferred one egg and were lucky that it implanted itself and started to grow. Our other two eggs are waiting for us in a freezer at our clinic.

Finding out I was pregnant was one of the most emotionally charged moments of my life. After a year and a half of disappointments, a doctor finally said those magic words to me. While I was happier than ever, I knew that moment was just the beginning of a long and difficult road ahead.

During my pregnancy, my husband and I had many hypothetical debates about what we would do if we found out they transferred the wrong embryo to my uterus. We also debated what we would do if we found out that our embryo was transferred to someone else's uterus. The debates often became heated and emotional, neither of us able to agree on what was the 'right' thing to do. After our baby was born, we again asked each other those questions. But at that point, we realized that what each of us thought was 'right' was ever grayer than what we thought before.

Many of the thoughts and events that Cameron and Avery experience in this book come from my own experiences going through IVF, pregnancy, and labor. While every woman experiences childbearing differently, I hope that some of you will be able to identify with their struggles.

Acknowledgements

While this book has one author, there are multiple people who contributed to making this book what it is today. First, a big thank you to my husband Ori who spent hours brainstorming with me, listened to all my thoughts, and helped me develop the story. I would never have written this book, or any other, if it weren't for his constant support and encouragement. I also want to thank him for being an amazing father and husband and for taking care of our daughter while I wrote.

I also want to thank my parents. Thanks to my dad Nahum for reading the first draft and giving me multiple ideas on how to improve the story, as well as proofreading. A big thanks to my mom Linda, who got so engulfed in the story, she forgot to do any editing. I also want to thank my mother for being my target audience and answering all my annoying questions about her response as a reader. Another big thank you to my parents for their support and for constantly advertising my books to everyone they speak with.

I would also like to thank my grandmother Dorothy and my aunt Gail and uncle Mark for reading the second draft and providing invaluable feedback. Gail, an oncologist, and Mark, also a doctor, helped me to ensure accuracy with the medical aspects of the book.

Additionally, I want to thank Dr. Ariel Weissman for not messing up my IVF procedure (to the best of my knowledge!) Thanks to him, my beautiful daughter was born and I received the inspiration to write this story.

I also want to thank those who helped work on the book. Miranda Larrison, a book reviewer I met via Instagram who read an early draft and provided very helpful feedback. Marianna Cohen, an extremely talented graphic designer who created my cover. Kate Allyson who did the final proofreading of the novel.

The biggest thank you goes to all my readers, especially those who leave me reviews on Amazon and Goodreads. Reviews (and recommendations!) are the best way to give back to an author you like. They help other readers decide whether to read a book and encourage writers to keep going.

Learn more about me by following me on Instagram

@aviva_writes

or check out my website, www.avivagatauthor.com

Made in the USA
San Bernardino, CA
27 August 2019